TITLES BY RANDY WAYNE WHITE

RANDY
WAYNE
WHITE

DEEP
BLUE

G. P. PUTNAM'S SONS   NEW YORK

PUTNAM

G. P. PUTNAM'S SONS
Publishers Since 1838
An imprint of Penguin Random House LLC
375 Hudson Street
New York, New York 10014

The Library of Congress has catalogued the G. P. Putnam's Sons hardcover
edition as follows:

Names: White, Randy Wayne, author.
Title: Deep blue / Randy Wayne White.
Description: New York : G.P. Putnam's Sons, [2016] | Series: A Doc Ford
novel; 23
Identifiers: LCCN 2016006512| ISBN 9780399173516 (hardcover) | ISBN
9780698186866 (ebook)
Subjects: LCSH: Ford, Doc (Fictitious character)—Fiction. | Marine
biologists—Fiction. | BISAC: FICTION / Crime. | FICTION / Suspense. |
GSAFD: Suspense fiction. | Mystery fiction.
Classification: LCC PS3573.H47473 D458 2016b | DDC 813/.54—dc23
LC record available at http://lccn.loc.gov/2016006512

First G. P. Putnam's Sons hardcover edition / March 2016
First G. P. Putnam's Sons premium edition / March 2017
G. P. Putnam's Sons premium edition ISBN: 9780425280256

Printed in the United States of America
1 3 5 7 9 10 8 6 4 2

To Ms. Emerson Elora White
with love and best wishes for a
joyous, productive life well lived

An ocean without its unnamed monsters would be like a completely dreamless sleep.

—JOHN STEINBECK, *Sea of Cortez*

It is not the strongest of the species that survives, nor the most intelligent that survives. It is the one that is the most adaptable to change.

—CHARLES DARWIN (VIA JIM CUTLER, STAFF SCIENTIST, MOTE MARINE LABORATORY)

Sanibel and Captiva Islands are real places, faithfully described, but used fictitiously in this novel. The same is true of certain businesses, marinas, bars, and other places frequented by Doc Ford, Tomlinson, and pals.

In all other respects, however, this novel is a work of fiction. Names (unless used by permission), characters, places, and incidents are either the product of the author's imagination or are used fictitiously. Any resemblance to actual persons, living or dead, or to actual events or locales is unintentional and coincidental.

Contact Mr. White at www.DOCFORD.COM.

AUTHOR'S NOTE

In 1989, just for luck, I summoned my sons, Lee and
Rogan, into the garage, where I wrote in those days, and
asked them to type the last two words, respectively, of the
final sentence of the first Doc Ford novel, *Sanibel Flats*.

They did; banged the words out on my old Under-
wood typewriter, just like Dad.

Lee was nine; Rogan seven.

Talk about good luck! That was more than thirty
books ago, and each book has gained a larger, more devoted audience. My sons have continued to humor me
over the last twenty-six years. Every book I've written
remains unfinished until they have typed (copied and
pasted, these days) the final two words of the final sentence.

I shared this bit of family history to explain why the author's notes always contain some variation of this line: "Finally, I would like to thank my sons for helping me finish another novel."

Superstition isn't silly to those of us who fly in small planes and know their way around a baseball dugout— not if it produces results.

Before acknowledging others who contributed their expertise or good humor during the writing of *Deep Blue*, I want to make it clear that all errors, exaggerations, or misstatements of fact are entirely my fault, not theirs.

Thanks go to Jim Cutler, staff scientist, Mote Marine Laboratory, for his expertise (and an excellent video) on the Captiva Blue Hole. Others who provided technical information were Tom Renn, director of Government Sales for American Technologies Network, Ken Cope (formerly of ASP) for tactical advice, Kenneth Levin of TruGlo Optics, and Christopher Combs of JW Fishers Underwater Search Equipment.

Insights, ideas, and medical advice were provided by Brian Hummel, Judd Miller, my brother Dan White, and my nephew Justin White, Ph.D.

Pals, advisers, and/or teammates are always a help because they know firsthand that writing and writers are a pain in the ass. They are Gary Terwilliger, Ron Iossi, Jerry Rehfuss, Stu Johnson, Victor Candalaria, Gene Lamont, Nick Swartz, Kerry Griner, Mike Shevlin, Jon Warden, Davey Johnson, Barry Rubel, Mike Westhoff, and behavioral guru Don Carman.

Special thanks go to a pair of Iowa high school baseball coaches I much admire: Bill Freese (Davenport Central) and Tom Souchrada (Davenport West). Bill and Helen Wundrum of Davenport have also been guiding forces.

Expertise on bushwhacking via a Maule seaplane was provided by my two fearless python expeditionary brethren, Captain Mark Futch and historian/writer Jeff Carter. (You'll learn more about our adventures via the next Hannah Smith novel, *Seduced*, which I am working on now.) A special acknowledgment goes to Jeremy D. Carter, a fine man.

Bill Lee and his orbiting star, Diana, as always, have guided the author safely into the strange but fun and enlightened world of our mutual friend, the Reverend Sighurdhr M. Tomlinson. Equal thanks go to Donna Terwilliger; Wendy Webb, my wife and trusted friend; Rachael Ketterman; Stephen Grendon, my devoted SOB; the angelic Mrs. Iris Tanner; and my partners and pals, Mark Marinello and Marty and Brenda Harrity.

Much of this novel was written at corner tables before and after hours at Doc Ford's Rum Bar and Grille, where staff were tolerant beyond the call of duty. Elizabeth, Greg and Bryce Barker, Madonna Donna Butz, Capt. Jeffery Kelley, Chef Rene Ramirez, Amanda Rodriguez, Kim McGonnell, Ashley Rhoeheffer, the Amazing Cindy Porter, Desiree Olsen, Gabby Moschitta, Rachael Okerstrom, Rebecca Harris, Sarah Carnithian, Tyler Wussler, Tall Sean Lamont, Mowtown Rachel Songalewski, Boston Brian Cunningham, and Cardinals fan Justin Harris.

At Doc Ford's on Fort Myers Beach: Lovely Kandice Salvador, Charity Owen, Johnny Goetz, Brett Vermuel, Dan Howes, Dave Werner, Nora Billheimer, Meliss Al-

leva, Christa Case, Ali Pereira, Daniel Troxell, Chris
James, Molly Brewer, Taylor Recny, Justin Vokuhl, Nick
Howes, Eric Hines, Dustin and Meredith Rickards, Tim
Riggs, Sandy Rodriguez, Netta Kramb, Mark Hines, Astrid Cobble, Angi Chapman, Kelsey King, Brandon Patton, Stephen Hansman, Kylie Pyrll, Deon Schoeman,
Lalo Contreras, Bronson Janey, Ethan Janey, and Reyes
Ramon.

At Doc Ford's on Captiva Island: Big Papa Mario
Zanolli, Lovely Julie Grzeszak, Shawn Scott, Joy Schawalder, Adam Traum, Alexandra Llanos, Chris Orr, Erica
DeBacker, Heather Walk, Jon Economy, Josie Lombardo,
Josh Kerschner, Katie Kovacs, Mary Head, Natalie Ramos, Patti Tesche, Ryan Body, Ryan Cook, Sarah Collins,
Shelbi Muske, Scott Hamilton, Tony Foreman, Yamily
Fernandez, Cheryl Erickson, Heather Hartford, Stephen
Day, Anastasia Moiseyev, Taylor Erickson, Ashley Doyle,
and Chelsea Bennett.

Finally, thanks to my sons Lee and Rogan for finishing
another book.

—*Randy Wayne White*
Telegraph Creek Gun Club
Babcock Ranch
Central Florida

DEEP
BLUE

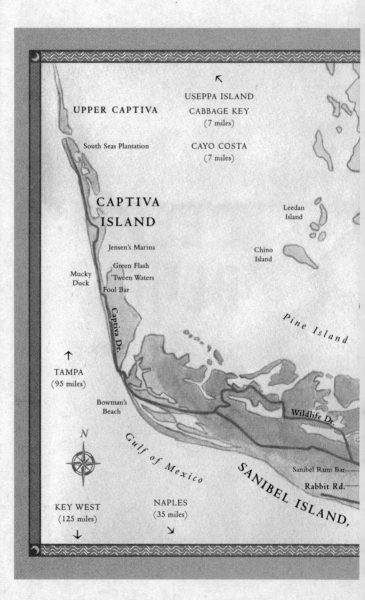

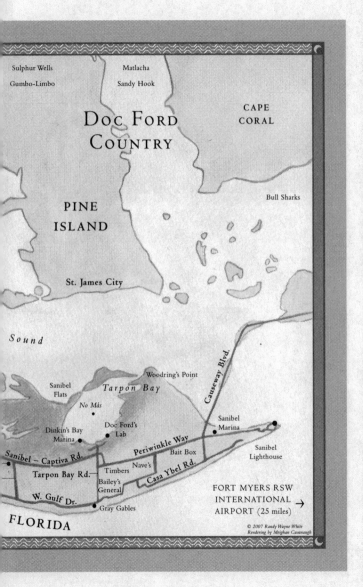

1

SITTING IN HIS LAB, MARION D. FORD ENTERED A numerical password and watched a hooded man execute three hostages with a ruby-handled knife. Different victims, different locations, and months apart, but always the same knife, never pausing to sharpen the blade.

How could that be?

The video had been edited by a pro, that's how.

The knife was of interest. He zoomed in. It had a curved blade like an antique sword, with a single ruby embedded in the hilt. On the pommel was a crowned triangle of silver, the symbol of Persian assassins from the time of the Crusades.

Ford opened a second link, entered a series of codes, and this time watched raw footage of the first two executions. This video wasn't available to networks or politicos—possibly, not even the White House, but Ford wasn't sure about that. He concentrated on the man wielding the knife: he was tall with corded forearms, but not muscular, his technique honed by video games and religious fantasies. He was a Muslim convert via Chicago, no name provided.

An egomaniac, Ford thought, *who played to the cameras but revealed himself in scenes that would be omitted— one where he used a cleaver.* Another: an adolescent yowl when he lofted his trophy, a severed head. Weird, the sound he made. A wild warble produced with a fluttering tongue. Like crows trapped in a cave.

There were two cameras from different angles, video rolling throughout.

The third video was different. The cameras had been paused several times, yet their POV remained unchanged. The scenes were choppy and sometimes blurry, which wasn't typical of raw footage. That struck Ford as odd. Digital cameras had autofocus. The hostage behaved differently, too. He was an aging Caucasian male, professorial-looking, who had to be dragged to the chopping block, unlike the others who had shown no fear.

Why?

Ford hadn't been supplied with his name either. That would come later—or wouldn't. It wasn't his job to care. He opened a notebook, pocket-sized, and wrote, in ciphered shorthand: "Victims #1 & #2 believed they were participating in a rehearsal."

He erased and revised: ". . . believed they were participating in *another* rehearsal," then paused to reflect before adding, "Victim #3 might not be dead."

He made more notes while he watched the footage again.

The link was time-sensitive. When the screen went blank, he rebooted his computer—a security precaution—before exiting the room, which contained rows of lighted aquaria, a microscope, shelves of beakers and chemicals, and, on the counter, a cylindrical Plexiglas tank in which a dozen sea jellies pulsed.

It was a moonless night on Sanibel Island, Florida, and breezy on this first eve in December. A good place to stand on the deck of a house built on stilts and piss over the railing into the water—a glittering stream that connected him, briefly, with the bay ten feet below.

Back at his desk, he sent an encrypted message that read *When?*

For the next several days, Ford began each morning with a long sunrise swim and sprint intervals on a butt-kicking machine called a VersaClimber. Pull-ups usually came next, but he'd broken a hand and torn his rotator cuff on a recent trip to Cuba. Only a partial tear, but he couldn't do the job he'd been assigned if it got much worse.

Still no word on Wednesday, so he tended to business, which included signing documents that made him half owner of a small seaplane, a Maule M-5 with a four-cylinder turbo. The fuselage was blue on white; leather seats and Plexiglas doors. The co-owner was an old friend, and, to celebrate, they flew to Shark River in the Everglades and caught snook.

There was another good low tide on Thursday. He was wading the flats with a fly rod when he finally received an encrypted reply to his question via satellite phone.

That night, on his bed, while his dog watched, he laid out two passports, an olive drab travel kit, a bug jacket, a hammock, $15,000 in cash, and some other things, including a knife, a laser pointer, and a small pistol, a Sig Sauer P938.

He'd returned from Cuba with that, too.

There were other weapons in a safe built into the floor—esoteric items, but better to travel light.

Ford was cleaning the pistol when a knock at the door shifted his reality from the covert life he had led for many years to the realities of a small marina, on a small island, where oddities (such as the odor of Hoppe's gun solvent) became an eager topic of gossip. So he stashed the pistol kit and offered his friend Mack, who owned Dinkin's Bay Marina, a chair and a cold bottle of beer.

Mack had some gossip of his own to share: a story that, under different circumstances, might have earned Ford's full attention.

"Our mystery Santa struck again," Mack said. He held the bottle to the light, then took a drink. "This time, he left five hundred bucks under the console of Eddie's boat. No idea who did it."

"Our Eddie?" Ford was dubious. Eddie DeAntoni, from New Jersey, was called Fast Eddie for a reason.

"I'd think it was gambling winnings, too, or somehow illegal, if it wasn't for the money Marta's little girl found on their houseboat. Same thing: a red candy-cane sort of box filled with old bills. Stacks of hundreds; all of them stiff, like they'd been soaked in water, then bleached. Nothing written on a card, just money. It's no accident, Doc. Sort of an early Christmas present, that's what Eddie thinks."

Everyone at the marina, and all of his friends, called Marion D. Ford "Doc."

The story about Marta Estéban and her daughters was true. Ford had helped the family escape from Cuba, which was why, two days ago, he'd been their unanimous choice to arbitrate on what ten-year-old Sabina had discovered in an anchor well and claimed as her own: $1,000 in cash. A big boost for a family in a strange country, not that their adoptive marina family wouldn't have looked after them anyway.

"He didn't make up a story just to con the IRS," Mack added. "There's a lot of eccentric rich folks on these islands. That's why I always tell our guys, 'Be nice even to the assholes, 'cause you never know who they'll mention in their will.'"

"Bleached bills left in the sun," Ford mused. "Or hidden underwater. Someplace shallow. I figured Sabina found a stash of old drug money."

"Bloody well possible," Mack, who was from New Zealand, said. "It couldn't have come at a better time for Fast Eddie. The fool gave away most all his lottery winnings, and his dive business has gone to hell 'cause of Hello, Dolly! Another few weeks with no charters and a cracked power head, he'd be bugger all."

Ford touched the stem of his glasses. "Dolly who?"

"Are you kidding? They quoted you in a newspaper story about her last week. Dolly, the shark. Some are calling her Hello, Dolly! like you're in the water, look around, and there she is. What are you gonna say? It's all anybody talks about."

"Why people need to give animals names—" Ford shook his head, mystified. "It's no different from some poor dog wearing a hat or scarf or sunglasses. I probably blocked the stupid name on purpose."

Dolly was a twenty-five-hundred-pound great white shark who'd been named by the biologists at Ocean Search who had tagged her. Ocean Search had tagged dozens of great whites with satellite chips that could be tracked via the Internet. Three weeks ago, the shark had surfaced off Sanibel Island, and might still be in the area, but sightings had not been confirmed. National headlines about her presence had affected tourism, and all but put local dive operators out of business.

Normally, Ford would have been happy to spend a beery evening with Mack discussing the subject. The marina's day-to-day problems—even when they included a great white shark—seemed sunny and manageable when compared to the cutthroat realities of the outside world.

He had a lot to do, though, so dropped a hint, saying, "I'm leaving for a conference in the morning or I'd offer you another beer."

"Anyplace interesting?"

Ford's eyes landed on the marina's black cat, curled in the corner, then moved to the cylindrical Plexiglas tank. "I'm presenting a paper on sea jellies. Near Orlando at one of those big no-name hotels that have a name. If you think about it, remind Jeth to tend to my aquariums after you lock the gate tomorrow. He's been more forgetful than usual."

"Jellyfish, that's what you'll talk about?"

"It's a misnomer. They're invertebrates, not fish."

Mack's expression asked *Who could possibly care?*

"Worldwide," Ford explained, "there've been megablooms of sea jellies and no one has figured out why. They thrive in polluted water, so that might have something to do with it. I can show you the data, if you're interested."

Mack's eyes dulled. He got up. "A hotel full of scientists," he said. "I've seen those female academic types. Like talking to textbooks with tits. But then, no one goes into your line of work for the excitement, do they?"

"I'll be back in a few days," Ford said, "but don't worry if I'm not." He got up. "Oh, and Hannah might stop to check on things. I told her she's welcome to overnight, if she wants."

Captain Hannah Smith, a top fly-fishing guide, was Ford's on-again, off-again lover.

Mack felt an obligation to remind him, "I hear she's been dating someone. Understandable, of course. That girl's a tough one to read—but aren't they all?"

Ford, moving toward the door, told him, "I've got to find my dog," and went outside.

The next afternoon, he landed in Mexico, near Tulum on the Yucatán Peninsula, and traveled south to where a resort the size of a cruise ship was anchored to a silver beach. A Florida biologist wouldn't be noticed among the eager tourist throngs, even if he loaded camping gear into a boat and didn't return for several days.

Ford paid cash for a locally built dugout—a *cayuca*—with an outboard. He pushed off before sunset.

South of the resort was the Bay of Ascension, a small inland sea pocked with islands and blue craters called cenotes that were openings to underground rivers. The craters tunneled far into the earth and exited—if they did—no one knew where.

Ford liked that. Along with sea jellies, he had been researching cenote formations in the Gulf of Mexico. Next week, he planned to dive a spot called the Captiva Blue Hole with a hipster friend of his, a boat bum mystic named Tomlinson, who was among the smartest men he knew. Also among the wealthiest, which is why some at the marina believed he was the mystery Santa.

Cenotes were a pleasant coincidence that Tomlinson would have interpreted as a karmic omen.

Good luck or bad?

Marion Ford didn't believe in either, for the same reason he had never believed in Santa Claus.

The resort was a five-star destination, a white concrete bluff encircled by bamboo-shack poverty where its employees lived—Mexican peasants the resort depended upon to keep tourists smiling. A typical worker-to-guest ratio was three to one. A typical income-to-income ratio wasn't available, but probably obscene.

Ford made use of the inequity, and the cash he'd brought, to create a loose safety net of goodwill. A very loose net, true, but worth the effort in an area where the resort was an island unto itself. Beyond the eastern fence was a hundred miles of jungle. Forty kilometers to the south, through littoral swamp and withering poverty, was Belize, once called British Honduras. Lying between was this shallow bay, with its islands and blue holes, where he had fashioned a remote base camp, as well as a separate spotting post, only a quarter mile from the hotel and beach.

Ford had done some exploring. He knew more about the area, he suspected, than the corporate bosses who'd built the place. But the bosses, by god, knew their clientele. The wealthy jetted in from around the world for the sun and sex and gambling, and the illusion of limitless excess, which, in the minds of some, equaled freedom. What the guests didn't realize was, despite the fixed smiles and amenities, the resort was an isolated outpost; a fragile life-support system for those who could not, would not, survive for long outside the property's gate.

Why would they bother? There was a long list of organized activities: yoga, golf, horseback riding, scuba trips to nearby atolls, billfish charters, and day trips to archaeological sites.

There were many such ruins. This was Mexico's ancient region of Quintana Roo, home of Mayan kings and gods, and temples that, amid choking vines, mocked them both, but were still worth the hundred-euro excursion fee (with a "traditional" lunch included).

Ford was more interested in solitary activities. Hopefully, the man he'd been sent to find would not be afraid

to go out alone. There was unsupervised snorkeling, kay-
aks and paddleboards for rent, a two-mile "nature trail"
that featured caged toucans and monkeys, and a lookout
pavilion over a pond where caimans—a variety of
alligator—waited patiently to be fed.

The pavilion was an ideal spot. Better yet, catch the
man alone while he was snorkeling the reef that lay midway between the beach and Ford's spotting post hidden
by trees.

It didn't happen.

He had been assigned an anonymous assistant; a "facilitator," housed somewhere on the resort property. By
the third day, he or she was getting antsy, too. Via encrypted phone, Ford received a text in Spanish: Máx is
leaving Wednesday, not Thursday. What now?

Máx, as in Máximo, the maximum bad guy. It was
code for the man he had been sent to find. Three days
ago, more information had been provided about the videos, including details about the victims and their killer.
The man with the ruby-handled knife was a failed actor
named David Abdel Cashmere, who'd converted to Islam
in 2010 at a Chicago mosque and was considered "homegrown." It was an important distinction to law enforce-
ment and terrorist organizations. *Homegrown* meant his
conversion was so profound, he would do anything, including harm his own country, to advance his cause. He
attended training camps for Lashkare-Taiba, a Pakistani
militant group, and for the Islamic State of Iraq and
Syria—ISIS. By 2013, he had emerged as an occasional
spokesman for an al-Qaeda cell in the UK. ISIS came to
power at about the same time.

In 2014, the FBI added Cashmere to the Most Wanted list, citing his involvement with a dozen bombings. They included Marriott hotels in Bali and Singapore, and several Christian day care centers in the Middle East—346 children killed.

In 2015, ISIS amped up Cashmere's status by naming him "American Senior Operative and Media Advisor," but under the name of Máximo al-Amriki. Soon afterward, the group began to release videos of far superior quality to the cell phone variety the group was known for. Beheadings took on a Hollywood polish.

Cashmere, the anonymous assassin, was becoming a star.

No surprise there, but the news about Cashmere's schedule change gave Ford only two more days.

He was sitting, cross-legged, in muck and mosquitoes, across from the beach, binoculars nearby. It was noon; had to be eighty in the shade. He threw back the hood of his bug jacket and jabbed a question into the phone: What's his afternoon schedule?

His ally, who went by the initials KAT, replied, Golfing w/financial backers. Tonight SOP: gets drunk, gambles, gets drunker, hires whores.

SOP stood for "standard operating procedure." KAT's meaning: *The man was never alone.*

Ford asked, Tomorrow?

> Breakfast meeting; massage; lunch
> meeting. Booked sunset parasailing;
> cocktail reception, more whores.

The unnecessary use of the word *whore* suggested either disapproval or contempt. Ford already suspected his ally was female, not that it mattered. He'd never worked with an assigned "facilitator"; didn't trust the concept or the judgment of anyone naïve enough to be involved. For that reason, he had led KAT to believe he was thirty miles north, staying in the touristy village Playa del Carmen, awaiting more intel before showing his face at the resort.

Now this.

The obvious move: wait until Cashmere was drunk, then pay an early-morning visit to his room. He would need a key and a diversion of some sort . . . And what else? While he considered that, he reread the text. A phrase jumped out:

>Booked sunset parasailing . . .

Hmm . . .

Ford mulled that over. All day, every day, a twin-engine boat towed a steady stream of thrill seekers belted to a parachute that soared two or three hundred feet into the air. One solitary person at a time. The boat was out there now, making the same damn boring circle, taking care not to stray too close to the bay, where there were shoals and reefs and thickets of mangrove trees laced into limestone.

Ford typed Stand by and picked up the binocs. The boat was the go-fast variety, a yellow V-hull with twin inboard engines built for ocean racing or running co-caine. It would be useless in shallow water.

Aboard was a crew of two, a Mexican driver and a spotter, and several European-looking passengers whose eyes were fixed on the sky. They reminded Ford of happy children flying a kite.

He swung the binoculars and tracked a hundred meters of yellow rope upward to the parachute. It was a massive scarlet umbrella attached by threads and a harness to a miniature person, who, when the binocs were focused, became a laughing blonde in a bikini. Laughing because she'd removed her top to taunt her male companions far below.

Ford lowered the binoculars but continued to observe. He'd been wrong about the boat steering a circle. It followed a triangular course because of prevailing winds; a steady northeasterly breeze. Steer downwind, even for a minute, the parachute might collapse. Apply too much throttle while steering across the wind, the rope might break.

He got to his feet, ducked through some brush, and exited bayside into quiet sunlight. The water was gelatin green, seldom more than a meter deep, and formed a waxen bond with distant islands and nearby hedgerows of rock and mangroves that separated the bay from deeper water.

No breeze here on the leeward side. At his feet was the spiraled egg casing from a whelk shell, dried and brittle. He returned to his spotting post; waited until the parasail swung to within a few hundred meters, then used segments of the egg casing to gauge the wind. One after another, he tossed segments into the air and watched them flutter to earth like miniature parachutes. With his boot, he marked off a grid. With his index finger, he measured variations of descent. All proportions were rough estimates, but close enough for what he had in mind.

His shoulder pack was a high-tech tactical bag, made by Vertx. In a hidden pocket, next to the Sig Sauer pistol, was the pocket laser. It resembled the gadgets used by college professors but was thicker, heavier, constructed of military-grade aluminum and carbon fiber. More like an LED flashlight, but with a security lock aft because it was to be used only in an emergency. The laser was powerful enough to signal an evacuation chopper, or even a satellite, sixty miles overhead, although it was designed to pinpoint targets for high-flying planes.

But was that all it could do?

Ford flipped up the tiny peep sight, twisted the lock to activate a sizzling green beam, and experimented on a nearby twig . . . then a mangrove root twenty meters away.

"Geezus . . . thing's dangerous," he muttered, then engaged the lock and hid it away.

Ford sent two messages, one to a man he trusted; another to his facilitator, which read Must meet tonight.

2

THAT EVENING, KAT, WHOSE LAPEL PIN SAID HER name was Astra, sat within a circle of tiki torches, legs crossed, silky blouse buttoned, waiting for him at the pool bar. All guests wore green wristbands. Hers was black or dark blue. She was an *Ecotour Advisor*, according to the badge over her breast.

Ford, thirty meters away, was hidden by bushes and shadows. They had agreed to meet at eight. It was now eight forty-five. Using binoculars, he watched KAT check and recheck her watch. Watched her drum glossy fingernails on the table. She signaled the waiter and ordered another daiquiri. The bartender poured double strength and served it without making eye contact.

The woman, an exotic-looking brunette, was accustomed to third-world deference and other perks of the ruling class. But she was not accustomed to being stood up. She opened her purse, retrieved what appeared to be an iPhone but wasn't, and typed a message in Spanish. The satellite phone in Ford's pocket vibrated in response. He read, You're late. I have a car if you need transport.

Instead of responding, he continued to observe, no longer using the binocs. Between the hotel and patio bar was a courtyard where, on this tropical night, small brown men on ladders wove lighted icicles through the palms, a shimmering umbrella effect. It was a reminder that even here, near the equator, Christmas was only a few weeks away.

Ford changed into tourist garb and hid his bag and swim fins in the bushes while the woman finished her drink. When she left in a huff, he followed. She made two stops before returning to a row of luxury cabanas that overlooked the beach. She was in Cinnamon Cottage— the buildings were named after spices or flowers—and her movements inside the cottage could be tracked by the lights she switched on. When he was convinced she was alone, he responded to her last text in English.

Mission scrubbed.

Through the window, he saw her hurry into the kitchenette, blouse unbuttoned, hair wrapped in a towel, and pick up the phone. Frustration; disapproval. It was in her mannerisms. She used her thumbs to type Why?

He didn't respond.

She demanded, On whose authority?

Ford wrote, End contact, and powered off his phone. A satellite log, which she might be able to access, would confirm that he could no longer receive messages. The same satellites would also confirm his location was in Playa del Carmen. He had stashed a little GPS transmitter behind the bumper of a public bus after syncing, then disabling, the GPS in his own phone.

Security cameras were a concern. In his pocket was a night vision monocular, or NVG, the newest incarnation made by American Technologies Network. Generation 4. No more halo glare around lights, and precise resolution. From his hiding spot, he could see details of the woman's face that weren't visible even after cleaning his glasses. Also visible was the until-now-invisible strobe of an infra-red camera in the courtyard. Two more cameras were mounted high atop an inland wing of the hotel.

A wall of jasmine separated the pool bar from the beach. Ford used the cover to move to an unlit shuffle-board court beyond the view of the cameras. From there, he could see the front entrance of the woman's cottage. Giant moths beat themselves against a porch light. Bats carved meteoric shadows; the siren throb of frogs regis-tered in the brain as silence.

KAT stepped out, wearing a white skirt and blouse with sandals, and walked briskly toward the main build-ing, which housed the reception area, shops, and a restau-rant. In her rush to leave, she failed to lock the cottage door. Ford slipped inside the room with its ceiling fans. The air smelled of shampoo and wicker. He planted a stickpin transmitter in the bedroom, another in the sitting room, where KAT's laptop was on a table but closed. Next to it was a pad of paper, with the resort's logo, the top sheet blank but veined from previous notes.

He tore off the top sheet, left the cottage, then jogged to catch up. The woman was just entering the lobby, up the steps through the double doors and past a security guard. A minute later, she reappeared on the terrace of the main bar. Soon she was joined by a tall man, wearing a white dinner jacket, no tie, and wire-rimmed glasses. A wisp of hair was combed across a head that was bald and unusually large.

The guy was a moneyed businessman, Ford guessed, but looked more like a professor from some elite liberal arts college. Twenty years older than KAT, which would have meant nothing under different circumstances, but the timing and contrast set off alarm bells.

There was something familiar about the guy.

He retreated to a safe place and used Gen-4 optics to confirm what his instincts wanted to deny: the man in the dinner jacket bore an uncanny resemblance to a kidnap victim in the videos, an Australian named Shepherd.

Unlikely, but a closer look was required. Twice, he moved to get a better view; used optical contrast and focus to study facial features that are difficult to disguise: earlobes, chin, eye sockets. Without digital analysis, there was no way to be certain, but the guy sure as hell looked like the aging Caucasian who had been dragged, kicking and screaming, to the executioner's knife.

Why would a kidnap victim conspire with terrorists to fake his own death?

Ford let the question go and skipped to something more important. If it was Shepherd, this was a setup and there could be only one reason: days ago, in the lab, he had written, "Victim #3 might still be alive."

That observation had been shared with only one person. Not that that meant too much. Procedure required the information to be passed along to at least a few others for analysis. If true, someone on the inside had leaked his notes about the videos. Or . . . their communications had been hacked.

That's what Ford wanted to believe, but, either way, this was serious.

He switched off the NVG monocular. In his career, no assignment had gone exactly as planned. The need to adapt was a Darwinian component that, in his mind, vindicated whatever action was required. If war—or life—were easy, the weak would have been eliminated from the gene pool eons ago. But this was *different*. This was the first assignment that had the feel of an elaborate trap.

The man in the white dinner jacket was laughing, a wineglass in his delicate hands. Ford watched them interact until he was convinced they shared a professional bond and, if they hadn't yet shared a bed, they soon would.

That was a plus. Emotional ties were a potential weakness. The bedroom required an investment of time. People talked. They let their guard down. And the stickpin transmitters he'd planted in the cottage were all but invisible.

He grabbed his bag and slipped away. If KAT and her colleague—or colleagues—hadn't figured out he wasn't in Playa del Carmen, they soon would.

The question was, should he run? Or sidestep the trap and kill the bait?

At ten p.m., security lights dimmed when the resort's generators switched to eco mode. Ford headed for the bayside marina, indifferent to the few vacationers who roamed the docks where yachts and trawlers were moored. His tourist disguise consisted of baggy shorts, sandals, a wristband fashioned from tape, and a golf visor, even though he didn't play golf and hoped he never would. The effect was as expected: security guards and guests ignored him.

Near a boat ramp where Jet Skis and paddleboards were stacked, a sign read

PARASAILING ADVENTURES
CONTACT OUR RECREATION SPECIALISTS!

Ford allowed the sign to lure him closer to the twin-engine go-fast boat that was empty but uncovered, afloat in a sheen of oil. A storage shed was nearby, door ajar: a room crammed with parasails and rope. Atop the mess, rolled into a ball, was the scarlet canopy he'd seen earlier. The parasail's harness, however, was still on the boat, looped over a winch that held several hundred yards of yellow braided nylon.

Ford didn't risk stepping aboard. There were rope samples enough in the shed.

His attention moved to the Jet Skis, then the stack of paddleboards. None of the boards approached the quality of his own favorite, an 11-foot carbon fiber Avanti, but there was a decent touring board hidden off to the side that was probably used by instructors. Ford claimed it with his eyes and did the same with a paddle.

He waited. From the direction of the pool bar came laughter and the tentative notes of a steel drum. A party was getting started.

Good timing.

When the docks emptied, he traded his tourist disguise for khaki shorts and paddled the board to his little dugout, anchored two hundred meters off the beach. He secured the board lengthwise, with barely room to sit.

The *cayuca* had a quiet little two-stroke kicker. A simple crank start, like an old lawn mower's, but powerful enough to rocket him back to camp through the silence of stars.

Behind, in the boat's wake, reggae music thrummed. The resort became a balloon of light that gradually deflated and was soon consumed by nightfall in Quintana Roo.

Ford's base camp was miles from his spotting post—a cave of buttonwoods and palms up a winding creek where the Maya had quarried limestone.

In the morning, when the sun was high enough, he carried snorkel gear into the creek to an abrupt drop-off and spent half an hour exploring the walls and bottom— uniformly fifteen feet deep, squared like a box. He saw pottery shards and at least one unbroken bowl that, beneath a film of algae, was decorated with designs of deepest azure. It had been a thousand years, perhaps two thousand years, since a human hand had made contact. Tempting, but he left the bowl and pottery shards undisturbed.

What he could not resist was retrieving what had been recorded in KAT's cottage last night. He dialed a thirteen-digit number, entered a code, and stared into the ancient quarry while the data was downloaded onto his phone. Ironic, the contrast in time and place and technology.

KAT had not brought the man in the white dinner jacket home, but she'd made a phone call. Perhaps to him, but maybe not. Ford listened to the one-sided conversation several times. It was only a minute long, but packed an emotional punch.

"Bitch," he said as he put the phone away. It was a word he seldom used.

Using the broad edge of a pencil, he shaded the sheet from the notepad he'd taken from the woman's cottage. Words began to emerge, amid much doodling, and sketches that might have been self-portraits.

Winslow Shepherd 802

Okay. This was proof. The man in the white dinner jacket was the Australian who'd supposedly been executed.

Pieces were taking shape.

Breakfast: wild bananas, instant coffee, and military lasagna from a box of MREs. While his jungle hammock and clothes dried in the sun, he experimented with the laser and lengths of rope he'd stolen the night before. What was the maximum distance a six-watt tactical laser would burn nylon? How long would it take?

After that, there was time to rig the paddleboard for an extended trip and hide it. He hoped the board wouldn't be necessary, but success favored those who devised options in advance of need.

The wind was of constant interest. At first light, it had freshened from the northeast, steady and dependable. Far out to sea, though, perhaps over a coral bank, or some unknown island, clouds of violet threatened rain before the day was done.

A storm would change everything, but it was pointless to fret. Around noon, he puttered to an isolated cenote; a black hole in the Earth sealed beneath luminous turquoise. The water was so clear, he tensed when he nudged the dugout over the lip of the crater, as if gravity would suck him downward.

He felt the same pleasant tension when he slipped over the side and jackknifed toward the bottom, but there was no bottom, only carousels of fish—barracuda, giant pompano, amberjack. They parted with predatory indifference to reveal limestone walls that spiraled into the inner blackness of the Earth.

At twenty feet, Ford latched onto a chunk of rock and gauged its weight before dropping it into the abyss. The rock tumbled in slow motion, with the resonance of skulls colliding, and started a brief landslide.

He looked up and imagined the little boat's anchor hooked to a larger boulder, the bitter end lashed to a dead but buoyant body. How far would the boulder tumble? At what depth, and for how many days, would a man's body dangle in suspension before predators reprocessed protein into fuel?

Adrift at the edge of the cenote was the largest predator thus far. It was a translucent blob the size of a garbage bag rooted to the tide by venomous strands, some of them twenty feet long. To sailors, it was a Portuguese man-of-war, but only a "jellyfish" to those who had not experienced the animal's sting. Each drifting filament was an arsenal of microscopic harpoons. They fired upon contact with living tissue, injecting doses of neurotoxin.

Sea jellies of all types were common here: bell domes and thimblesized dwarfs called sea lice, because they could slip under a swimsuit and cause a maddening rash. The animals—and they were *animals*—had no head, heart, eyes, brain, or ears; they were seawater-fueled by hunger and light, all highly efficient hunters. Man or beast, if sufficiently entangled, would soon be consumed.

In the afternoon, Ford dozed, or tried to, with the bug jacket pulled to his knees, hood drawn with only his nose protruding. Heat was a vaporous weight. It herded insects into the shade, so he zipped himself into his jungle hammock. His fear of being without reading material bordered on phobia. He had allowed himself only one sodden paperback, *Sea of Cortez*, by John Steinbeck. When he skipped to the part about biologist Ed Ricketts, a swatch of onionskin paper dropped free. Unfolded, he saw that it was a page written by his boat mystic pal, Tomlinson, who, apparently, had used it as a bookmarker. The man's elegant nineteenth-century penmanship was unmistakable.

What a goofball, Ford thought. The page was from the original manuscript of Tomlinson's best-known book, *One Fathom Above Sea Level.* The book had earned his pal an international following and a limitless supply of fawning devotees, many of them the bespectacled, pottery-throwing Berkeley types who were prone to sunburn yet seldom wore bras.

Ford had time on his hands. It wasn't his kind of book—he'd tried to wade through it before—but, what the hell?

He read:

My inner voice tells me I have no worth beyond the kindness I show strangers. It claims I make clown faces, and have no power to escape the puppeteer's strings.

Bullshit. The truth is this: my inner voice lies to me. The same is true if yours whispers that you are not worthy of happiness, or sufficiently attractive, or smart enough, or lack the strength to live without fear.

All lies.

Deep in the brain is a coward's crevice that values safety above all else. Why try? Why bother? Why risk any small success if failure is guaranteed?

Our silent voices are more trustworthy guides— bell note sounds that favor action over inactivity, and a life fully lived rather than a life of gray complacency.

How do I know this? Three weeks in an insane asylum have erased all the murky lines regarding

life, death, shit, and Shinola. Thus I take rubber
pencil in hand . . .

Enough. Ford slapped a mosquito; yawned while re-
folding the page and stored it in a hammock pocket provided for personal items. Another high-tech anomaly in
this ancient place was googling the name Winslow Shepherd.

There was much to learn.

He broke camp long before sunset and policed the
area until he was certain no modern spoor was left behind.

The little motorized boat—or the stolen paddleboard—
would be his last base camp before he fled Mexico.

3

WITHOUT A HOOD, THE MAN IDENTIFIED AS DAVID
Abdel Cashmere had the face of a bird; delicate, predatory, and vaguely reptilian, eyes framed by black hair. Surfing shorts, and shirtless, too, contrary to religious tenets, yet his pale ears signaled a devotion to modesty. In his adopted home of Indonesia, he would have worn a cap beneath a prayer scarf, a keffiyeh.

Quite a change for a failed actor from Chicago who had killed children with bombs and cut off human heads.

Yesterday, KAT had sent several candid snapshots for Ford to study. It was the same man, but was it the *right* man? This guy looked bigger, stronger, than in the videos. Maybe a substitute target was part of the setup, too.

Ford steadied the binoculars and messed with the focus. He was looking into the sun; glare blurred details. Aboard the towboat, the same Mexican crew was strapping the suspected assassin into a parachute harness. Also aboard were three Asian men, probably Chinese. This made sense if Cashmere and his group were here to secure funding. For decades, China had been quietly buying property—and loyalty—in third-world countries while the other major powers squabbled nose to nose.

Arming terrorists would be a solid investment in China's future.

With the Chicagoan, or whoever it was, kneeling on the launch deck, the boat idled into the wind. Ford focused on the boat's captain while the captain focused on the weather. Miles away, the squall, after building all afternoon, had grounded itself to the ocean with tentacles of rain. In high cumulus towers, lightning popped in silence. A slow, freshening wind rumbled ashore with the scent of tropic rain.

Ford knew what the captain was thinking: ocean squalls can linger for hours, then sprint landward. If you can see lightning, it can kill you. The trip should be canceled, but that would mean no pay, no tips. The captain probably had a family to support, and his boss would be pissed. Might even fire him for doing what was right instead of returning with smiling clients and a chunk of cash for the resort.

Ford empathized with the guy. He swung the binocs to the Asians, none of whom were smiling, nor did they appear aware of the squall. They were busy snapping photos of a jungle sunset, a ginger backdrop infused with jade. There was the illusion of osmosis; a siphoning of light. Slowly, the bay separating Ford from the resort was filled with a phosphorescent glow while the Earth darkened.

He scanned the beach, where a few vacationers, mostly couples, strolled. Nearby, he suspected, KAT and Winslow Shepherd were also watching. Perhaps with other confederates, but where and how many?

Down the shoreline, a rock jetty led into the harbor. Three men on Jet Skis were there in a tight little pod. Not moving, just sitting, as if enjoying the sunset. But they weren't there for the scenery. Their attention darted from the go-fast boat to the string of islands that separated the deep water from the bay where Ford waited. Serious, their manner, if not their expressions. The distance was too great for detail.

He let the binocs hang and cleaned his glasses. It was too late in the day for tourists to be on rental Jet Skis. Hell . . . it was too late in the day for parasailing, for that matter. Not with a squall building.

They're baiting me, he thought. *Or they want David Cashmere for themselves.*

He argued it back and forth. In any environment where there's a potential for danger, instinct is a more reliable guardian than intellect. If something doesn't feel right, it's not right. Ford knew this was true . . . sometimes, at least. Yet, he distrusted any behavior driven by emotion, and his uneasiness bore striking similarities to fear.

Vanity played a role, too. Last night, before midnight, KAT had told someone on the phone: "Mission scrubbed—you believe that? Whoever they sent is just another old-world hack; a dinosaur without a clue how things have changed. So"—the woman's laughter was irksome—"we'll just keep on keepin' on. His type is always so predictable."

Ford thought, *We will see.*

He focused the binocs on the man in the chute harness, who was still on the launch platform, a tad wobbly in the gusting wind, even with the mate helping to steady him.

A decision had to be made. Was the man actually the killer or some innocent bastard being served up as a target?

The captain gave a sudden thumbs-up and hit the throttle. The parasail blossomed huge over the boat and swept the man upward in a graceful arc. Ford didn't hear the familiar warbling cry, but he saw it: David Abdel Cashmere, mouth open, sailed high into the sky with his tongue fluttering.

In the video, the assassin had done the same while lofting a severed head.

Ford shouldered the bag and bulled through the mangroves to his boat, where he stopped long enough to cup his ears and listen. Wind freshened in gusts; mangrove leaves clattered, while, offshore, the squall rumbled.

No noisy Jet Skis, though.

He motored three hundred yards downwind to an island he had chosen earlier and dragged the *cayuca* out of sight.

*   *   *

From this new vantage point, he couldn't see the resort, or the beach, or even the towboat. But the parasail was there; a scarlet blossom in the twilight sky, high above the trees where Ford waited, the Vertx tactical bag at his feet.

A tree provided a leaning post. He braced the laser, snapped open the peep sight, and found the dangling appendage that was the Chicagoan-turned-terrorist. The rope linking Cashmere to the boat was a gray thread on a gray-green sky. Even at this distance, almost a quarter mile, the laser's beam would have permanently blinded the man if it swept across his eyes.

That was an option.

Ford lowered the laser and looked at the ground to confirm the weapon he'd selected was there. It was a twelve-inch sliver of wood from a black mangrove or lignum vitae tree that had been crystalized by salt and sunlight. No coroner would question how it had punctured the brain of a man who'd fallen from the sky.

Ford, wearing gloves, secured the stake in his belt and used the binoculars.

The parasail was still laboring into the wind. He could tell by the angle. It moved toward the squall clouds that sailed landward; black towers fulminant with rain and the day's last green light. After several seconds, lightning popped. Cashmere, in his harness, saw it, or maybe heard a sudden sizzle that spun his head around. Long seconds later, the thunder reached Ford, who took pleasure in the man's scared-shitless reaction. The failed actor began a frantic waving, motioning for the captain to bring him down.

Ford retrieved the laser and got ready.

The parasail appeared to pause. It tilted briefly, lost altitude as if threatening to collapse, then ballooned round and taut. This indicated the towboat had turned and would soon cross abeam the wind like a sailboat on a long reach.

The captain was preparing to reel in his client. First, he would have to circle into the wind and gradually slow while the boat's mate did the grunt work. It was a process that required several careful minutes because running across the wind put a tremendous strain on the chute's tackle.

Ford released the laser's safety lock, pressed the activation switch, and used the tree to steady his aim. Instantly, he was linked to the parasail by a needle-thin beam of light that was the same luminous green as the sky. A Star Wars character with an infinity sword—that image came into his mind.

Using tiny sawing strokes, he painted an area midway between Cashmere's feet and the water below. Even with the peep sight, there was no chance of cutting the rope. Ford was well aware of this fact. That's why he had packed to leave in advance. But if he got lucky, if the megawatt laser melted only a few nylon strands, then the combined force of wind and engine torque might do the rest. If the laser failed, nothing was lost. He would retreat unnoticed, undiscovered, and, hopefully, allowed to pursue terrorist converts—and KAT—another day.

But it happened. One instant, the parasail was aloft . . . the next instant, it was a deflating balloon that spiraled crazily toward the peep sight while Ford's eyes widened in surprise.

Holy shit.

He grabbed his bag and started through the mangroves toward where he guessed the parasail might impact. Foliage blocked his view, but the escalating sound of slapping canvas and Cashmere's screams kept him on track. Halfway across the island, limbs suddenly exploded en masse.

Ford stopped. An instant later, the tree canopy parted, as if cleaved by a plow, and the sky was displaced by a scarlet cloud that was the parasail. Tied to the end, like the tail on a broken kite, was David Cashmere.

Christ—still fifty yards to go. He confirmed the wooden stake was in his belt and charged ahead, while wind bubbled beneath the chute and dragged the man inland, where the rigging finally snagged. When it did, the guy suffered a hell of a jolt, then he hung there, legs dangling, dazed but conscious enough to hear someone crashing toward him.

The look on Cashmere's face when he saw a human being coming to his rescue—shock and child-like hope. He even managed a smile when he yelled, "Praise be to God—help me, brother."

Ford hollered back, "Don't unbuckle that harness," and kept going; vaulted over roots and used branches for support. He couldn't hear the Jet Skis yet, but knew they would come.

The failed actor recognized an American accent when he heard it, so he switched roles. "Goddamn, man, am I glad to see you. My face is bleedin'; arms, too. Help me get down from here."

Above, a branch snapped and tilted him in his harness.

Only then did he realize he was thirty feet off the ground. "Oh my god . . . help me, man. I can't—"

A rumble of thunder blotted whatever came next.

"Grab a limb," Ford yelled, and kept repeating advice while he battled the last few yards through the brush.

Cashmere tried; reached and kicked his legs, but lost his nerve when the parasail lifted several feet higher, then bounced him as if on a trampoline. "Oh . . . shit. Man, I'm gonna die up here if you don't—"

More thunder.

A tangle of yellow nylon snaked along the top of the tree canopy, the last of it draped among low branches. The guy was too far off the ground to reach without climbing trees too frail to climb, so Ford turned toward the rope. When he was halfway there, another gust dragged the parasail into the air while the man screamed, "Dude . . . do *somethin'*!"

Ford did. He trapped the rope, secured it around his waist, and began tractoring in line. Soon he was pulling at the ankles of the killer he had watched behead two innocent people—Cashmere, still in his harness and tangled in a shroud, while a storm tried to pull them both off the ground.

In the distance, the hornet whine of Jet Skis was now audible. Ford locked his hands on the harness and let his own weight pull the man down until they were nearly eye to eye, but it was a battle. The wind was getting stronger.

"Shut up and listen," Ford said, which didn't do the job, so he slapped the man—not hard—and nearly lost his grip on the straps.

Check Out Receipt

Regina - George Bothwell Branch
306-777-6091
http://www.reginalibrary.ca

Thursday, January 2, 2020
10:54:02 AM
25867

Item: 39085600600270
Title: Deep Blue
Material: Book
Due: 23/01/2020

Item: 39085401073834
Title: The agency
Material: Book
Due: 23/01/2020

Total items: 2

Thank you! If you would like to
update your library notification to
telephone, email or text message,
please contact your local library.

**Regina
Public
Library**

Support your library.
reginalibrary.ca/donate

**Regina
Public**

Eyes the color of almonds sparked. "Asshole. Why the hell you do that?"

No acting. This was the real David Abdel Cashmere.

Ford replied, "Do what I say, you'll be okay. First, dump your pockets."

"Pockets?"

"Do it."

"The hell I will. Get me down from here or I'll—"

The parasail shot upward. Ford had snaked an arm through the harness, so it lifted them both into the trees, where they spun, then yo-yoed.

"*Shit*." Ford got his legs wrapped around the guy's waist, then emptied the pockets himself—nothing but a plastic room key, a guest wristband, and some change that spilled to the ground, falling farther than expected when he looked down.

Some of the fight went out of the Chicagoan. "I'll do anything, man; *anything*, but don't let that wind take me again. Okay? Money—you want to get paid? Seriously, I'm rich . . ."

The temptation was to use the wooden spike and get it over with. Instead, Ford let the man talk while he switched his grip from the harness to the dragline, which trailed to the ground. When he got both hands tight, he pushed away, then swung close enough to grab a tree limb. After that, getting down was like descending a ladder, just slower, because he had to get a wrap, then pull the parasail down hand over hand. Finally, he dropped free, still holding the yellow line.

On the ground, he tied a quick-release loop around a sapling, then pulled Cashmere to within a few feet of safety. The whole time, the man had been hollering threats and orders, but suddenly realized what had happened.

"Hey—why'd you stop? I'm gonna get this damn harness off before—"

Ford yanked the rope free and let the parasail jolt to a tenuous stop a few feet higher. "I'm going to ask you a few questions. If you lie to me, I'll let you fly away."

The man's breathing changed. "Sure . . . anything. What do you want? But pull me down first."

Ford did—almost.

What he wanted was an answer to four questions, but he had to settle for three. That's when, through a montage of leaves, the first Jet Ski streaked past, followed by two more. The parasail was visible from the water. That was obvious from the sound of the engines. The skis slowed, and turned back, which is when Cashmere lost it and began screaming to the drivers for help.

Ford popped the quick-release knot and let the chute kite upward. If he let go, the Jet Skis would follow the parasail, not him. But he didn't let go. Instead, hand over hand, using the sapling as a brake, he hauled the man almost to the ground and looped another knot. Then he reached for the harness as if to unbuckle it. "David," he said. "That's your name, right? Your real name. David Cashmere. Where's your ruby-handled knife when you need it, David?"

Hearing his name frightened the guy more than the stream of wind battling to lift him skyward. "No. Really . . . it's not, you've got it all wrong. Who are you?"

Ford held the harness with one hand and moved the

other to his belt. "Those men you decapitated a few weeks ago—did you bother to tell them it wasn't a rehearsal?"

Cashmere looked away.

"What about the day care centers? More than three hundred dead children; body parts scattered for their parents to find. That doesn't bother you?"

Cashmere turned and said, "Fuck you. If you want to get paid—

Ford swung the wooden stake then, but it skipped off the man's temple. It took another glancing blow with the wind gusting, then a third try, this stroke cleaner—maybe—before the stake wedged deep enough to stick.

Strange . . . in those wild seconds, Ford heard no screams nor the thunk of wood seeking purchase. He heard nothing at all until the wind ripped the parasail from his hands.

After that, he stepped back and watched as the man was dragged through the high tree canopy into the sky, still kicking and screaming—but cognitive enough to pull the stake out of his face or temple and hurl it.

A very sloppy job.

Ford didn't want to think of that.

The northern point of the island offered a better view. From the bushes, he watched Jet Skis chase the parasail. David Cashmere became a rag doll that banged across the bay at an incredible speed. In half a mile, he would collide with trees on another island. If that didn't kill him, a twilight squall and open sea awaited on the other side.

No one could live through that.

Could he?

*   *   *

Ford waded the *cayuca* into the bay and started south, using islands to screen him from the beach and Jet Skis.

If he's not dead now, he soon will be.

In his head, he repeated that like a mantra.

Water had lost its turquoise glow to clouds overhead. Wind remained a goading force. It pushed him away from what some might refer to as the scene of the crime—if that twisted bastard survived.

He won't, impossible. He's drowned by now.

But what if the Jet Skis got to him first?

Ford was a rational man and had to admit it was possible. That led to a new level of reasoning: even if Cashmere was found dead, there were at least two people at the resort who might claim a crime had been committed.

KAT and Winslow Shepherd.

Maybe *that* was the setup.

Shit-oh-dear.

It was an expression used by his pal Tomlinson to denote any unexpected quandary that should be dealt with but was beyond control.

Shit-oh-dear, indeed. KAT and Shepherd could blame the murder on him—not that they'd seen him. They hadn't. But even if they accused a faceless, nameless American, it would make it difficult to get out of Mexico or even to cross the border into Belize.

Ford slowed the boat and argued with his better judgment. The rules of his profession could be summarized in three words, *hit-and-vanish*, meaning *Leave no trace and do not linger*. He'd never had to return to cover his tracks, so why start now?

Because of the damn woman, that's why. One of the three questions Cashmere had answered was about her.

KAT was a double agent. Or, at the very least, a traitor. More irksome was her condescending tone. He was a dinosaur, according to her, incapable of understanding how the world had changed. Even more offensive, he was predictable.

Bitch—he nearly said the word again but didn't. Emotion could not play a role in the decision he was about to make. No . . . a decision he had already made.

He stopped the boat, shifted his bags to adjust trim, then turned into the wind. Ahead was a waterfall of rain and sparkling lights that, in the far distance, marked the hotel resort.

An hour passed. The squall swept the bay clean of waves and flooded into the jungle, where clouds and rain were absorbed by foliage. Lightning tracked the storm's path with a silent strobe. A couple of times, he almost changed his mind. But then a medevac chopper landed, sat for twenty minutes with lights flaring, then banked away toward Playa del Carmen or somewhere on the Yucatán where there might be a hospital.

This suggested that Cashmere was still alive.

A short time later, a second, larger chopper buzzed the resort, then settled into a methodical search pattern miles to the south and southwest, which was the likely path of escape for an American agent on the run.

Ford knew they were looking for him.

Okay . . .

After that, there was no turning back.

He anchored the little boat a quarter mile off and swam to shore, carrying the gear he needed. In his head was a plan. Winslow Shepherd was in Room 802, according to the notepad he'd found near KAT's phone. She might join the professor there or they would rendezvous at her place.

This was all hopeful guesswork. Even so, he followed that linkage methodically. He used the laser to fry the sensors on two security cameras and entered Cinnamon Cottage. It was empty. He removed the thumbtack transmitters he'd planted and hurried on, destroying three more security cameras along the way.

Lightning strikes could be blamed for all sorts of technical failures.

There was only one building with eight floors—a stack of luxury suites set back from the beach and away from the noise of the pool bar, although the bar was closed and quiet after so much rain.

Ford took the stairs, rather than an elevator, and checked out the seventh floor to get a feel for the layout. These were the big-money suites, two to a floor, each with the requisite bedroom with a view.

Ocean views guaranteed balconies.

He went up the stairs to the eighth floor and stopped in a corridor that separated the suites and was open to the sea. No windows, no screens, just vaulted stucco supports with a railing that was within reach of each balcony.

He placed an ear against the door of Room 802. Quiet

inside. By straddling the railing, he crossed over to a back sliding door and entered Shepherd's apartment. The man had been a math professor, according to the Internet, and the professor had left a desk lamp on and the television.

Ford went through, then came back to the balcony. There was no need for additional light to inspect the balcony railing. It was made of wrought iron with a polished wooden banister, all anchored solidly in concrete.

From the tactical bag, he took a multi-tool and a stainless Randall survival knife that was strong enough to pry bolts out of walls. Not all the bolts; not even most. Just a few key supports to scare the hell out of them both, if needed. The rest, he would play by ear.

There was a closet off the kitchenette. That's where Ford was hiding when, around midnight, the professor and KAT entered. They locked the door behind them, then tumbled themselves into an embrace that carried them, both panting, to the floor, then a couch.

The next half hour was awkward but informative because they talked afterward. Talked a lot; some of it loud enough to hear.

Finally, the lovers walked naked out onto the balcony, where there were stars above the deep ocean gloom and where they lit what, from the vantage point of a closet, smelled like a joint.

The professor was offering the joint to KAT when Ford stepped out with a flashlight in one hand, the little 9mm pistol in the other.

He asked the professor, "Aren't you supposed to be dead?" then spoke to the woman, saying, "Okay. Tell me what happens next."

4

MACK WAS IN THE MARINA OFFICE ON SUNDAY,
the second week of December, when Tomlinson entered,
holding a leash attached to a large dog. The dog, a retriever of some sort, was prone to destructive behavior if
his owner, Marion Ford, left the island for more than a
few days.

It had been eight.

Mack tilted his bifocals up from *The Wall Street Journal.* "Instead of fidgeting, just go ahead and give me the
bad news."

Tomlinson had a habit of chewing strands of hair when

he was nervous or using a finger to doodle designs on his temple. He was doing both. "Whoa. Whatever happened to a simple 'Hello'?"

Mack frowned at the dog. "What did he do this time? No, get to the important part. If insurance won't cover it, how much is this gonna cost me until Doc gets back? I've about had it with pets and children around here. Did he chew the lines off a dinghy or drag in more canoes?"

Tomlinson said, "Shallow up, man. Yeah, he took something, but unless someone called the cops, no one has to know. Doc's what I came to ask about. Any word from him?"

Mack swung around in his swivel chair. "I *knew* it."

The marina office was in a two-story building with large windows overlooking Dinkin's Bay, a brackish lake ringed by mangroves and oyster bars; a few houses, way out there on Woodring Point. Outside the windows, on the pine deck, was a walk-in freezer and a fish-cleaning table that serviced the little restaurant next door. The deck narrowed to make room for more mangroves, then branched off into dockage, where, in the deepest part of the basin, vessels large enough to live aboard sat in a neat row. That was A dock. Docks B and C fingered away from the shoreline.

"Nothing missing," Mack said, then paused while his eyes lingered on a small man, shirtless, all bone and muscle, out there alone, standing in a canoe.

Standing?

Yes—the silly fool. The bay was a submerged plateau of turtle grass and sand potholes, seldom deeper than a person's head, but deep enough if the person was only five-four and couldn't swim.

"What the bloody hell is Figgy doing out there without a life jacket?"

Tomlinson didn't have to look. Mack was talking about Figueroa Casanova, a Cuban whose size and IQ had been stunted during childhood but who was still smart and funny in odd ways. He, too, had come to Florida with Marion Ford's help.

"He's fishing. Using a handline. Don't worry about him. Figgy used to paddle out in an inner tube and fish the Gulf Stream."

"Well, someone should tell the crazy fool that six feet of water is as good as a mile for a man who's barely five feet tall." Mack's eyes refocused. He stood. "I'll be damned . . . a boat *is* missing. See? The Brazilian's boat. It's gone from its slip."

The Brazilian was Vargas Diemer, a jet-setter who owned *Seduci*, a 55-foot Lamberti custom yacht. Tomlinson chuckled. "Are you high? It would take a tug to tow that thing. Vargas probably went for a sunset cruise. What about Doc? Have you heard from him? We're supposed to go diving tomorrow, and that guy has never missed an appointment in his life without calling ahead."

Mack had other things on his mind. "If it floats, flies, or isn't tied down, that dog is the devil with fur."

On the counter was a black cat, Crunch & Des—named for two characters in novels by Philip Wylie. The cat stood and arched his back to invite a scratch, but Mack ignored him.

"Thieving dingo," Mack muttered and tossed his cigar on the counter as if his day had been ruined. He exited the side door and reappeared through the front, his head bobbing above shelves that were stocked with hats, fishing tackle, peanuts, peanut butter crackers, and a mannequin wearing a T-shirt that read

SANIBEL ISLAND
ZEN CITY

"I give up," he said and took his seat behind the counter. "Get him out of here before he shakes water all over everything."

Tomlinson gave the leash a couple of tugs, then backed out the door, coaxing, "Come . . . Come on. That'a boy," speaking in a respectful tone until the dog sprinted past him, ripped the leash from his hand, and vaulted over a railing into the bay. A dozen gulls spooked to flight, screaming as they soared overhead.

"I've got a shock collar," Tomlinson yelled from the door. *And I know how to use it!*

Mack turned away. "Now, for the last time—what did the dog steal?"

"It's not like it's grand theft . . . Come on, I'll show you." He stepped back so Mack could exit, then spun a section of *The Wall Street Journal* around. A small headline, inside page, appealed to his taste in conspiracy theories:

**CHINA CLAIMS
TWO U.S. SPIES
KILLED IN MEXICO**

Speaking to Mack's back, he said, "Did you read this?"
"No . . . just the stocks."

"You should. I'm telling you, people of the world are fed up with America's bullshit. Fascists will blame the Muslims or—" Tomlinson stopped to rescan details because it occurred to him the name Marion Ford might appear.

It did not. Even so, he dropped the subject.

"I hope you don't spout that hippie political drivel around the guides," Mack said. "Especially if you plan on stealing their beer. Very patriotic, those buggers, and not in the best of moods. Hello, Dolly! may have hurt the dive business, but she was a boon to the fishing guides."

"What do you mean?"

Dolly, the great white, had faded from the headlines over the last three weeks, but Tomlinson felt like he'd missed something. "I thought tourism was way off."

"Haven't you noticed? Everyone *thought* it would kill tourism, but it was just the opposite. The guides were booked solid just on the chance customers might get a look. Same with the hotels and restaurants. Now they all miss her.

"On the other hand," Mack added in a kinder tone, "I have a pretty good idea who's giving away those stacks of hundred-dollar bills. Our mysterious Father Christmas deserves a pass, I suppose, to say any damn thing he wants. For a while anyway."

Tomlinson didn't understand that either, nor the wink in Mack's voice. "Has to be a very generous citizen. Who is it?"

Mack chuckled.

"Seriously. Tell me his name. Or her. Who are you talking about?"

More laughter.

Tomlinson, looking at Mack, shrugged, and said, "I need to start paying attention."

They were approaching the bait tank. It was a wooden reservoir covered by screens on hinges, all connected by white PVC to a pump that chugged and hissed and filled the air with ozone.

Behind the tanks, near a picnic table, was the ice maker where the guides stashed their beer. Tomlinson opened the lid, dug around, and pulled out two green bottles of Steinlager. "Anyway, the dog—I hid what he took in there." He indicated the tackle shed. "Want one?"

"Nope," Mack replied but accepted a bottle by rote, then leaned his bulk against the wall. "Well, open the blinkin' door and show me."

It was five p.m. The sun was low in the west, a bland hole in the sky that meant the cold front was nearly gone. It was breezy; a bite of autumn in the air, to Tomlinson, who was the unlikely progeny of Long Island industrialists. He stepped out of the shed carrying two figurines, both of them plastic cows. Not life-sized, but big enough.

"What the bloody hell?"

Tomlinson placed the figurines side by side on the deck. "Until I checked, I figured the dog snatched them from that restaurant on Periwinkle."

"The Island Cow?"

"But I was wrong. I talked to one of the managers. All their cows are where they belong."

Mack was relieved—sort of. "Who else around here has plastic animals?" He hefted one off the ground. "Feels like pretty good quality; commercial-grade, I'd say.

What's this, a Holstein? Holsteins are black and white. Back home in New Zealand, folks raised them for milk in the Southland." He turned the figurine upside down. "Yep . . . must be a Holstein."

Tomlinson had a theory, but his attention had swung to the mouth of Dinkin's Bay, where a vessel was entering. Elegant lines, a bone-white hull, and a flybridge taller than the palms that grew in clusters on Woodring Point. It was the Brazilian, Vargas Diemer, on his million-dollar yacht.

"There he comes," Tomlinson said.

Mack misunderstood and checked the parking lot, where, coincidentally, outside the gate, an old Chevy pickup was backing into its usual place. "I'll be damned," he said. "Doc's finally home from Orlando."

"No way."

"Yeah. There's his truck."

Tomlinson perked up a little when he saw the familiar blue Chevy, but he'd meant there was no way Ford would spend a week in Orlando. But he played along. "Goofy World is a heck of a place to hold a conference on jellyfish. Some find that hard to believe."

"I don't put much stock in what anyone says around here," Mack said. "Bunch'a gossips, talking about how he packs his bags and disappears. Doc, I'm sayin', like, he deals in marijuana or something."

Tomlinson mouthed the question, *Marijuana?*

"Or he has a wife and family somewhere. You know how these stories get started. Or he's doing volunteer work for some church. Goes off on retreats or service missions."

Tomlinson was shaking his head now. "*Our* Doc?"

"Personally—I know we've talked about this—I think it has something to do with the way he behaves toward women. Doc's a good man; he's got a chivalrous streak, so he keeps the details to himself. Plus, he's still got a bad case for Hannah, so he doesn't want her to know he's screwing around." He was inspecting the other figurine, a brown plastic cow with white patches. "Jersey, you think?"

"Naw," Tomlinson said. "The only friend he has from Jersey is Fast Eddie." He was watching Ford shoulder two khaki bags from the truck, limping a little like he was tired. "Let's give him some time to settle in before we hit him with downers about the dog."

"Downers? Oh. The dog's not a problem unless he leaves you in charge. She'd be a better choice." Mack pointed to the docks and gave a little wave. "Animals have a sixth sense about who they should mind and who they shouldn't. No offense."

"Totally out of sync, the two of us," Tomlinson agreed. "Most animals, I have like a telekinetic link, but that curly-coated bastard has the sensitivity of two buckets." He looked to where Mack had waved.

Moored midway down A dock between a gleaming Grand Banks trawler and a soggy old Chris-Craft was a small houseboat, with curtained windows and wash hanging on a line. A little girl, with black braids and jeans, stood at the railing. She acknowledged the men with a dismissive wave, then returned to watching the dog swim in what appeared to be pointless circles. It was Sabina, Marta Estéban's younger daughter, the ten-year-old who'd found a pile of cash in a boat that wasn't worth what had been hidden there.

Tomlinson checked on Ford's progress. The man had disappeared down the path to his stilthouse but had left a truck door open. "Think I'll go say *Buenos días*," he said.

"Tell him welcome back for me. Oh—the fishing guides radioed in and they're bringing a couple of buckets of oysters. And pen shells. I know Doc likes pen shells. I'm going to start the grill now."

Tomlinson replied, "Sure," even though he'd meant to say *Buenos días* to the girl, Sabina, not Ford. Without her help, there wasn't much chance of getting that damn dog hosed, washed, and dried.

Plus, the girl's mother, Marta, might be home.

Tomlinson liked Marta. Everyone at Dinkin's Bay liked Marta, even the women, which was approval of the highest sort. Marta, late thirties, had labored in Cuba's tobacco fields before her husband ran off—a survive-or-wither life that was visible in her rough hands and the depth of her eyes. Yet she exuded a smoky vitality that, in Tomlinson's mind, promised a lushness of flesh akin to tropical fruit. Mangoes came to mind.

"Would you mind calling the dog?" he asked the girl when he got to A dock.

"I don't speak English," she replied in English. "Call him yourself. You're lazy."

Tomlinson stroked his goatee to cover his amusement. He was fond of Sabina, too. Like most difficult children, the wisdom she possessed was at war with the lack of wisdom in others. Especially adults.

"I'll give you a dollar. Two dollars, if you'll help me wash and dry him before Doc comes out."

"Profiteers," she said. "Is everything about money with you?" She paused to study Ford's house, which was an old house with a tin roof built on stilts a hundred yards down the mangrove shore. "Marion has"—she had to search for the right word in English—"is delivered?"

"Returned, delivered. Yeah, he's back. And you couldn't be more right about the money thing. Sabina—" Tomlinson waited for the girl to look at him, but she didn't.

"How about five dollars?" the girl countered and flung a bony hand in the direction of the stilthouse. "I was rich until Marion interfered. A thousand U.S. dollars; piles too big to carry. Then he made me share with my idiot sister, but what he really did was give it to Mama, because I haven't seen that money since. Now I'm poor and want five dollars."

"Deal," Tomlinson said, while the girl talked on in a mix of English and Spanish: "I will call the dog and make him sit. But you'll do all the work and pay for my shampoo. And if he growls when I tie ribbons around his ears, you have to hold his mouth closed. Promise?"

This was asking a little much. "Uhh . . . I should probably speak to your mom before we make any legally binding agreements. Is she around?"

"Marta is none of your business, so stay away from her. You make Mama nervous. When she's nervous, she changes into her new dress or takes a shower."

"Marta?"

"I'm old enough to call my mother by her name." Sabina turned an ear to the houseboat, which was old and motorless, but had a fresh coat of blue paint. "Yes . . . showering, like she's doing now. I'm surprised there's water left because Maribel spent an hour primping before her rude friends came with bicycles."

Maribel was the older sister who shared her mother's beauty but not Sabina's sharp edge.

"Marta gets nervous, huh?" Tomlinson tried to conceal his interest by feigning interest in the bay, where the dog was chasing the shadows of birds that soared above. "I suppose it's only natural she gets a little flustered when a man comes calling. That's probably true no matter who it is. Some tall, handsome hombre, or—"

"Not handsome," Sabina said. "I'm talking about you. And Marion, of course." She peeked up at the sun, fought off a sneeze, then looked at the water and made a circular motion. "Round and round and round," she said. "He's chasing an airplane that he thinks is a fish. That dog is no smarter than certain adults I've met."

This close to sunset, all the rental boats were in, and the guides would be back soon to fillet sea trout and mackerel and whatever else their clients had iced for dinner. Already a cloud of gulls and terns battled for air supremacy above the docks and the panting dog.

"He's chasing bird shadows," Tomlinson said, "not airplanes."

"I'm not a child. I know what a bird is. Perhaps I can teach you." She pointed at the sky. "Birds flap their wings and have feathers. But *that's* an airplane. See? No feathers."

Tomlinson shielded his eyes from the sun. It took him a moment to locate an object that flew higher than the gulls, but still low enough to cast a shadow on the water. It wasn't an airplane. It was round and flat, about the size of a coffee table. "I'll be go to hell," he said. "What the . . . it's a freakin' flying saucer."

"Stop your swearing," the girl warned, "and admit you were wrong. It's been flying in circles above our boat for the longest time. What I've been wondering is where they found a pilot small enough to drive such an airplane."

"Not your boat. It looks like it's hovering over—" Tomlinson pointed to Figgy, who was still fishing from a canoe midway between the marina and Ford's house. "But that doesn't make sense, so it's probably—" He got his bearings so he wouldn't fall off the dock, then strode toward the object, hands shielding his eyes. "Hey . . . it's a drone. A goddamn drone."

The girl pirouetted onto the dock, and followed. "It makes no noise," she said. "That's why only the dog and I saw it. How can an airplane fly without an engine?"

"Damn thing's no toy," Tomlinson remarked. "It's circling the marina, probably shooting video." He took another few steps. "Sonuvabitch, yeah. Sending video to some narc hidden around here someplace. Goddamn feds, I bet. They've had their noses on my act for years."

Sabina's good instincts told her it was a bad time to scold the man again for profanity.

"Unless . . ." Tomlinson was thinking out loud. He thrust his hands out, a signal for the girl to stop. "Whoa. Don't say a word for a second. Just watch."

Sabina followed the man's gaze and understood.

Down the shoreline, partially screened by trees, the back window of Marion Ford's lab opened, but not wide. Ford's face filled the space long enough for him to adjust his glasses, then only his hands were there, a small dark object in one of them.

"What's he doing?"

"Quiet."

"Is that a . . . ? What's he holding, a flashlight?"

Tomlinson pivoted and shooed the girl away. "We're going back to your houseboat."

"But I want to see!"

"Call the dog," he told her. "The dog will stay with you until I talk to Doc and see what's up." He spoke in a tone Sabina had never heard him use before. Not mean, not bossy, but serious, like one adult speaking to another.

Sabina started to reply when one of the tourists hollered, "Oh my god . . . look at that!"

She turned; Tomlinson turned, too, and they both watched the flying saucer tumble down, down, down until it smacked the water with the sound of sheet metal falling from the sky.

It hit close, very close, to the little Cuban, Figueroa, who, surprised by the sound—or the sudden wake—tumbled backwards out of the canoe.

The dog saw it all, and took off through the water. He cut a beeline wake, only the animal's head and rudder-tail showing until he had crossed forty yards of open bay. By then, the drone had sunk, but Figueroa was still fighting to keep his nose above water.

For a second, it looked like the dog was going to rescue the Cuban. Instead, he ignored Figgy and went after the drone, which had gone under a couple of canoe lengths beyond, where there were bubbles. The dog tilted his butt high and clawed toward the bottom. Three times he dived to search for the thing, spouting water from his nose like a dragon when he resurfaced.

The fourth dive, the dog went down and didn't come up.

"This is bad," Tomlinson said, kicking off his Birkenstocks.

Down shore, Marion Ford hit the water, and was swimming before his face cleared the surface.

5

FORD KNEW THE DOG WAS ALIVE, STRUGGLING ON the bottom, because the surface boiled where he'd gone down. Trouble was, not far away, the Cuban was struggling, too, slapping water the way children do when they can't swim. He was trying to get to the canoe, which had drifted just out of his reach.

Ford knew Tomlinson was behind him, swimming hard but not fast. His pal had too much hair, and those baggy shorts created drag for the elegant windmill strokes of someone who'd participated in water ballet until it got too competitive. He would have to let the dog drown unless he could yell some sense into the Cuban.

Ford yelled in Spanish, "Figgy. Stand up, for christ's sake, it's shallow!"

The Cuban made panicky gurgling sounds and managed the word *shark* a couple of times, even though the great white was too big to enter Dinkin's Bay, or most other bays in Southwest Florida.

"Goddamn it, take a deep breath . . . use your feet." To demonstrate, Ford speared his legs down in what was maybe five feet of water, stood for a microsecond, then used the bottom to dolphin forward, almost to the dog. When he looked up, Figgy had done it; was staggering like a drunk in water up to his chest.

Ford eyeballed the spot where the dog had gone under—only remnants of a surface boil left—and did another dolphin dive. He used his hands to feel along the bottom, which was sandy, spiked with sea grasses and tunicates. Visibility was never great in the bay, but it was better in winter, which was the dry season. Even without a mask, he could make out blurry images.

Finally, there was the dog: a black shadow on a plain of gray marl. Ford's hands found fur; got his arms around a bony chest, but the dog's body resisted when he tried to lift. He got his feet under him and used his legs to heft what felt like a great weight, which was mystifying because the dog weighed less than eighty pounds. All bone and muscle, true, but why the hell . . . ?

When he got the animal to the surface, he understood. The dog's collar had looped around something, the landing gear of what looked like an aircraft. The object was not heavy, but wide and round and solid, which had turned it into an anchor.

He yanked the aircraft free and let it sink, then took stock. The dog lay limp with his mouth open, long tongue dangling; eyes closed, and he wasn't breathing. Warm, however, the animal's furred weight, and dense with muscle. He cradled the dog, tilted his head, then squeezed but not so hard that ribs broke. Water and bubbles vomited from the mouth. He repeated that until there was nothing more to jettison.

"Come on—wake up." Talking in the stern way of a trainer giving commands while he thumbed open one eye, then the other. No gleam of consciousness looked back.

Ford knew CPR. But on a dog? He tried anyway: mouth and airway appeared to be clear. A bear hug allowed several quick chest compressions . . . then he cupped his hands around the retriever's snout and exhaled mightily.

The furry chest inflated a little, but not much. He checked for a heartbeat. None.

Several times, he repeated the process while the dog sagged in his arms, warm, dense, and still. So close to life, yet not alive. Many a night, that warmth had caused irritation when the dog demanded bed space, particularly on summer nights—a breach of conduct to which Ford provided stern words, but ignored when the lights went out, or the temperature dropped.

He'd lost track of time. How many minutes had gone by? Four . . . six?

More time passed before he finally told himself, *Stop*.

As he knew better than most, the demarcation between life and death is a fragile veneer; a thread parted by
a single breath. On one side lay the present; on the other
the past, irreversible.

"Is he okay?"

With all Tomlinson's splashing, Ford shouldn't have
been startled, but he was. "Not breathing."

"What?"

Ford realized he hadn't actually spoken those words.
He'd tried, but they hadn't made it past his lips. "He's,
uhh . . . he's not . . . his respiration stopped."

"Give him to me, I'll do it."

He thrust out the dog so Tomlinson could take him,
then busied himself using his feet to relocate the sunken
drone.

Tomlinson was near tears. "Cripes! This is like Batman
drowning . . . he couldn't . . . *Damn it*. Wake up, boy,
come on now. He'll be okay, Doc, you just wait." The
man was silent for several seconds, then yelled, "Figgy,
get your ass over here!" He went silent again.

The Cuban had overtaken the canoe. "This boat is a
worthless turd," he called over. "It won't let me in."

Tomlinson's Spanish was good enough to say, "Walk
the freakin' thing over here, you dumb shit. Get the lead
out."

Ford's toes found the drone. He kept his back to the
marina and lifted the thing to the surface, but just for a
quick look. It was an expensive, high-tech piece of ma-
chinery. No obvious markings. The carapace was carbon
fiber. It bristled with eight propellers and the appendages
of telemetry. Two . . . no, three mini-camera eyes were

mounted on robotic cams, and a cockscomb of antennas along the spine.

The genius of technology, as always, was in the parroting of nature. In this case, a flying crab.

Eight days he'd been away, the last three nothing but buttbusting travel, not one minute of sleep. Now to return to this?

A reasonable way to refocus was to haul the drone ashore and give it a careful inspection. Where had it come from? Why had a military-grade drone—an unmanned aerial vehicle; UAV—been circling his house?

The problem was, Ford knew the answer and he didn't want anyone—especially Mack or others watching from the docks—to figure out the truth. Someone—an organization or its hireling—had sent an aircraft to monitor his lab. They wanted to know if he was still alive and if he'd made it back to Sanibel.

His eyes moved to the marina, where Mack stood apart from a cluster of tourists. A few locals had been alerted, too. Rhonda and JoAnn, middle-aged women, were on the bow of *Tiger Lilly*, an old, ornate Chris-Craft that was their floating home. Marta Estéban and her daughter Sabina watched from the dock. A couple of other familiar faces were there, too. All friends.

A UAV required a pilot linked via a computer. He focused on the unfamiliar faces, presumably tourists. There were eight . . . no, nine. Young parents with a couple of kids; some mom-and-pop retirees; a fit-looking threesome dressed in stretchy cyclist outfits. A male cyclist and two others: one of them, unmistakably female; the other, no clue.

None carried a briefcase of the sort necessary to house a computer control system. And only the woman cyclist was concerned enough to jog across the deck, where she jumped down among the mangroves to get a closer look.

Maybe she was a UAV hobbyist and it was her aircraft. Ford hoped this was true.

He kept his back to Tomlinson and tuned out a monologue that oscillated between wild profanities and gentle spiritual negotiation. By then, the Cuban, Figgy, had gotten involved, saying, "Brother, I don't think you're doing that right unless you're kissing the dog good-bye. You never been to a cockfight?"

The absurdity of this caused Ford to turn. The two men had laid the retriever across the bow of the canoe, Figgy holding the dog's rear while Tomlinson did compressions and blew air into the dog's mouth. His pal looked up long enough to say to Figgy in Spanish, "Do you mind? I'm trying to concentrate here."

"Just a question, man. I never liked this dog much. He growled and pissed on my foot once. Why you think a dog do that? Trotted up, sniffed, and pissed right on my—"

Tomlinson said, "Hold the damn canoe steady. Check his heart. Do you feel anything?"

Figgy continued talking. "Yes, and me wearing my new shoes."

"His heart's beating?"

"No. Yes, he pissed on my shoe, so I don't like this dog. But if you trying to breathe life into an animal, brother, you not doing it right. That's why I ask about cockfights. You never been to a cockfight?"

More compressions, another attempt to blow air into the retriever's mouth. Tomlinson, exasperated, said, "If you know something I don't, show me."

"Ain't no roosters around to show you, man. I'm talking about fighting cocks. I had a bunch one time. They didn't fight worth a damn, so I had to breathe lots of them back to life."

"You breathed *roosters* back to life."

The Cuban asked, "What else you gonna do? They too stringy to eat, man."

"He's all yours," Tomlinson said and waited to trade places.

Ford had had enough. "Carry him back to shore—but not in front of those kids. Into the mangroves by my place, take him there." He pretended to kick around with his feet. "That little plane—whatever it was the dog was chasing—I can't find it. So to hell with it."

Tomlinson gave him an odd look while the Cuban, slogging around to change sides, said, "Okay. But if he bites me, it's your fault."

Figgy's CPR technique was unorthodox. He clamped the dog's jaws shut and opened his own jaws wide enough to insert half of the dog's snout into his mouth. First time, he damn near gagged. Pulled away, saying, "Dog snot . . . *mierda*, man," but went right back at it, blowing air while Tomlinson worked the dog's ribs like a bellows.

How long had it been?

Ford wondered about that, irritated with himself. When something of potential importance occurred—a gunshot, a scream, a lightning strike—he automatically looked at his watch. It's the way he was. Not this time. It felt like a lot more than five or six minutes had passed. Add to that the minute or two the dog had been trapped underwater.

If true, further efforts to revive the retriever were futile. Worse, it struck him as a pointless indignity to man or animal—in this case, a dog who, while not spectacularly bright, had possessed quirks that Ford, like most dog owners, found endearing because they either were qualities he lacked in himself, or mirrored strengths that appealed to his own vanity.

"That's enough," he said finally. "The dog's dead. Don't make more of it than it is."

The UAV was on its side between his feet. He squatted, pretending to adjust a shoe, and picked it up, but kept it beneath the surface when he started toward shore.

"Marion?" Another odd look from Tomlinson. "You okay? How long has it been since you got any sleep?"

Ford didn't respond. Slogging toward them in a hurry was the woman cyclist in blue-and-gold racing tights, no helmet, chestnut hair tied back. Tall with broad shoulders, and busty enough to give the illusion of narrow hips until the water deepened. Without stopping, she called, "Hey. Hey! Someone said there's a dog out here in trouble."

No mention of the drone.

"Slide your feet," Ford called back. "Even if you're wearing shoes, slide your feet. A lot of stingrays on the bottom out here."

She kept coming, but took longer strides like a skater. "What about the dog?"

"It's too late unless you're a veterinarian. Too late even if you are."

"I am," she said. "Are you sure?"

This was unexpected. "You're a vet?"

"My office is in Sarasota, but maybe I can help. Are you sure he's gone?"

Ford floated the UAV drone behind him, even though it was underwater. "No, he's right there. He drowned; got snagged on something and was down too long."

That struck the woman as insensitive. She stopped and squinted, looking beyond him to the canoe—nearsighted or her contacts weren't up to the task. "Thank god, the owner hasn't given up," she said, then abandoned her skating technique, got her knees up, and ran past him. Stumbled only once; kept her balance and covered a lot of ground. An athlete. Soccer or track; possibly, a hurdler.

She didn't hear him respond, "I am the owner."

Ford watched the woman until the angle threatened to bring the dog's body into view, then turned away.

Where could he hide the UAV? He focused on the problem as he waded toward shore. More people had gathered on the docks, and the fishing guides were back, idling their skiffs, beneath flocking gulls, into the boat basin. Vargas Diemer's yacht was in the channel, too, the Brazilian standing at the flybridge wheel looking svelte, crisp, and confident.

Too many eyes. Ford would have to drop the drone before he got ashore. But it had to be the *right* place. As he knew, if you sink even a sizable object in a small area of water, it's still damn hard to find. Years ago, he'd hopped into a rental boat with Jeth, one of the guides, to test a small outboard. Jeth had failed to tighten the transom bolts; the motor had vibrated off, not far from the dock, in less than six feet of water, yet it had taken them hours to find the damn thing.

Another example was . . .

He stopped. Why was his mind wandering? Strange, the way he felt; a sudden inability to focus that might be caused by days without sleep. On the other hand, it might also be a way of distancing himself from what had just happened to the retriever.

This was unusual for Ford.

Dogs, insects, fish, people, the old, the very young, died by the billions each microsecond of every new day. Some men died with a stake in their brain; others, on patios after a fall. Death was as necessary as it was inevitable. It was a chemical process unsullied by sentiment.

Sometimes, death was also a tool.

But, damn it, this was Sanibel Island, not the back of beyond . . . the dog was, after all, *his* dog. He about-faced and plowed toward the canoe, which wasn't far.

Tomlinson had the animal in his arms, holding him nearly upside down, while the woman worked on the dog's abdomen. Massaging it, perhaps. Every few seconds, Figgy did that weird thing with his mouth as if trying to swallow the dog snout-first.

Geezus, this time when the Cuban pulled away, the dog's tail thumped the water a few times.

Had the tail really moved? Or was it just a weird spasm? Ford began to jog.

A moment later, when Figgy leaned to brave another breath, a long, sloppy tongue slapped his face, then his ear. Feeble paws tried to swim; the retriever's tail whacked the canoe. It made a wooden drumming sound that didn't stop until Figgy, trying to dodge the tongue, hollered, "Hey-y-y, man, stop that shit."

"You're one lucky owner," the woman was saying to Tomlinson when Ford came up. "Not many people know canine CPR; a large dog, especially. But it's basically the same for small animals. Your friend's obviously a dog lover."

She shot a look at the Cuban, who was shirtless, all sinew and muscle, blue and red Santeria beads around his neck. "I'm Ava," she said to him. "What's your name?" Then, because of Figgy's blank response, she asked Tomlinson in confidence, "Is he hearing-impaired?"

"Figueroa? Dude's got impairments you would not believe." Tomlinson was scratching the dog's back, his ears, grinning. "He doesn't speak English, but he's a hell of a shortstop. And he knows quite a bit about roosters, as it turns out."

Figgy, not so confidentially, requested a translation, before explaining in Spanish, "I like her *chichis* and her ass. In Key West, a gringa once told me I was delicious. Think she'd like to smoke a *pitillo*?"

The woman liked the rhythms of his voice. "My Spanish is terrible, but I know he asked a question. Something about me in Key West?"

"He's concerned the dog might bite you because you're a stranger, uhh . . . which happens a lot in the Keys," Tomlinson replied, then addressed the Cuban in Spanish: "You sick, twisted little pervert. Mind your manners. This woman's a freakin' veterinarian."

"I like gringa soldiers. Of what army?"

"*A médico de animales*, you sex fiend."

"Even better," Figgy said while the dog squirmed in his arms, "tell her to take this crazy bastard." He cringed, pulled away. "Stop your shit, doggy. I'll drown you myself."

Ford stepped toward the canoe. "Give him to me."

"I want to check him over first," the doctor said to Tomlinson. "He's not the owner, you are, right?"

"No way, it's his"—he indicated Ford—"the damn dog won't listen to a word anyone else says. Hey, Doc. I think the big fella's gonna be okay. Isn't that great?"

The woman said, "I'm not so sure," with an edge that offered a couple of meanings. She helped Figgy transfer the patient into the canoe; the dog, so woozy, couldn't stand when he tried. She checked his eyes, his gums, felt the pads of his feet, then waited in silence with three fingers on his chest, her growing concern visible.

She checked his eyes once again before saying, "He's not out of the woods by a long shot. His breathing's way off. We need to get him to a clinic. Do you have a vet? One of the guys I'm with, he owns a building complex, and a vet has an office there. This late, though . . ." She took out a phone in a waterproof case and used her thumbs to send a text.

Ford ran a hand over the retriever's head and started pushing the canoe toward shore. "He was underwater for a long time. Four or five minutes . . . But, yeah, a vet, of course. A couple of months ago, I had a vet check him out . . ." He lost the thread and spoke to Tomlinson. "Any idea how long before he started to respond? He had to have been under for at least five minutes. Hell, maybe more. It seemed longer."

The woman said, "You're exaggerating, I hope."

Ford's expression: *Why would I?*

"That's bad; very bad." She sent another text, or read one, in a real hurry now. "We've gotta move, guys. My friend will open the clinic. We had a taxi waiting, so our bikes are already loaded." She splashed up beside Ford. "Get out of the way. It'll be faster if I do it."

"Do what?"

"Move."

He did.

They watched her take off running, pushing the canoe, the dog's head visible amid geysers of water, his expression a look of addled surprise. Over her shoulder, she yelled, "At least one of you try and keep up. I'll call the marina with . . ."

They couldn't make out the rest.

Ford arrived onshore ahead of Tomlinson, who'd stopped when the Cuban fell into a hole, but the woman and her friends were already buckled into a van—a Sanibel Taxi—that was leaving the parking lot.

It was a while later that Ford remembered the drone. He had dropped it out there in the bay when he'd seen the dog's tail move.

6

AFTER SUNSET, WHICH WAS EARLY, ONLY SIX P.M., the man Ford trusted called and said immediately, "You dropped the ball, but I don't want to hear details. Not here. Understand what I mean?"

In all his years of clandestine work, this was the first Ford had been warned not to trust their supposedly high-tech, cutting-edge, "impenetrable" communications system.

I'm screwed—that's what he thought, but said, "Then why did you call?"

"It's a sports metaphor. Dropped the ball. Instead of

going one-for-one—which is what you were *supposed* to do—you went one-for-goddamn-three. Baseball. Are you with me so far?" There was silence, the man controlling his anger.

Ford's take on this gibberish: David Cashmere had not survived his parasailing adventure. Great. KAT and Winslow Shepherd were still alive and that was okay, too. But then he realized that "one-for-one" might not refer to Cashmere, his actual target. If so, no telling who was dead.

"I haven't slept in a bed for quite a while," he told the man, "and I haven't slept at all going on thirty-six hours. So I'm going to take a chance here—" He was about to just say it, come out and ask, *Did I kill the right guy?* but his eyes moved to the kitchen window, the dark bay beyond. The UAV was still out there somewhere. Its owner had yet to appear. Ford, staring out the window, asked, "How did you know I was home?"

"You'll recognize the sound of me hanging up when you check your messages. You were overdue, so I called. Tell you the truth? You ever make a call and hope someone doesn't answer? That's me calling you. One-for-three," the man said again. Then he lost it. "Where the hell do you get off going rogue? Engaging our own assets when you knew—"

"*Our* assets?" Ford interrupted. "Look up an Aussie named Shepherd. While you're at it, find out KAT's real name and who's—"

"No details," the man warned. "Jesus Christ. There's a word for what you did. In fact, whole books on protocols and laws, but the word I'm thinking of begins with you-have-screwed-the-pooch, buddy. I didn't okay any of this shit, not a single directive from me. And you didn't bother asking. That's the truth, isn't it? I want to hear you say it."

The conversation was being recorded, Ford realized. Months from now, it might be played at a hearing if Congress ever figured out who to subpoena.

"I understand," he said.

"That's not what I wanted to hear."

"Hang on," Ford replied and put down the phone before he lost his temper. He'd been making ceviche because Mack had invited him and some others to discuss a real estate deal—some old cottages off West Gulf Drive. On the counter were limes, an onion he'd been slicing, and a superb chunk of mangrove snapper. He placed the knife in the sink, opened a beer, then returned to the phone. "My dog almost drowned today," he said.

After a long silence, the man replied, "Who?"

"The vet's keeping him overnight for observation."

"So what?"

"That was my reaction, too. At first anyway. Weird, huh? I think back, I see the last ten, fifteen years of my life in double vision. Separate jobs, memories. In fact, separate personalities, but just one guy: me. That's what I'm getting at. No complaints—I signed on the dotted line and I'm proud of some of our work. But one of those personalities I mentioned is a cold-blooded asshole."

"No shit," the man said. He was loosening a little.

"I'm talking about myself, not you."

"Do I sound confused? Asshole; of course you are. With the personality of an ice pick. Like going rogue without any input from—"

Ford decided to get it over with. "I take full responsi-
bility for doing what I felt was necessary. At no time did
I receive a directive or instructions or advice from—wait.
Should I say your name?"

"Take it easy, Doc. Jesus Christ. We've been at this a
long time together."

This was true. They could bicker and bluster and
sometimes draw blood, but the rock-bottom measure of
trust was this: who would run toward the gunfire to save
your ass if your ass was on the line?

Ford sensed his ass was. "I'm not going anywhere."

"Oh?" The man was suddenly paying attention.

"I'm trying to make this work. It would be easier if I
had more details. That name I mentioned. Shepherd. You
recognize it?"

"We're not getting into that. The best I can do is"—
the man had to think about what he could or couldn't
say—"Well, put it this way. I wish you'd gone three-for-
three. But, Jesus Christ, not without . . . you know . . ."

This was a surprising admission. "Then you understand."

"About the thing we're not discussing? Or the overall
situation?"

"The keyhole view," Ford said. "Something has
changed, a serious breach . . . I can't say here. I don't read
newspapers. Maybe you remember I avoid them for a
reason."

"That's almost funny. There are no newspapers. Not
really. Just the Internet. Fewer and fewer countries, too.
Cybernations instead. The last guy in charge almost
brought the house down. Still might. Some think inten-

tionally, but I don't buy into the conspiracy crap. You really don't know any of this?"

"I was talking about the business."

"Ah, that. What's left of it. The pros are suddenly scared of politicians. Some are even choosing sides. That's a first; unprecedented, in my experience. As long as the wings don't fall off, the ship's supposed to stay in the air, right? That's all changed. And you, ol' buddy, are up to your ass in something I don't even want to think about." The man let that sink in. "The cavalry's not coming if you call, Doc. I'm not even sure who controls the cavalry anymore. The major players change every four—"

"Whoa, back up. You honestly don't know—"

"I said it, didn't I?"

"Geezus." Ford took a moment to process this. "I'm surprised you bothered to call."

"Don't change the subject." The man cleared his throat, which was a signal to listen up. "You're not quite a movie star, but close enough, and no one wants to be in the movies. With me so far?"

"Keep going," Ford said.

"You're not the autograph type, so I'd think about closing shop, if I were you; a nice vacation, maybe. But don't stray too far from home. About that other matter . . . Are you listening?"

"Yep."

"It's about their head guy, not ours. Their boss, if you want to call him that. He can have his backers cut you out of the deal. Or do it himself, if he wants. Not now, but a week or two down the road. It's possible—depending on how fast he recovers."

A lot of information was cloaked between those lines. Some obvious; the rest had to be extrapolated. Ford had been photographed or videoed, presumably at the resort, and identified. The religious crazies and another party—the Chinese, most likely—were looking for him, probably building a case for extradition. He should leave the country, but don't choose a place that had ties with China, or Mexico.

The bad news: the "head guy," David Abdel Cashmere, was alive and well enough, or still sufficiently in control, to have Ford killed. Or to use his ruby-handled knife up close and personal.

During three days of hard travel, he'd had time to anticipate variables, some of these included. He sniffed to signal subtext. "Sanibel's nice this time of year, plus it's the holidays. Like I said, I'm staying right here. I've got research projects—"

The man interrupted, then went silent. If Ford wanted to give away his location, there had to be a good reason.

"Too much work to do," Ford continued, "and I hate quitting a project before it's done."

The man knew what that meant. "Tell me about it."

"In the Gulf, there are what geologists call blue holes. Well, actually, they call them remnant archaic springs. So, most days, I'll be offshore in my boat. Diving spots as far north as Tampa, maybe Crystal River."

He added details; islands, towns where he might put in for the night. Then went on for a while about blue holes and jellyfish to camouflage what came next. "I don't know if you're interested in any of this."

"I figured you were intentionally trying to piss me

off," the man said. "Scuba diving in December—we've got three feet of snow up here."

Yes, he was interested.

"Tomorrow," Ford replied, "the weatherman says low eighties, but a little too windy to dive. A friend and I were supposed to go out, but we postponed. Next week, there's a nice four-day window; calm, mid-eighties."

"Why I put up with this shit, year after year," the man said. "This morning, way below zero, I sat on the Beltway for an hour, traffic all backed up because of sleet. That's what I thought anyway, but turned out some third-world dignitary needed extra security. It's always either them or the White House screwing things up." He gave that a beat. "Then almost fell on my ass when I hit a sheet of ice on the steps."

The White House?

Ford played it straight. "Sounds like you're the one who needs a vacation. Why not come down for a few days of fishing while I work? Pick a place, I'll meet you."

"Did you say as far north as Tampa?" the man asked. "I still have friends there. We went to a couple of Rays games; some of the women in the stands, they were worth the price of a ticket alone."

Rays stadium was in St. Pete, not Tampa, but Ford replied, "Send me a couple a dates."

On the Internet, he checked news summaries, dateline: Washington, D.C. What dignitaries had been to the White House recently? He had already started a file on KAT and Winslow Shepherd, but he would do more on that later.

Next, a cursory search on unmanned aerial vehicles. He'd heard rumors that the Special Ops base at MacDill could pilot a UAV from Tampa to the Mediterranean, carry out a mission, then land it safely again at the little runway near Raccoon Creek—more than ten thousand miles fueled by solar energy.

The missing drone had solar panels but didn't seem stout enough to weather a squall, let alone the Atlantic Ocean. What was a more reasonable operating distance?

Ford preferred books or charts to Google Earth, so he got out the atlas. Using a draftsman's compass, he drew radii of fifty, one hundred, and two hundred miles, then focused on possible launch sites. Due east, two hundred miles away was Freeport, Bahamas. Cuba was 210 miles south. The Yucatán was nearly four hundred miles southwest. A hell of a lot of water and unstable weather separated those spots from Sanibel. Ford had to admit it was possible, but it was more likely the aircraft had been launched from somewhere in Florida.

Twenty minutes later, he put the atlas and compass away and was back in the little galley, working on the ceviche, despite a hundred other things that demanded his time. What he had told the man about living dual lives was true and never more evident than when he had just returned from an assignment overseas.

Like now: there were stacks of mail and phone messages to answer, a dozen email inquiries from school biology departments regarding specimens they needed.

All would have to wait. He'd been through this transition too many times not to consciously reboot by focusing on some small, pleasurable task.

It was a process: jettison recent events by reminding himself he was *here*, not *there*. He was no longer paddling his ass off to put distance between himself and what had happened at the resort. There had been bribes and boats and jungle roads, then more bribes to slip across the border into Guatemala. Outwit the hunters; a fight-or-die mentality that required behavior not acceptable in the gentler enclaves of Florida.

The islands of the Gulf Coast among them.

He was *here*, not *there*. Sanibel's weekly shopper's guide provided confirmation. On the front page was a list of holiday activities. Tonight was Luminary. The bike path would be lined with candles in paper bags. Next came the Marching Mullet Parade, with Junkanoo dancers, then the Lighted Boat Parade, and a whole long list of church activities and potlucks. Next week, South Seas Resort would host its annual Holiday Stroll. At Dinkin's Bay, a community known for excess, the Twenty-six Days of Christmas were already under way. Tonight was Day 13. At the marina, they were roasting oysters near a keg of beer, awaiting Ford's arrival with ceviche.

In contrast, two days ago . . . no, three, he had been confronted by a couple of teenage thieves carrying machetes. This was Belize, south of Placencia, near some mud-and-junkyard village off the Monkey River. A defenseless ecotourist, they'd assumed. No idea who he was.

Not true of the border patrol cop who had motioned him into a room later that evening. Both were *What to do?* moments; sources of an adrenaline rush that even now, thinking back, caused his stomach to knot, but also sparked in his brain a sensation of purest clarity and purpose. Soaring but in control. It was a little like that.

The sensation was much different from the way he'd felt in Mexico, that night on the balcony, after saying to the woman, "Tell me what happens next."

Ford didn't want to think about what had happened next but couldn't help seeing the contempt on the woman's face when he stepped out, pistol raised.

"Predictable," she had assured Winslow Shepherd. According to research, the Australian math professor was a political *activist*, a word that had many connotations but usually referenced a person who was a pain in the ass, yet had noble intentions.

That wasn't true of Shepherd. When applied to him, *activist* was a euphemism for anti-anything that had to do with Western society, particularly the United States.

In the intelligence community, the activist label was assigned to people with all sorts of political agendas. It denoted passionate concern without violent intent.

For the destructive ones who hid behind that banner, more accurate labels were assigned. There were *thug opportunists*, *TV radicals*, *Sunday militia*, and *revolutionary socialites*. *Anarchist* was still used to signal those who were intelligent, methodical, and truly dangerous. The word had biblical linkage but an updated credo: to start anew, first destroy the old.

Shepherd was a mix of both. Working under the radar, he'd done his share of damage. He was Australia's version of Weathermen founder Bill Ayers, a rich kid who despised the source of his own good fortune—and probably himself as well. He'd become a self-styled guerrilla; an underground fighter who preferred mail bombs to putting his own ass in the line of fire. The world of academia, and his university tenure, had provided a shield while he tried to destroy the very political system that guaranteed his own freedom.

Shepherd was not a very good guerrilla fighter—the seventy-nine bombings with which he was associated had managed to kill only three. They were high school kids who had had the bad luck of being in a post office at the wrong time.

The young professor had been indicted, found not guilty, and released back into the system.

"Kill all the rich, kill your parents, bring the revolution home," he was quoted as saying—but only after he was safely back on university soil.

Despite his best efforts, Shepherd had never achieved the Hollywood cachet of Ayers, but he'd come close by accomplishing something Ayers had been unable to do. Shepherd had fathered a like-minded son who was a genius. A true genius, not the suburbanite variety. The college prof had named the kid Julian Caesar Winslow Shepherd.

Julian had taken their game to a whole new level. By age sixteen, he had hacked the computer systems of the Pentagon, NASA, U.S. Naval Intelligence, and others.

Presumably, with his father's help.

The son—or the pair of them—had damn near broken through into the National Security Agency's files when the kid was arrested by Australian Federal Police. Dad came to the rescue and the teen was released after paying $500 in reparations. Over the next few years, that error in judgment allowed several Western intelligence agencies to be compromised—intel that was shipped straight to terrorist organizations.

The Australian Federal Police issued arrest warrants for both men, as did seven other world powers.

The duo disappeared into the underground while rumors bubbled here and there. Father and son were feuding. The son sued the father through a team of Swiss attorneys for a long list of wrongs, including copyright theft and slander. A series of news stories were fed to Reuters, presumably by the outraged father. The son, by then a computer wizard, took his case directly to the world via cyberspace.

Then they both vanished again.

The kid, Julian, now twenty-four, was rumored to be holed up at some embassy in South America, but continued to raise Internet hell worldwide. He had changed his legal name to Julian Solo—an intentional slap at his father, who, even now, claimed to be the real genius behind his son's burgeoning software enterprises and his "activist" ventures. The whole long while, the FBI, MI5 out of the UK, and Interpol were hot on their trail.

No wonder Winslow Shepherd had behaved like a coward when asked, "Aren't you supposed to be dead?"

Ford still had a lot to learn about Julian, but if he'd known about Shepherd's bombing spree, he would've handled matters differently that night on the balcony.

A damn sloppy job.

Ford took a breath and reminded himself, *You're home.*

Yes, he was. He should have been tired yet felt like he was caffeine-buzzed. It was always that way. Finish the ceviche, he decided, then wander down to the marina; try to resume his role as the kindly biologist who was thoughtful, dependable, and always on time.

On the cutting board was the superb chunk of mangrove snapper. The fillet was cold in his hand and possessed the density of cheese. He set aside a piece for the marina's cat and diced the rest into a bowl that had been chilled in the freezer. With a clunky old lever press, he juiced a dozen limes. Then added Spanish onion, garlic, coarse sea salt, a whole bunch of cilantro, and diced half of a mild jalapeño.

After fermenting in lime juice for an hour, the fish would no longer be raw but had to be kept chilled. On his way to the fridge, his eyes landed on the pocket laser near the window. Stupid to leave it out, even if it looked more like a flashlight than a weapon that could shoot a military-sized UAV from the sky.

That is exactly what he'd done. He'd made a snap decision; no thought as to what the fallout might be if the aircraft tumbled into the water. The laser had probably fried the electrical system, or gyro sensors, or . . . hell, who cared? It'd worked.

He stood at the window. Dinkin's Bay was a dark canvas with a halo glow from the mainland. No boat lights, or anything else out there, to cause concern.

Except for the drone. Someone would come looking for the damn thing. If not tonight, soon.

The path to Ford's house exited through mangroves into the parking lot, just outside the gate, which was open, but only a few vehicles were inside. Fast Eddie, who was doing dive charters again now that his engine was fixed, was talking to Vargas Diemer, the Brazilian. Both lived at the marina; both were commercial pilots, although Eddie had lost his license or been grounded for some reason.

At a marina where an anchor was the only tether, it wasn't the sort of question one asked.

They had been talking about the drone. Ford could tell by the way they went quiet as he approached; then Eddie, a little too cheerfully, said, "Welcome back to the land of coconuts and money. What's shakin', professor?"

Any other time, Eddie would have first asked about the dog. Vargas knew enough about Ford's clandestine life not to bother. A safer subject was the dive business, which transitioned to great white sharks.

"People say Dolly ain't a problem no more? Hell, not two hours ago, Mack was complaining; said he wished she'd come back. You believe that shit? Said business had never been better; and the local chamber of commerce types, they want her back, too. Know what I told that fat Kiwi? Told him, 'Come to the next meeting of dive operators and we'll stick all the money we're losing up your ass.'"

Vargas was laughing while Ford said, "Take it easy, Eddie. Mack's the one who helped you get into the business. And he's also a friend."

"Aw . . . I know; sorry, Doc. I get carried away. But it's been almost four weeks since that big bitch pinged. She's gone, right? Does that make headlines? Hell no. Now the rumor mill is killing us, too. Like that bozo drunk who claimed he saw Dolly cruisin' the beach—turned out to be a freakin' kayak. Then, last week, some guys on a head boat claimed they saw her thirty miles off near the *Mohawk* wreck. Total bullshit. Forty people on that stinkpot, but only a couple see her? Did you see the video that asshole shot?"

Ford had seen the blurry footage. "I couldn't tell what it was for sure, but it certainly wasn't a shark."

"Exactly," Eddie said. "Great whites don't hang out in the Gulf." He looked to Vargas. "You ever seen one out there?"

"I've never seen any fences out there either," the Brazilian replied, his accent not thick but evident. "Sharks, they do what they want. I used to fly a C-5 for an oil sheik. He had a mistress on an island off Africa. Réunion Island—Doc, you know that island. Name one place in the world I wouldn't swim, that's it. Tiger sharks and bulls mostly, but probably white pointers, too. Réunion is the tip of a volcano in the middle of nowhere. Understand what that means? All around the island the ocean's black, it's so deep; no reefs or structure, so what's a shark going to eat? *People*, that's what, because sharks are animals and animals learn. Go where the food and sex is. They're no different than us."

Eddie had learned to dive off the New Jersey coast; was a member of an outlaw group, the Hell Divers, who pirated deep-water wrecks. Crazy deep, sometimes, all for trophies and the beer parties afterward. He had too many shark stories to allow the Brazilian to have the last word.

Ford listened, thinking, *It's good to be back*. Didn't say much, which was typical, until Eddie asked, "What was a great white doing in the Gulf, you think?"

"Vargas has a point—she was after food. But it could be more of a genetic memory thing. When the Spaniards arrived—fourteen, fifteen hundreds—this coast had a big population of monk and blue tip seals. That's what great whites eat. It's been a hundred years since a seal was sighted off the Florida Keys, but maybe—I'm theorizing here—maybe in the mind of a female great white the memory is still fresh. Not her memory, but inherited; a feeding route passed down through who knows how many generations."

There was more he could have added. Throughout central Florida, the fossilized teeth of Megalodon, a massive prehistoric shark, were commonly found, some larger than a man's hand. The peninsula had contained a shallow inland sea that flowed into the Gulf south of what is now Tampa—a primary feeding transect for sharks the size of a Greyhound bus.

The connection was tenuous but made sense. In the 1960s, when biologist Eugenie Clark started what is now Mote Marine Laboratory, her team caught several great whites on shark lines set off Boca Grande Pass near Fort Myers. They weren't common, but they were out there.

Another seldom seen animal was out there, too—a swimming predator even larger than a great white, but Ford, who had seen blurry video, kept that to himself.

"Food and sex," Vargas said again. He started toward the marina, where there was music and Christmas lights. Gave Fast Eddie time to get ahead of them before saying to Ford, "Whose was it, sport?" No accent, now that it was just the two of them. And no need to explain he was talking about the UAV.

Vargas was too good-looking, too wealthy, and too dangerous not to have enemies and too cautious to have friends. That's precisely why Ford trusted him enough to dispense with the bullshit. "You saw it happen?"

"I'd just rounded the marker into the bay, but I saw enough. What did you use? Not a rifle. Even with a suppressor, a guy like you wouldn't risk hitting someone he didn't want to shoot."

Ford shrugged that away. "Let's say it crashed and leave it at that. It's still out there. If I wasn't so tired, I'd go out and look tonight."

"Need help?"

Maybe, but the Brazilian wasn't the help-his-neighbor type.

"What do you get, these days?" Ford asked. "A couple thousand an hour?"

The Brazilian shook his head, amused. "I have the occasional Christmas special," he said, meaning *I get a lot more than that.*

7

WHEN MACK SAW FORD AND THE BRAZILIAN COM- ing, he felt a tension not unfamiliar to a businessman who owned a small marina where people with big personalities, and sometimes big egos, lived hull-to-hull in boats. Mix in alcohol and love affairs, there were bound to be conflicts.

For Mack, that meant doing his best to defuse issues or get the hell out of the way so he didn't share the blame later. It meant pretending to be cheerful when he wasn't and likable to a few—a very few—residents he didn't like or trust.

Vargas Diemer topped the list.

There was *something* about the Brazilian.

Ford, on the other hand, was a local favorite. Not Mack's personal favorite, but among the general population. The biologist was a bit too aloof, as if shielding something, and his disappearances were a source of unease. More than once, Ford had returned with blood wounds that did not mesh with a science symposium or a lecture on jellyfish, as he'd claimed.

Running a successful business also meant keeping your damn mouth shut.

Mack had seen the drone tumble from the sky. He'd seen Ford aim something from the window of his stilthouse—not that he would bring it up. Violent history was implied, like now: the biologist was limping a little when he and the Brazilian passed the bait tank, where decorations were swagged above the purloined plastic cows, each cow aglow with a lightbulb in its belly.

Tomlinson's idea, no doubt.

Mack stood over a grill piled with oysters. He put down the tongs and surveyed people socializing on the docks. A couple of dozen; plastic beer cups and laughter, Cuban music clattering from speakers; rows of boats decorated like Christmas trees.

But no Tomlinson.

This added to the tension, which was unusual since Tomlinson's presence usually caused more problems than anyone's in Dinkin's Bay. The man was a boat bum hipster, an avowed pacifist, and a shameless womanizer. This made him a lightning rod for political arguments, jealousy, pissed-off husbands, and at least two fistfights.

Tomlinson never participated, of course. As an ordained Rienzi Buddhist monk (supposedly), violence was beneath him. Instead, the troublemaking bugger vanished like smoke from a spent bullet.

He was a good egg, however. Mack couldn't deny that. The strange bastard was decent and funny but could not be trusted with another man's girlfriend, wife, or daughter—hell, a man's grandmother, for that matter.

The same was true of Vargas Diemer.

That's why Mack was concerned. While Ford had been away, his most recent love interest, Hannah Smith, had had sunset cocktails and dinner aboard the Brazilian's yacht. Twice, Mack had seen Tomlinson climb into her little fishing skiff, and they'd been gone all day.

Hannah was not a promiscuous person, but she was a tall, healthy woman in her thirties and she was human.

Morality wasn't the issue. No one was more aware than Mack that people led secret lives, and that those secrets were guarded for a reason. He himself was having affairs with three women simultaneously, one who lived aboard *Tiger Lilly*, another from Cleveland, Ohio—an Internet match that required a camera and an imagination, but she would be visiting Florida soon.

The third woman, a widow, owned rental cottages off West Gulf Drive, a nice little property that she'd agreed to sell to Mack—if she and the other two ladies didn't somehow meet up.

Talk about an old fool asking for trouble.

Get through Christmas without a blowup, that was his goal. Timing was all-important. Recently, he had been diagnosed with prostate cancer. Surgery was scheduled for the day after New Year's, which gave him only a couple of weeks to live it up and enjoy the pleasures of his stupidity. *Peacefully*, though. That's why he hadn't told anyone about the diagnosis.

Love was love and friends were friends, but, damn it, Mack had a marina to run, and important things to accomplish, before he ran out of time.

Ford loaded a toolbox into his pickup truck because Mack asked him to do it, then made room for Tomlinson, who was returning from somewhere on his bike.

"This island is a floating candelabra," Tomlinson said, slamming the door. "Sometimes, I'm sorry I swore off acid. Beautiful out there, man. Like riding through stars. All the way from Blind Pass, I just sort of let my eyes blur."

"Swore it off, when, an hour ago?" Ford asked, then said, "Oh."

Brown bags aglow with candles lined Tarpon Bay Road clear to West Gulf, about a mile, including Lilly's Jewelry, the parking lot at Bailey's General Store, and the new rum bar across the street. Christmas Luminary. He'd forgotten.

"You missed the oyster roast," Ford said. "The guides brought in some pen shells and I made ceviche."

They talked about that; mentioned the dog and the pretty veterinarian, then their plans to dive the Captiva Blue Hole, Ford saying, "Let's give the wind a few days to die down. The viz will be better." He glanced over at Tomlinson. "Where were you?"

"On my bike? I bought a farm not far from here."

Tomlinson was fiddling with the truck's ancient AM radio: right-wing talk shows, Mexican accordion music. "You don't actually listen to this crap?"

"That's what you call them now? Farms?" Ford asked. His pal grew marijuana on a couple of backcountry islands where there were shell middens high enough to plant. For a decade, he'd sold boutique weed, but had recently claimed he was leaving the business because legalization had taken the fun out of it.

"A real farm where I can plant things legally. Almost four acres. Wait 'til you see it—just this side of Blind Pass Bridge. There's an old rain cistern there, built, I don't know, late eighteen hundreds, maybe. You know that old kind of concrete they made using seashells? It's big. Big as a small swimming pool and five feet deep. Plenty of high ground. I was told Thomas Edison paid islanders to grow goldenrod on the acreage. Either for synthetic rubber or some kind of weird-ass experiment. You know, kill it and study it. The white man's way."

This was news to Ford. "You already closed on the property or made an offer?"

"Dude, believe it or not, time doesn't stop when you leave the island. You were gone for, what, a week? It came on the market, so I snapped it up. Hannah thought it was a good deal. Her mother, Loretta, she's a master gardener. She's been giving me advice. The Smith family's been farming these islands for more than a hundred years."

Ford told himself, *Don't react,* but couldn't stop himself from asking, "How's she doing?"

"Full of piss and ginger, that woman. People think

she's nuts after they cut that clot out of her brain, but I think she's been elevated to a whole new level of consciousness. It happens that way sometimes. When I stop by, Loretta will smoke the occasional doobie and tell me about conversations she has with a chieftain. A big guy, really handsome, Loretta says. He lived on the islands more than a thousand years ago." Tomlinson waited, anticipating a reply, then realized, "Oh . . . you meant Hannah, not her mom."

Still no response. Tomlinson cut to the chase. "I haven't gotten Hannah's knickers off, if that's what you're asking. She's made it clear: don't even try." He snapped off the radio. "How can you live without music, man? You could buy a tape player cheap at Goodwill. Or skip ahead a few decades and install a CD player." Tomlinson folded his arms.

Ford, looking at rows of glowing paper bags, said, "Yeah, Luminary is kind of pretty."

End of subject.

Ahead in the lights of the truck, Mack's beat-up Lincoln Continental turned left onto West Gulf at the beach access and drove past the Island Inn, almost to Shalimar, where they turned left again into a shell drive shielded by palms.

A wooden sign, not visible from the road, read

GRIN N BARE IT
BEACH COTTAGES

"Where we headed?" Tomlinson asked.

Ford put the truck in park. "We're already here. Mack's

thinking about buying this place." He got out, the night dense with salt mist and jasmine, and spoke over the truck's roof. "I must've jogged past this driveway a thousand times but never noticed the sign. You ever hear of it?"

"How much they asking?" Tomlinson, using his fingers, combed his hair back while he got oriented. "Love, love, *love* the name. A nudist colony, I bet. But"—his eyes took in six mini-cabins, windows dark beneath an awning of coconut palms—"doesn't look like it's been open for a while. Hell . . . hasn't been open since the sixties, maybe. Wow." He tilted his head and sniffed. "Time warp, man. I bet this is where Elvis lives."

"Mack didn't mention a price," Ford replied. "If it's more than a couple of acres, the land alone's worth a bunch. So maybe he wants us to invest. Hey"—he was thinking about the UAV, worried someone might come looking, plus he was tired—"I'm not going to stick around. Do you mind catching a ride back?"

"Shallow up a tad, man. Why you so jumpy? Never mind—I don't know why I bother asking. You're always warp speed when you get back from one of your *lecture* tours." It was mild sarcasm to preface what came next: "Want to talk about the flying saucer that buzzed your lab? If someone's after your ass, you can tell me. Or are we just gonna pretend it's business as usual?"

Ford, looking toward the cottages, said, "I didn't know he was bringing them."

In a shell parking area, the Lincoln's dome light showed Mack and two passengers getting out—the ladies from *Tiger Lilly*, Rhonda and JoAnn. Middle-aged; JoAnn thick and busty, Rhonda the opposite. They'd been partners, business and romantically, for a long, long time. A few months ago, Rhonda had begun slipping out to meet Mack when JoAnn was away.

Tomlinson lowered his voice. "The big guy's been dipping his willy in the family fun pool. Think she knows?"

"You're the expert on double-dipping," Ford said and checked his watch. It was a little after nine. "Better yet, I'll jog back to the marina and leave the keys in the truck."

The property consisted of six tiny cabins built around a commons area—gas grill, a shuffleboard court, orange trees heavy with fruit—and a large one-story clubhouse, CBS brick and stucco, with linoleum floors and tables for potlucks and bingo. Plenty of room to seat fifty or more people. Mack needed a flashlight to find the breaker box because the power had been switched off.

They toured the cabins one by one, the doors padlocked. Kitchenettes, dusty bamboo furniture, outdated TVs. Single beds, unmade, in a space so small that they took turns having a look.

Mack led them to a tiny swimming pool, which had been drained. There was a tiki bar on an artificial beach where weeds had battled their way through a foot of white sand. Then back to the clubhouse, which smelled of Pine-Sol, where they sat at a folding table while Mack stood as if calling a meeting to order.

"Remember a few years back when the feds tried to close Dinkin's Bay to powerboat traffic?" he said. "It didn't happen. Still hasn't, but the day's coming. You can delay the feds, but you can't win if they want something. And they want control of that bay."

Tomlinson's eyes took in the space around them. "A last lifeboat. Yeah, I get it, man. Is there deeded beach access?"

Mack continued, "Almost five acres, this building, the cottages, and there's a small house at the end of the drive. The owner—she's a widow—she lives there part-time and is desperate to sell. Well . . . she's willing. The property's been through the foreclosure process half a dozen times and she's always managed to keep the dogs away. Old-time repeat clients who've been holing up here since her husband—he was a lot older than her—since he built the place back in the sixties. He died a few years back; now most of her repeat business is either dead or dying, so she closed the place to save on utilities. That was almost two years ago."

JoAnn, sitting next to Rhonda, asked some of the right questions—price, zoning, taxes—then added, "Are you out of your goddamn mind? So's the seller at the price she's asking. With a name as tacky as Grin N Bare It? That would have to go, but why even bother? This place is a teardown. Developers will pay twenty, thirty percent more and build condos." She focused on Mack. "What's the catch?"

Rhonda, oddly subdued, opened her purse, took out a packet of tissues, then put the tissues away.

Tomlinson exchanged looks with Ford while Mack explained, "Cash, that's all. She wants a clean deal, and keep it simple. What I'm thinking is, we fix the place up and run it at a profit."

He motioned vaguely to include the concrete walls, beige paint peeling, and a tiny kitchen, where there was a counter piled with old phone books still in plastic. "If someone at the marina has friends visiting, or their boat's being hauled, we'll book them here instead of a hotel. Hire a manager and a handyman—Figgy is just the guy, I think. We can do the work ourselves in our spare time. I know, I know, the cottages are tiny, but think about it. Who knows more about living in cramped spaces than people who live on boats? We're all set as far as zoning." He craned his head back. "A little patch and polish . . . probably redo the wiring; the right furniture and an entertainment system would really liven up this place. And it comes with a license to sell wine and beer."

Tomlinson, wearing shorts and a tank top, stood and walked barefoot to the stack of phone books, and began shuffling through them. "Beer—rehydration's important in the tropics, but why not buy a liquor license, too? I picture a seafaring motif: antique charts, serving wenches in low-cut dresses. And over there"—he pointed—"big-ass speakers for bands we can hire. I say we run the place as a private club. No suits or pinheads allowed . . . But seriously, ladies, you really want to change the name?"

JoAnn was asking Mack if he needed investors, or had the cash, while Tomlinson continued with his thread. "How about we call this"—he had to think for a moment—"call it the Float On Bar. Or . . . the Déjà Vu Inn—yeah, the little hideaway so friendly, you could swear you've been here before. But to change a classic name like Grin and"—he plucked a magazine from the stack, saying, "Aha! Here's proof. What did I tell you,

Doc?" He held up the magazine. "This is why we never heard of the place. Nudists don't advertise for the same reason they don't need pockets."

International Naturists, the publication's name; lead story, Ford didn't bother to look when it was passed around.

Mack answered a few more questions before getting down to it. "None of us are getting any younger. Down the road, five or six years, if the feds kick us out, we'll have a place to go. A sort of a—what do you call it?—family compound. That's a perk. What I didn't tell you is the owner has accepted my offer. I want to get this place up and running before the season's done. With me, it's strictly business. If the buildings are structurally sound, if there's no mold, and if the title's clear, I'll sign the contract. Mold is a hell of a lawsuit risk. Doc? That's why I asked you to bring your tools. Let's check behind some of the drywall and have a look inside the vents."

Ford helped for a while, then left his tools and the truck with Tomlinson and jogged home.

What kept going through his head as he lay in bed was Mexico and the procession of events after he'd stepped out, pistol raised, and said to the woman, "Tell me what happens next."

Ego had made him do that. It was his reply to the charge of predictability.

KAT—*Astra*, her name tag had read. Who the hell was she? And why was a supposed asset working with people like Shepherd and Muslim radicals?

More likely, she'd been turned by the Chinese.

A striking woman. In his mind, Ford saw her face in profile but winced when he imagined how her face must look now. That started an unfolding scene, the way it had happened, and he couldn't stop the slow-motion details flashing behind his eyes.

The look of contempt on her face—KAT, naked, a smoldering joint in her fingers, yet she did not attempt to cover herself, but the man did. He had stepped back to use her as a shield, both his hands fanned low, a fig leaf to hide his genitals.

KAT's voice had remained calm while she ignored the gun and looked into Ford's eyes. "*Really?* Just how dumb are you? Pull that trigger, even if you shoot us both, our security people will be all over this place. You ever even seen the inside of a Mexican jail? That's what's going to happen *next* unless . . . are you drunk? Is that the problem? Or just stupid?"

Ego; another spark. KAT's gray-green eyes had bored in while Ford stepped toward them. Winslow Shepherd, then the woman, took a step back, the balcony railing only a meter away. She'd kept talking. "What's your name? If you're going to kill us, it can't hurt for me to at least know your name."

Ford, lying in the void of a late waxing moon, remembered thinking, *She's had hostage negotiation training.*

Then came a momentary distraction: the woman irritated by Shepherd, who was cowering behind her. "For god's sake, Winslow, take your hands away from your dick. This man's a jock—*look* at him. He certainly doesn't care. He's been in"—gray-green eyes, black in starlight, followed the joint's ember when she flicked it away, then pivoted to him—"you've been in lots of locker rooms, haven't you? Football? You're from the U.S., and you've got the size." A glance over her shoulder; laughter with an edge. "Poor, scared Winslow—neither one of us cares about your dick, so please just stop."

Oh, she was good. Tough under pressure. Ruthless, but her veneer began to crack when she heard the metallic clack of a pistol hammer. It caused them both to retreat another long step, palm trees, a tiled deck eight stories below. Suddenly, they both became talkative, chattering away about how unnecessary this was, they could make a deal.

Then Shepherd, who had begun pleading, did something Ford hadn't anticipated. He clamped a hand on KAT's shoulder while he reached blindly, blindly, for the railing with his other hand. Finally, found it; assumed the heavy wood would support his weight when he pulled the woman closer as a shield and he leaned back . . .

Goddamn it . . . that wasn't supposed to happen.

Ford threw the sheet off and stood, aware of an odd humming noise outside. A rain cistern blocked the bedroom view, so he went to the galley, where the windows opened out onto the marina and the bay. A cool breeze huffed through the screens; the house, on pilings, seemed to lean, with the tide running below.

Huz-z-z-z-z-z-z . . .

Again, he heard it . . . each thrumming chord in sync with a slow-gusting wind. He followed his ears into the moonlight and found the source: two fishing rods, lines taut, had been left in rod holders clamped to the railing.

Ford remembered loaning them to Jeth Nicholes, one of the fishing guides, who had returned the rods while he was away.

End of alarm, but he wandered around the deck anyway, checking the area from different angles. His nerves, sensitized by lack of sleep, made it difficult to sleep. A twitchy, sand-under-the-skin feeling.

On nights like this, he sometimes anchored his boat in a quiet spot and dozed beneath mosquito netting on the bow. Maybe that's what he would do—guess where he'd lost the UAV and anchor there to guard the area. It wasn't that late, just a little after midnight. The quarter moon told him the time. Its craters, rust-colored behind clouds, tilted low in the west. Moonset on this early Monday morning was twelve twenty-two a.m.

It was the sort of thing Ford checked daily.

Bayside, he stopped at the railing. A white anchor light bobbed near the mouth of the bay. It was a mile or more away, but distance was tough to judge over water, especially at night. A mullet fisherman, probably. He cleaned his glasses, let his eyes adjust, and saw two fast shadows cross the sky—flitting images, like bats flying out of the moon.

Were they late-roosting birds or more drone aircraft?

He grabbed his equipment bag, a pillow, and went down the steps to the lower deck, where his boat was cradled on a lift.

"Damn," he said, but welcomed the diversion.

8

THE DRONES DIDN'T ARRIVE UNTIL TWO HOURS later. Ford, who had been unable to sleep, found it damn near impossible to wake up until he realized what was happening.

He had anchored a quarter mile from the marina, almost parallel to Tomlinson's sailboat, *No Más*, but a long distance away.

It was a sleepy, breezy, starlit night, once the moon vanished. In his dreams, he was adrift on a jungle river, gliding toward a waterfall that, instead of roaring, made an oscillatory hum like propellers. The propellers whirred

louder, ever closer, as the falls sucked him toward obliv-
ion—an eight-story drop, a tiled patio below, that was
shattered by KAT's scream when the rail gave way. Then
Winslow Shepherd, with his arms locked around the
woman's neck, rode her down, down, down to cushion
himself from the bone-on-concrete crunch that silenced
them both for a few seconds.

Then came the agonized cries.

Ford sat up and realized he was awake. He scooped
saltwater into his face, but the electric hum of propellers
continued. He found his glasses, then opted for the NVG
monocular, which he'd left within easy reach along with
a flashlight and the laser.

The flick of a switch transformed night into fluorescent-
green day.

It didn't take long to locate the source of the noise.
Two small aircraft, one elongated, the other more like a
multi-bladed helicopter, hovered low over the water a
football field away. His first reaction was to grab the laser,
but then he realized it might be wiser to sit quietly and
observe for a while. No rush. Somewhere, in a darkened
room or vehicle, computer pilots were monitoring live
video from cameras that were their surrogate eyes.

Had they seen him? Probably not—or the pilots were
so fixated on finding the missing UAV, they didn't give a
damn about anything else.

Another factor was Ford's unusual boat. The hull was
Kevlar encircled by inflated tubes of black carbon fiber
that looked bulletproof—and maybe were, considering
the agency that had commissioned the design. To mini-
mize radar signature, the boat was built low to the water

with few right angles or vertical surfaces. Covering the
bow was a hood made of neoprene polymer sheeting that
was radar-absorbent. When opened, the hood made a
nice little tent to sleep under.

Ford checked the time. It was almost three in the
morning. In Europe, the computer types were already at
their desks. It was possible the operators were there, but
this was a clandestine op and stealth was more important
than punching a clock.

He settled back . . . then gradually got to his feet,
thinking, *I wish I had video,* because what he saw sur-
passed his assumptions about drone technology.

They were golf-cart-sized aircraft with multiple propellers that made them immune to gravity. In his mind,
he designated one as the saucer, because that's what it
resembled, the other a helicopter, but shaped more like a
canoe. No lights at all; invisible without NVG optics.
They hovered for a few seconds . . . separated in a slow
search pattern, then hovered again minutes later.

The laser fried the drone's telemetry, Ford thought. *They
can't find it. If they do, they'll mark the spot and send a
recovery team later. Nothing to worry about now.*

Even so, he crawled aft, found his dive bag, and laid
out mask and fins. The laser was waterproof, but a poor
choice if he had to act fast. That afternoon, it had taken
a full minute to bring down the UAV. He added the laser
to the pile anyway. Then, after thinking a moment, he
pulled anchor, too, but quietly.

Wind had settled; his boat—27 feet of Kevlar with a
rigid inflated collar—caught what little breeze there was
and drifted toward the unmanned aircraft.

They were still hovering, but lower, only a few yards above the water. Ford used night vision to watch until the belly of the helicopter emitted a blinding light. The saucer switched on lights, too, and became an amphibious vehicle that kicked up spray when it landed in five or six feet of water. Then it did the impossible—the vehicle tilted itself, using some kind of jet propulsion, and dived like a miniature sub.

They had found the missing UAV.

Geezus . . . the laser wouldn't be fast enough to stop what was happening. He looked around for another weapon. A fish gaff—a short pole with a steel hook—was within easy reach.

He grabbed it and went over the side with mask and fins.

Cameras on the helicopter spotted Ford swimming on his back, low in the water, when he was a few body lengths away. A beam of hot light, or an electrical charge, found him and stabbed a sizzling jolt through his temple.

Damn.

He submerged and nearly panicked, worried he'd been blinded or that a high-tech laser had seared the synapses of his brain. No . . . he could still see, and he was so pissed-off, his anger proved all brain circuitry was working.

The saucer was nearby in five feet of water, illuminating a chunk of bottom with its LEDs. The lights provided a point of reference. He spun around, used his fins, and skimmed over tufts of sea grass and sand until the helicopter's lights were above him. No telling if it was still hovering low, but he wasn't going to linger and risk getting zapped again.

To hell with the laser. Ford crouched on the bottom, then rocketed upward and swung the gaff. He made contact. He swung again—a glancing blow that spun the drone around and sheared off a couple of propellers. The machine battled to right itself, and nearly succeeded, while Ford dolphined in pursuit.

He breached the surface a second time and made solid contact before splashing down like a whale. When he came up, the aircraft was in the water, circling like a duck with a broken wing and showering sparks.

"Bastard!" He drew back the gaff to finish the job but was knocked sideways by a searing pain in his thigh. For a crazy second he thought, *Stingray*, but then understood: the saucer UAV had zapped him from underwater. Worse, it was coming after him, lights blazing.

Ford started toward his boat, then thought, *It's too far*, and launched himself toward the saucer instead. It was only a few body lengths away and appeared to be surfacing.

Whap.

A bead of light hit him in the shoulder.

Whap. Another grazed his ear; the drone so close, the glare was blinding.

He struggled to stand—never easy with fins—and swung the gaff before his feet were under him. The impact of aluminum hitting carbon fiber sent an electric jolt down his arm. Again he swung but missed, and momentum carried him face-first into the water. This time, he stayed under and used the fins until he was near the boat before he surfaced and looked back.

The saucer had either sunk or flown away, but the copter was there, still plowing wounded circles. Ford kept his anger in check until he was close enough to use the gaff and swung it like an axe three times. The crunch of carbon fiber was satisfying, but the machine's power source wouldn't quit.

He looked up in frustration. "Where are you sons of bitches?" he yelled and hit the machine again . . . then again.

From a sailboat in the distance an unexpected voice hollered back, "Doc . . . ? Hey, Doc! If the sonuvabitch isn't dead yet, don't kill him, man. At least until I get there."

When Tomlinson heard a wild splashing in the distance, he grabbed binoculars and hurried topside. When he saw Marion Ford's boat, then Ford himself hacking away at some poor bastard in the water, he turned and spoke to the pretty veterinarian. "This appears to be one of those family emergencies that's personal and, no doubt, ugly. Would you mind tossing your clothes in the dinghy so I can take you ashore? We're a little pressed for time here."

"What did you mean *don't kill him*? Who's out there?" The woman, naked, her breath sweet with the odor of good herb, poked her head out the companionway. "All that splashing, you said it was probably dolphins."

"Could be. Yep. Entirely possible. On the other hand, I'm not exaggerating when I say the less you know about me and my friends, the better. I'm talking about people at this marina. Oh, sure, they might appear to be normal, even semi-sane, but you don't want to peek behind the curtain when it comes to this crowd."

"Oh my god—you're serious."

"You betcha. I might write another book."

"Are you saying they're criminals?"

"Worse. High-ranking government employees, some of them—but you didn't hear that from me. Sex fiends and deviants are a walk in the spring rain compared to a few of my neighbors, but we all manage to get along." He pointed to A dock. "Every boat has a story that would curl your hair. Come on . . . get dressed. We've got to go."

The woman, with a fresh huskiness, said, "Instead of just vacationing, maybe I should move here."

She ducked into the cabin, where the flame of an oil lamp cast exotic shadows. Tomlinson feasted on various intersections of her body: soft underbelly of breasts, chines of ribs, a shaved mound, the joining of thighs and luxurious lips.

"Look at you," the woman grinned. "You're ready again. I had no idea older men were so much fun."

This was a surprising thing to hear. He'd never thought of himself as older or younger than the women he had loved, but only said, "Pay no attention to that heartless bastard. My brain is in complete control." His eyes swept the cabin. "Any idea where your bra ended up? Or I can bring it along, if you'd like to meet for breakfast." He paused. "I know your first name's Ava—Dr. Ava—and you have a Scandinavian sort of last name. What was it again?"

"I'm sleeping right here," the woman replied. "This is the first time I've been stoned since vet school and I'm going to savor every moment." She turned her backside to him and crawled into the V-berth on hands and knees, a sprig of mistletoe on the hatch above as her butt disappeared. It was a Yuletide tableau that squeezed the heart and damn near brought tears to his eyes.

"God bless this life and all the lives to come," he said. "Oh—later, if you hear me talking to someone—a guy, most likely. No matter what we say, we're either lying or making shit up. You're a doctor. I refuse to drag you into whatever sinister scheme a pal of mine might be cooking up."

No time for an explanation.

He started the little four-stroke on his dinghy and sped away.

"A blimp?" Tomlinson said to Ford. "Why are you out here at three in the morning beating the shit out of someone's toy blimp?"

What Ford had thought of as a helicopter did, indeed, look more like a motorized zeppelin now that he was in his boat, engines idling, with the spotlight on. In the white glare, insects and exhaust spiraled above the little aircraft's hull, which was partially submerged. It was the size of a garbage can, but sleek, carbon-colored, no markings save for solar panels and jagged tears in the fuselage caused by the gaff. A line had been secured around the thing and cleated off at the stern.

Ford, aiming a flashlight at his thigh, asked, "Do you

see a bruise there? And on my shoulder?" He craned his neck. The spots throbbed as if he'd been burned. Then he was done with it and put the flashlight away. "I'm going to tow it in and take a closer look. No need for you to stick around."

Tomlinson, in his dinghy, looked up at his pal, who was standing at the console, putting stuff away—an obsessive neat freak. "Not until you explain what's going on. Wait—shine the light on the blimp again. That's not the same one you shot down this afternoon. Or whatever the hell you did."

"Keep your voice down," Ford said. "You know how sound travels. It's up to you, follow me or don't, but there's not much more I can tell you."

Tomlinson, thinking, *Why am I not shocked?* followed his pal anyway, neither of them saying much until their boats were secured and they were in the lab, where Ford, wearing soggy shorts, no shirt, switched on a desk lamp next to the computer. "Do me a favor and look up a guy named Winslow Shepherd. I'm going to get some dry clothes on."

"The Australian activist—that Shepherd? If it's the same one, I—" Tomlinson stopped midsentence, looking at his friend's leg. "That's one bad-ass bruise you got there, pal."

"You know him? He's a math professor . . . or used to be."

"*Knew* him," Tomlinson replied. He took the desk lamp and held it out like a torch. "Wow . . . I've never seen a bruise like that before. How'd it happen?"

Ford looked at his thigh, where there was a welt with

radiant lines of green and purple. It resembled glass that had been shattered by a bullet. "Tell me about Shepherd. Or his son, Julian—do you know him, too?"

"Turn around, dude. Come on . . . just do it." After a moment, Tomlinson returned the lamp to the desk. "There's another bruise just like it behind your shoulder blade. And . . . Geezus, your ear's all screwed up, too. Did you get shot, or speared, or . . . ? No—don't tell me, but, man, you should have a doctor take a look." He snapped his finger. "Hey, just so happens I was, uhh, consulting with a doctor earlier. She's asleep on my boat."

"Stick to the subject. How well did you know Shepherd?"

"She wouldn't mind if I woke her—"

"Tell me, damn it."

"*Okay*, but I barely knew the guy. Let's see . . . We dropped mescaline together a couple times and rode Harleys from north L.A. to Berkeley. This was years ago at a big peace rally in San Francisco. No—Winslow had this tricked-out Triumph, not a Harley. We were speakers at one of the venues. Otherwise . . . well, just one of those people you meet but don't get to know very well."

"Sounds more like you were runner-up for best man at his wedding."

"It was a tribal thing," Tomlinson explained. "Imagine thirty thousand intellectuals and hipsters all with the same goals. Freedom, equality, and Keynesian economics. Pure, you know? A family oneness, and, of course, the right to smoke weed. We weren't into the individuality thing, so there was no need to connect on a one-on-one basis."

Ford's turn to shake his head, meaning *Why am I not surprised?* He motioned to the computer. "There's a reason I need information on Shepherd and his son. Did you ever meet Julian?"

"I might have seen him. There were a lot of naked kids running around in those days. Later, I read he changed his name to Julian-something-Solo. Julian Caesar Solo? I don't know, my imagination might have added that. Anyway . . . there was an article in the *Times* or I would've never made the connection. This was a year or so back after he hacked the big boys and narced out the CIA—a couple of other agencies, too—for spying on private citizens."

Ford was interested. "What did you think about that? What Julian did, I mean."

"Right on, is what I thought. Who wouldn't? Our basic damn rights to privacy were being shit all over. The other famous hacker—was it Snowden? No, he was more of a whistle-blower . . . Anyway, Snowden was an *I'll do anything to be a rock star* dweeb. But Julian, man—Julian was raised with the same pure ideals that represent the very best of our movement."

Ford smiled to signal tolerance, but the smile faded. "Did Shepherd mention he sent a mail bomb that killed three high school kids? Or maybe that was after your joyride."

Tomlinson knew about it but only shook his head.

"I'll bring you a beer when I come back," Ford said and left the room.

When he returned, the marina's cat, Crunch & Des, followed at his heels, and on the screen was a mosaic of photos—all bruises similar to those on his shoulder and thigh.

"Sonic weapons caused these, man. It's the only thing I can find that explains that weird design. Ultrasonic or ELF sonic, according to this. It explodes the corpuscles; liquid in cellular tissue, the cells go *Boom!* Sound so far off the scale, only dogs can hear it."

Tomlinson turned to the screen. "Or maybe they can't. Speaking of which, I had a . . . well, a recent consultation with the vet from Sarasota. Your guy checked out fine, but Ava does have a couple of questions. Why not let her look at your leg?"

"Who?"

"The vet. She's asleep on my boat. I thought I mentioned that. Sonic wounds can be serious, dude. That shit can explode your eyeballs. You don't even want to know what happens to your brain." Tomlinson's gaze moved to his pal's swollen ear and he gulped. "Or . . . it couldn't hurt to call nine-one-one. How you feeling, ol' buddy?"

Ford stood there in jeans and a tank top, holding two bottles of beer. He handed one over. "Like I haven't slept in two days, but it's actually closer to three. I can't believe you've already got her in bed." He drank, removed his glasses, and squinted at the screen. "Sonic weaponry, huh? Whales and dolphins use the same thing. Prehistoric whales could hit their prey with a squeal that was more like a depth charge. Tunas, even seals—their lungs would explode. Air sacs, in the case of fish."

Tomlinson waited, but that's all the biologist said. "So that's why you beat the shit out of a midget airplane?"

"Something like that."

"Did it have, like, guns? Or was it the flying saucer that nailed you—the one showed up before sunset?"

Ford shrugged and scratched the cat's ears after it vaulted onto the dissection table.

"I'm trying to picture what sonic guns look like. The blimp, it's mostly solar panels and electronics. Were there more than two?"

Another shrug.

"Hey"—Tomlinson was getting frustrated—"is there something I'm missing here? Assholes send million-dollar drones to buzz-bomb a respected biologist with sonic warfare shit. That's not typical holiday fare. I think your neighbors have a right to ask for a few details. What if more of those bastards come back and their aiming system, or whatever, goes tits-up? They might start blasting boats out of the water. I never thought I'd hear myself say this, but maybe we should notify the cops."

"I'd have to answer questions," Ford said. "Did you bother doing a search on Shepherd and his son?"

"Forgive me for worrying about a friend with bruises that look like Key West tattoos done by a meth freak. Jesus—fross, man." He sighed. "I found a more recent article in *Newsweek* on those two, then sort of went down a bunny hole."

"Yeah?"

Tomlinson combed his hair back. "Why not just tell me what's going on? My guess is, there's nothing I'll find with a quick computer search you don't already know."

"Let's just say that one or both of them might have a reason to keep an eye on me," Ford said. "You didn't find anything?"

Tomlinson swung around in the chair, and the computer screen changed. "Julian's a multimillionaire now—a billionaire, in fact—from software he created, which led to him owning Internet businesses worldwide. The kid's a genius. He caught the perfect wave, technologically speaking."

"What about his dad?"

"I'm not done. Julian funneled a lot of his money into righteous causes up until two years ago. That's when the U.S. and a couple of European nations decided he was doing too much good in the world and tried to arrest him. So he went underground. Trust me, people raised in the movement *know* how the underground works.

"The bad news," Tomlinson continued, "is that he and his dad had a falling-out. Something about Winslow trying to take credit for what the kid did. Ego, man. I do remember that Winslow could be an egotistical ass. What I don't understand is"—Tomlinson spun back, eyes serious—"what this has to do with you hammering the crap out of a million-dollar blimp. Dude, I know you. There's a connection. At least, you believe there's a connection. In your mind, being frivolous means wearing your cap at a jaunty angle."

Ford put his glasses on and straightened them before meeting his pal's gaze. "We're about to cross a dangerous line here, if you really want to know."

"Shit. I *knew* it." Tomlinson got up and began to pace. "Less than an hour ago, I was just saying . . ." He let that drop. "I'm not sure what you're asking me to do."

"Potentially? Turn traitor against whatever cause you and Shepherd have in common. Or, possibly, just Shepherd . . . or him and his son. Or both. I'm really not sure about any of this, but certain elements are falling into line. I need to know where those two are. You know the guy. Is there someone you can call?"

"That was twenty years ago—another lifetime. He could be dead, for all I know."

"He's not. Shepherd's in a hospital somewhere— maybe Mexico or South America. I don't know his condition, but he's definitely not dead."

Tomlinson stopped and stared at Ford. "Jesus Christ. I just flashed on something so dark . . . my god. You weren't in Orlando. *Mexico*—that's where you disappeared to. Doc . . . please tell me I'm wrong about this."

Like he hadn't heard a word, that was Ford's reaction. "I've got to hide that drone somehow . . . and find the one still out there. They've got telemetry systems that can't be killed, from what I saw. You were right, they'll be back. Or they'll send someone. You mentioned a cement cistern on the property you bought."

"What about it?"

"That's not obvious?"

"Yeah—scary obvious. It's a beautiful little pool built for irrigation a hundred years ago, not hiding contraband. Twenty by twenty, and five feet deep. You know that old coquina-type concrete they used? But electromagnetic waves can pierce concrete, if that's what you're thinking."

Ford conceded with a nod. "Then maybe we'll carry it offshore when we dive the Captiva Blue Hole. No one knows how deep that hole is, and it's covered with a limestone lip. Or we'll sink it somewhere else and mark the location with the GPS." After a pause, he added, "I want to be fair about this, so no more questions about your friend Shepherd, okay? Not tonight or when we dive."

Tomlinson sulked and drank his beer. "Were you sent to Mexico to kill Winslow? At least tell me that."

"If I was in Mexico, whatever I did or didn't do was entirely up to me. And that's the truth."

"Geezus . . . a guy I hung out with. He was a pompous prick sometimes, I admit that, but his whole life has been dedicated to making the world better. This really sucks, man. No way he'd be involved with sending freakin' killer drones to hurt someone."

Ford gave Tomlinson's shoulder a reassuring pat. "Think it over," he said, then went out the screen door.

9

FORD LAY DOWN TO REST FOR A FEW MINUTES and woke up four hours later, his regular time: seven a.m. That quick, back on schedule, or so he believed—a man accustomed to travel and the exigencies of juggling two lives. Immediately, he rushed out to confirm the broken UAV was where he'd left it.

There it was, under the house on his boat, lying beneath a bow hood of neoprene polymer. The material resembled Kevlar but had been developed by stealth engineers to absorb, not deflect, prying technologies such as radar and homing devices.

An additional protectant from satellites was the house's floor of yellow pine and a tin roof.

At a more leisurely pace, he went upstairs for breakfast. This morning, he chose tea, not coffee, three soft-boiled eggs, and what was left of the snapper, which he seared in a cast-iron skillet, then shared with Crunch & Des, who was a lot friendlier now that the dog was gone.

On the fridge was a note from Tomlinson:

Friendship is the cement that binds destinies or drags our crazy asses into the deep blue sea, where fish will eat our dicks off and shit in our ears. But, what the hell—I printed all the pertinent data. (Signed) B-fucking-Arnold

Two folders there: DRONES, another labeled SHEP-HERD. Inside was contact information for Shepherd and his son, much of it outdated, but a start.

Drones. Ford intended to do a quick review but was drawn in by video of fantasy-world machines that were, in fact, real. The U.S. Marines had pack-animal drones that resembled headless oxen, only larger. They stomped along on four steel legs, bulled through brush and trees, impervious to obstacles, and never tired. Ford imagined the enemy's reaction when these monsters appeared on a smoky battlefield.

There were hundreds of other unmanned aircraft, or UMAs. Most were powered by four or more propellers, some disguised to look like hawks and crows, some that resembled oversized mosquitoes. Intelligence agencies had come up with those. More than once, he double-checked to confirm the videos were real, not Hollywood cartoons. That's how incredible some were.

Amphibious and underwater drones were more inventive because the sea contained a broader diversity. Robotic stingrays and shark clones that could operate deeper than any man. There were mini-subs, cannonball-style rovers, and even . . .

Ford cleaned his glasses, then zoomed in. *Jellyfish*, of all things, with Plexiglas domes and antennas for tentacles. Cameras affixed to gyros protruded from their bellies and resembled captured prey.

The landline phone rang. He reached, without looking, and answered, "Sanibel Biological. Ford speaking."

"Oh, good, this is Ava Lindstrom. Tomlinson gave me your number, I hope this is a good time."

His mind was slow to match the data: she was the veterinary from Sarasota who'd spent the night on Tomlinson's boat. "Dr. Lindstrom," he said and nearly added "you're up early" but didn't. "I intended to call you. Thanks for taking charge yesterday. How's he doing? Uhh . . . my dog, I mean. Not Tomlinson."

The woman chuckled with uneasy professional restraint. "That's why I'm calling. We skipped over a lot of the paperwork because it was an emergency. Now I'm trying to catch up. Do you have a sec?"

Ford turned to the screen door, his view of the bay blocked by the breezeway, pine planking painted gray. He couldn't see Tomlinson's sailboat. "You're welcome to stop by. Or I can pick you up in my boat."

There was an uncomfortable silence. "Unless your

boat has wheels, that would be quite a feat. Where do you think I am?"

Uh-oh. He shut down the computer. "No idea, but there's usually water access—"

"Not on Summerlin Road, there isn't. I'm at the clinic. You remember the clinic? Your friend Tomlinson can remind you. He just left—or maybe you two already had a nice little chat this morning. One of those locker room gossip sessions guys apparently like."

"Not at all," Ford replied. "I thought you were vacationing here. On Sanibel," which came off okay but could have been smoother.

"That explains it," she said, her tone chilly. "If it's all the same to you, I'd rather do this over the phone. I'm sure we both have better things to do."

She needed billing information—all the usual stuff— which Ford supplied while she typed away at a computer, then surprised him by asking, "What's the dog's name?"

He had never bothered naming the dog. "Why do you need that?"

"Because on the form, there's an open box. That's what I'm supposed to do, fill in the little boxes and complete these forms."

"It's okay with me if you leave it blank."

Her sigh signaled impatience. "Mr. Ford, in five years of practice, almost twelve years of dealing with pet owners, I've never had anyone refuse to tell me their dog's name. It's a fairly simple question. It's not like I'm prying into your personal secret history. Or is it?"

Ford's eyes moved from the cat with the literary

name—Crunch & Des, asleep on the dissecting table—to a shelf where the *Sea of Cortez* and the novel *Far Tortuga* lay in dust jackets, both dog-eared after many readings. "Peter Matthiessen," he said.

"Yes . . . What about him?"

"That's his name."

"The writer, I'm familiar with some of his work. What's he have to do with—"

"You asked for a name. That's it. Peter, ahh, Peter *Steinbeck*. That's what I meant to say."

The woman asked, "We are talking about your dog? You named a dog after—"

"Two writers," Ford said. "I call him Peter. Well . . . Pete—or Steinbeck. It's sort of a marina tradition."

"Pete," the woman said and cleared her throat. "It's better than Lassie, I guess. Wasn't Pete the dog in the Little Rascals cartoons?"

Ford hadn't had time to think this through. "I didn't want a name he'd confuse with the basic training commands. You know, *sit*, *stay*, *down*—"

"I'm familiar with the commands." She was typing.

"Or Steinbeck. That definitely works. Two syllables. Hell . . . put down whatever you want."

It was the wrong thing to say. "Yesterday, after you turned your back on that poor animal . . . are you sure he's really your dog? An AKC registration number, or some proof of ownership, would make me feel a lot better about this. If there's a legal issue, the clinic would need a copy in the files."

"How about a receipt from the previous owner?" Ford

asked. "And there's an ID chip implanted under the skin of his neck. You didn't scan it?"

"This isn't my clinic," the woman reminded him. "Do you remember the previous owner's name?"

"Why are you so concerned? I just paid my bill, that should be it. Tell me something—when, exactly, did I piss you off, Dr. Lindstrom?"

"I have no idea what you mean," she said, but then backtracked. "Okay, okay. Look . . . I'm no prude, but I'm not easy, so I guess I'm a little defensive. Tomlinson obviously told you about last night. Why didn't you just admit it?"

"If it's any consolation, he didn't share any details, and he wouldn't have even if I'd asked. It's a long-standing rule we have here. It lets us pretend we're decent and honorable and all that stuff. Truce?"

The woman replied, "Now you're scaring me," but laughed a little. "I actually am interested in the dog's background. In school, I did research for the Dog Genome Project. He's . . . unusual."

Ford said, "You noticed."

"I noticed he doesn't bark. That suggests an injury, and we did find significant scarring on the neck, but it could also be a trait that was engineered. Unlikely, but . . ."

"Genome Project," he said to nudge her along. "Haploid sets of chromosomes."

"Look at you," she said. "Single chromosomal sets, yes, exactly right. I'm suddenly convinced you really are a biologist—you never know what to believe in a beach town."

Ford had never thought of Sanibel as a beach town, but listened to the woman add, "A brain scan showed activity in the dog's frontal lobes that I've never seen before. Are you sure he was underwater more than five minutes?"

"You're going to like this," Ford replied. "The previous owner was a geneticist. A Ph.D. from Atlanta."

"You're kidding."

"It gets better. The guy got seriously into retriever trials, breeding and training both. *Obsessed*, is his son's word for it. He had one of those medium-sized RVs—a Winnebago, maybe—and he was killed in a crash on Tamiami Trail on his way to a show in Coral Gables. The dog survived . . . Well, it's a long story, but I noticed the same thing you did. He doesn't bark. And enough other behavioral—oddities, I guess—that I had some DNA samples analyzed."

"Oh my god."

"Yeah. I've got a whole file, but it's way out of my field."

"Oh my god," she said again but slower. "You think Pete's a specially engineered hybrid."

"Who?" Ford asked, then winced but pressed ahead. "I'll bring the results when I pick him up. Will he be ready sometime today?"

"He's with Tomlinson. I thought I mentioned they just left . . . well, about fifteen minutes ago. If you don't mind, I do have one more question. The geneticist—do you remember his name?"

*   *   *

It was calm this December morning, the air cool off the bay, but warmer when Ford exited the mangroves into the sunny parking lot where his truck was parked, the engine still ticking with heat.

Tomlinson had recently returned.

There were a dozen cars in the lot, and, outside the office, Mack was deep in conversation with Rhonda, while Figueroa, muscles shiny in the sun, lugged a heavy box toward the boat ramp. But no sign of his pal or the dog.

Ford did an about-face. He completed routine chores in the lab, then went into his bedroom to change into shorts and running shoes. He awoke an hour later, glared in the mirror, and told himself, *Your lazy ass is slipping* . . .

A fitting punishment was a tougher workout, which he modified to do double duty. Instead of jogging to the beach for a swim, he put on a mask, no fins, and crawl-stroked a quarter mile out into the bay. Maybe he would stumble onto the missing drone.

He did not.

Half an hour and three miles later, he sprinted the final hundred yards into the parking lot, then stood, panting at leaning rest, until he was able to walk without wobbling. As he made his way through the mangroves, he tried to convince himself *That's enough for today.*

No it wasn't. A few years back, he'd drilled holes in two joists under his house and mounted a wooden bar over the water. It had just enough spring to make pull-ups easier, but not enough to admit it was cheating. Because of a torn rotator cuff, he hadn't used the bar in months. Today, his lazy ass decided he would. Never mind the spectacular bruise behind his shoulder or the orthopedist's warning to let the damn shoulder rest.

You can do this, he told himself.

No he couldn't.

Four pull-ups into an intended set of fifteen, what felt like ground glass caused him to lose his grip and sprawled him into the water. He came up spouting more personal advice, but louder, and when he was done, a man said, "I've heard all those words, but never in exactly that combination. Do you need help getting out?"

On the walkway, near the gate, stood a guy who looked too young to be wearing a gray suit and carrying a briefcase. "Are you Dr. Ford? My name's Watts. I was told this is where you live."

"Give me a second," Ford said. He used the ladder, went up the steps, and came out with a towel and wearing a dry tank top. "What can I do for you?"

"Just a couple of questions. I've already spoken to a few others who live in the area. Friendly place, this island."

"Questions about what?"

"Is there somewhere we can sit down and talk?"

"That sounds official."

The man, smiling, shook his head and started toward the house. "More like a private discussion."

Under the house, hidden in the boat, was the broken drone. Ford went down the steps, but not in an obvious hurry, saying, "Most people see the sign at the gate. You're supposed to ring the bell before you come through . . . Watts, you said?"

"You were putting on quite a show when I walked up," the man replied. "I must have missed it."

"Not a problem. For all I know, the damn sign's gone. Come on. We can talk out here." Ford slid past the guy, where he got a whiff of shaving lotion and gauged his size: six-three, a hundred and ninety pounds, with ears and a face unscarred by wrestling or mixed martial arts. "Yep"— he stopped and held the gate open—"the sign's still here."

Watts—if that was his name—remained relaxed. He had the easygoing confidence typical of insurance sales-men and federal agents. "Why is it I get the impression I'm not welcome?"

Ford wasn't wearing his glasses but stared as if the man's eyes had come sharply into focus. "You aren't— until you tell me why you're here. You could be a con man or with a group that's offended because I sell marine specimens. Or pissed-off because I don't think manatee and snook should be on restaurant menus. Oh, don't laugh. I get my share of crazies. What's your first name?"

The man, still chuckling, let that go and opened his briefcase. "I've been retained by a company that lost one of these yesterday. We know it went down here, some-where in the water. There's a reward if you can help."

Ford accepted a color photo of the saucer-shaped drone. He studied it for a while, then handed it back. "I saw something that looked like this fly past yesterday af-ternoon. Propeller-driven—you could hear the propellers but no motor—so I remember thinking it must be fairly high-tech and expensive. Then, for no apparent reason, it crashed right out there." He pointed vaguely. "I was sur-prised the owner didn't come charging out and try to get to it before it sank. So was everyone else. Now, a day later, here you are. How do you explain that, Mr. Watts?"

"Like I told you, it's owned by the company that hired me. It's a production company out of New York, but they have offices in Miami and Naples. They were shooting B-roll for a national ad campaign—Florida's sunny, sandy beaches, something like that. And you're right, it's an expensive piece of equipment. They want it back."

Ford started to say, "If they launched the thing out of Naples or Miami . . ." which is when he saw the dog out there, in three feet of water, struggling with something heavy; a black, saucer-looking object he'd dragged half-way to the stilthouse, even though it sank whenever he stopped to get a better grip. Like now.

"Let's talk in the parking lot," Ford said. He waved for Watts to follow him through the gate.

"Something wrong?"

"I was just pointing out there are plenty of scenic beaches around Naples, so why would they send a drone clear up here? But if they did, they did." He pulled the gate wider. "Are you coming?"

Watts sensed Ford's uneasiness. "Where?"

"The guy who owns the marina, his name's Mack. Mack got a better look at the thing than I did, and he rents boats. If it's in the water"—he motioned again, getting impatient—"you need a boat, right?"

"Maybe they're shooting an ad about Sanibel," Watts replied. He turned and looked where Ford had been looking and saw a furry butt sticking out of the water. But he did not yet see the missing drone, which the dog was battling to lift to the surface. "What the hell's that?"

"It's a dog."

"I can see that."

"He brings me all kinds of junk from the bottom. It's what retrievers do. Do you like dogs?"

When Watts turned away, saying, "Not really," Ford released a long breath but didn't feel safe until they were in the parking lot, where he pointed to the marina office and said, "You'll find Mack in there."

"We're not done."

The temptation was to tell the guy, *The hell we aren't*, but he couldn't risk being followed back to the lab. Plus, he had some questions of his own for the man.

It didn't happen. After waiting fifteen minutes outside the office, Ford went in to find Mack alone at the cash register. "Where's Watts?"

"The guy in the suit?" Mack reached under the counter for something—a small brown envelope. "I don't know. He walked in, gave me this, and left. I told him you were around here someplace. Who is he?"

Inside the envelope, no writing anywhere, was a cheap memory stick.

Ford said, "I've got to go," and jogged back to his house, where the dog was still battling the drone. But there was no sign of Watts—if that was his name.

A stopwatch icon appeared on the screen, then a warning in red: Time Terminated: 30 seconds. Do not pause or attempt to copy.

The stopwatch began ticking when Ford opened the file. A document appeared that typed itself as if being dictated:

If you killed the lying fool, I might have thanked
you. Instead, I'm obligated. Your only option is
to cooperate. Reparations, etcetera, to be
decided pending the old man's death or
recovery.

The document vanished, replaced by video. It showed
a hospital bed, where Winslow Shepherd lay with his leg
in a cast elevated in traction. Otherwise, he didn't look
too bad when he turned to the camera and slurred, "Tell
him he won't get away with this. Show him." Then attempted to yell, "You can't hide from . . ." but the words
collapsed into a coughing fit.

Ford tried to do two things at once: note details that
gave away the location and also capture a screenshot to
study later. But too late—not for the screenshot but to
correct his first mistake, which was opening the memory
stick in the first place.

The screen went black; a fan inside the hard drive dou-
bled its speed. Ford realized his system was being hi-
jacked, or erased, or both. In a rush, he yanked cables and
power cords free and threw the memory stick across the
room. The hard drive went silent, but it took a while. If
his files were still being downloaded, would throwing the
hard drive in the bay halt the theft?

No . . . not if software mogul Julian Solo was behind
the attack. Ford believed he was. The phrases *lying fool*
and *old man's* were convincing.

Idiot.

He slid the computer under the steel dissecting table—
as if that would help—banged open the door, and

clomped down to the lower deck, where he tried to calm down by looking in a wooden fish tank there. He'd made it from a thousand-gallon rain cistern, added all necessary pumps, a sub-sand filter, and a hundred-gallon upper reservoir to improve water clarity. Pumps hummed a froth of fresh spray onto the surface. Pinfish and snappers and a little bonnethead shark darted for cover among a host of living, breath-filtering species. There were tunicates, scallops, and triangular pen shells.

The pen shells were the size and color of a turkey's wing. They produced iridescent black pearls, and their abductor muscles were sweet with a mild cucumber flavor and good to eat. Colonies of thousands lay not far off the beach yet were unknown to most chefs, thus an unused resource.

It was calming to stand there and observe a lucent microcosm of the sea. But then the missing drone popped into his head and he turned. The dog was gone, but the drone was there, abandoned at the edge of the mangroves. He checked behind him, glanced at the sky, then went after it.

Beneath the house, next to his boat, was a hose. He washed the carbon fuselage clean and inspected both sides. Six of eight propellers were gone. Four mini-cameras protruded on spindles. There were dozens of sensors embedded in the skin but no identifying marks.

The aircraft wasn't heavy, once the water had drained. Fifteen pounds, approximately, and the circumference of a garbage can lid. He hid the thing on his boat next to the other UAV, then decided the bow cover, which was engineered for stealth, wasn't safe enough.

Maybe there was no safe place. Not with Julian and his network of Internet wizards in pursuit. They obviously had their orders, and Ford suspected what those orders were. Julian wanted his drones back. And wanted revenge.

But after rethinking it, Ford wasn't so sure. The document had been ambiguous. *If you killed the lying fool, I might have thanked you,* the text had read. Or was he wrong about the wording? Then something about reparations, etcetera, to be paid pending the old man's death or recovery.

I should make notes while it's fresh, Ford thought, but, either way, he had to wonder if Julian had offered him a way out.

If you'd killed the old fool, I would've thanked you.

That wasn't quite right either, but close enough.

Ford stepped under the house and looked up at the floor. Stacked between joists were sheets of tin roofing he'd replaced after the hurricane of 2004. If he covered the drones with enough tin, maybe a satellite couldn't find them. That was easy enough but sloppy. There had to be a better way.

Somewhere he'd read about constructing a room that was immune to lightning strikes. A Faraday cage, the structure was called. The design was based on a theory regarding the flow of electromagnetic energy. The cage was equally effective at blocking electronic waves of all sorts. That's what had caught his attention—Ford, a man who loathed the intrusions of the Internet yet lacked the willpower to get rid of it.

These days, at least, he could rationalize his weakness

because there was no place in the whole damn world where satellites could not be accessed.

Winslow Shepherd's voice had reminded him, *You can't hide.*

Well . . . he could try.

He didn't remember enough about building a Faraday cage to start immediately, but metal sheeting was a key component. Later, assuming his computer was kaput, he'd borrow Tomlinson's laptop to do the research.

Ford stacked the tin at the edge of the deck, made notes in the lab, then went to find his dog.

10

ON THE WALL SEPARATING THE OFFICE FROM THE fish market was a VHF radio that scanned three channels used by the fishing guides, plus emergency channels monitored by the Coast Guard. Mack, and sometimes Jeth, who filled in behind the counter, kept the volume low unless they heard something of interest.

Mack, chewing at a cigar, reached for the knob now when an unfamiliar voice called out, "Shark! . . . Shark! . . . You wouldn't believe the size of this bastard. It's gotta be twenty feet long."

Seconds passed, then he heard: "A great white, I think.

Yeah . . . gotta be. A great white shark. Oh my god . . . it's coming back and we've got two divers in the water. Anybody copy? Shit . . . Stand by."

A burst of static followed. This suggested to Mack he was eavesdropping on a vessel that was close enough to Sanibel to bang in loud and clear, but not far enough offshore to communicate with vessels in deeper water. On the roof was an illegal antenna that, on a good day, reached twenty-five miles into the Gulf. Ten miles, though, was typical. The captain in trouble wasn't far off the beach.

Static . . . more static, then the same voice yelled, "A freakin' great white shark! I gotta get our divers up. Anybody . . . do you copy? I could use some help out here, guys."

Mack knew that Fast Eddie had left with a scuba charter at eight a.m., yet he looked to confirm Eddie's boat was gone. It was the man's first charter in weeks, but that wasn't Eddie's voice. New Jersey accents were unmistakable. Dive captains sometimes paired up offshore, so maybe Eddie's radio was the source of the static. A bad antenna, or too far out to be heard.

He reduced squelch and turned up the volume, then hurried to the door, which was always propped open. He wanted someone to witness this. Aside from tourists, all he saw was the big brown retriever and the little Cuban, Figuerito, who was in the parking lot throwing rocks for the dog to retrieve, pitching as if in a baseball game.

Mack hollered, "Hey, Figgy. Get in here. Hurry, man! Bring Tomlinson and Rhonda, too, if they're handy."

The Cuban said something to an invisible umpire and

came on the run. He didn't speak English, but he knew an emergency when he heard one.

Mack slid into his regular seat behind the counter and pointed to the VHF when the Cuban and dog appeared. "A dive captain out in the Gulf, he spotted a great white shark and he's got divers in the water. It's gotta be her, the one they tagged. Dolly. Damn it, I knew I should've made Fast Eddie cancel that trip."

Figuerito nodded as if he understood. The dog, panting, did a circle and collapsed on the linoleum floor.

"The captain, the poor bugger, he can't contact anyone. I'm thinking I should hail the Coast Guard and—" A burst of static caused Mack to hold up a warning hand: *Listen.*

Offshore, the unknown captain spoke to a passenger but had the mic key open. "Goddamn thing's bigger than my boat, man. You see it? I don't know where it went. Keep your eyes open." He clicked the mic key twice. "Hailing any vessel, any vessel off Lighthouse Point. We've got a big-ass great white circling us and we've got two divers down. I blasted the emergency recall until I'm deaf, but they haven't responded. Oh, shit . . . now what?" There was a pause. "I'm thinking about . . . Yeah, I'm gonna have to go in after them. Stand by." A wailing horn made the last few words difficult to decipher.

Mack got to his feet. "Did he say he was going in the water? That's what I think he said. Or did he? Geezus, I hope I'm wrong. Figgy"—he pointed in the direction of Ford's lab—"go fetch Doc. Bring him back as fast as you can."

The dog jumped to its feet and charged out the door. The Cuban, confused, followed.

Mack looked at the radio, saying, "You're a fool if you go in. Don't do it," then realized he could talk to the guy himself by picking up the microphone. He tried.

"Break, break, this channel, this is Dinkin's Bay Marina. Skipper? We've got you loud and clear. Do you read? State your location, we'll send out a boat now. Also suggest you switch to emergency channel sixteen. That's channel one-six. Do you copy?"

Static; more static, then a garbled mess when other vessels came on with offers to help—one off Vanderbilt Beach, another near Sanibel Causeway. The confusion went on for a while, which Mack tried to abate, saying, "Clear this channel. Do you read? There's a boat out there in trouble. He has two divers he can't locate. Someone hail the Coast Guard and tell them to switch over."

The guy in trouble was too busy to respond, or maybe didn't hear the calls. No . . . his radio was screwed up. That was the problem. He could transmit but not receive, which is why, when he returned to the mic, he was frustrated. "If there's anybody out there who gives a damn, there's a twenty-foot great white shark circling us. Freakin' wide as a bus, and close enough to the beach that someone should warn those dumbasses to get out of the water."

Ford came through the door in time to hear most of that. Mack shushed him and attempted to contact the vessel again. "We have you loud and clear at Dinkin's Bay. What's the status of your divers?"

Ford's forehead wrinkled. "*Divers?* Who is that?"

Mack, using the microphone, repeated the question about divers several times. No response.

"What's his location?" Ford asked. "If he's close enough to the beach to see swimmers, he can't be in more than twenty feet of water."

Mack started to explain but was interrupted by the captain, who pressed the mic key while shouting to someone, "She's coming back . . . see it? Jesus Christ, look at the size of that dorsal. Billy . . . Billy! Stop taking pictures and hang on to something, man. Bastard's coming right at us." Then remembered why he'd picked up the microphone and hollered, "If anybody can hear me, we need help . . . A shark, a great white, has to weigh two tons. We're off Lighthouse Point about . . ." The man's voice softened to a whisper. "No . . . it's still coming . . . coming faster. Oh my god . . . we should've brought a bigger—"

Slam a hammer into a wall, that's the sound they heard next. Then silence, except for the sudden garble of many vessels transmitting at the same time. A lot of people had heard what just happened.

Mack rushed to the phone.

"Who are you calling?"

"Nine-one-one. I'll have them contact Coast Guard and scramble a chopper. Doc, we'll take your boat. I'll supply the fuel."

Ford, standing at the counter, covered the phone with his hand. "It's a prank, I think."

Mack grabbed the phone anyway and dialed.

"At the very least, say you're not sure it's an emergency," Ford advised. "Just say what you heard. Think about it. That last line about needing a bigger boat. It's right out of *Jaws*."

Ford listened to a one-sided conversation, Mack talking to the 911 operator, while the Cuban went out, followed by the dog, and returned with a bottle of orange pop.

When Mack was finished, he asked Figuerito in English, "Did you hear the captain say he needed a bigger boat? I didn't hear him say that, and anyone could tell he was scared shitless. Guys who take dive charters, they all have decent-sized boats."

In Spanish, Figuerito asked Ford, "Is there a problem with the radio? Tell him I don't know anything about radios."

"Mack," Ford said, "who takes clients a mile or two off the beach to dive? There's nothing to see out there but sand. You told nine-one-one the guy didn't identify himself, so how do you know he was a charter captain?"

"His radio was screwed up. I know the difference between a guide and a bloody weekender by the way they bloody well talk. He had two divers in the water—I could hear his emergency horn in the background—but they didn't come up." The marina owner thought for a moment. "Damn, I left that part out about the horn. Maybe I should call them back."

"What channel are you on?" Ford leaned over the counter to look. "You're on seventy-two. If it was an emergency, why didn't he use channel sixteen? If I was going to try a stupid prank, I wouldn't risk pissing off the feds by tying up an emergency channel. They could arrest him for that."

Mack's mind had already skipped ahead. "I need to contact Fast Eddie. He's out there with a party of four: three divers and one along for the ride. He said they'd do a checkout dive at Belton Reef, then head out to the Rock Pile, depending on the wind."

Ford was about to point out it was too windy to be offshore, that he and Tomlinson had postponed their dive. Eddie's decision had nullified the argument, but he was still convinced what he'd heard was some drunk or smartass who was a pretty good actor.

Sharks seldom attack boats. Even great whites. When they do, they chomp a propeller or some dangling appendage. Only in movies do they use their heads as battering rams.

Mack switched to channel 68 and began hailing Fast Eddie but made time to say, "Maybe you're right, Doc. But what if you're wrong?"

Ford couldn't disagree with that. "We'll take my boat, but see what Eddie has to say first."

He waited at the door. Outside, near the fuel pumps, the owners of *Tiger Lilly*, Rhonda and JoAnn, were in animated conversation with a couple of others who lived on A dock. Observing from the flybridge of his yacht was Vargas Diemer, pressed and pleated in gray slacks and a collared shirt. The Brazilian appeared interested, which was unusual for a man who wore aloofness like a mask.

Mack noticed the ladies and covered the mic while he explained, "Rhonda's computer crashed."

"Just now?" Ford asked.

"JoAnn's computer, too, or they both got a virus, something that makes them think the world is about to end. Rhonda texted me not twenty minutes ago."

Ford was thinking, *Julian?* but said, "It's probably a coincidence."

Mack, with an *I guess so* shrug, continued hailing *Jersey Girl*, which was Fast Eddie's boat.

Vargas waved Ford aboard and met him aft, where the railings were stained mahogany red and brightwork glistened. There were no corny nautical icons on this vessel. It was 55 feet of oceangoing craftsmanship that meshed with what Ford knew about the Brazilian. Which wasn't much, but a lot more than anyone else outside a few embassies and enclaves of power around the world.

That's why Vargas didn't bother with a phony accent when they were alone.

"They think the Internet is down, but that's not the problem," Vargas said. He glanced at Rhonda and the others. "My system's designed to go off-line if it senses certain probes. That's how I know. No point telling them, but we've been attacked. At least six computers here at the marina."

Ford thought, *Shit—this is because of me.* "Are you sure? Could have been a power surge or—"

"The way my system works, there's a visual alarm; nothing audible. I wasn't at the computer when it happened, but the alarm's been tripped. Definitely a hacker tried but couldn't break through."

"If you're right," Ford said, "I did something so stupid that . . . Anyway, my hard drive was compromised before whoever it was went after the marina. At least, I think so. That bothers me. Why would anybody go after the marina?"

Vargas touched the back of a chair, meaning *Take a seat*. "I'll save the obvious question. This early in the day, I know it's bottled water for you." He crossed into the main salon with a leading man fluidity that Ford ignored but, in truth, envied.

The obvious question Vargas would ask was *Who was the attacker*?

Should he confide? He'd already admitted the truth about the fallen drone. Part of the truth anyway. Ford debated the pros and cons while he waited. When one is pursued by a powerful enemy, a savvy ally is an asset, and the Brazilian was an unusually savvy man.

If asked, the Brazilian would say he was a commercial pilot for Swissair. Or he'd offer a business card that said he was CEO of an import-export company that had offices in Rio, Luxembourg, and Dubai. Solid stories that impressed the ladies, but misleading. Swissair had changed its name to Lufthansa several years back, which is probably when Vargas had gone to work for himself. His import-export business existed, but its office was a P.O. box in Lauderdale.

Even a third-level background check had required some guesswork.

Ford's summary: Vargas was a big-time freelancer and very good at what he did. He could be trusted—if the fee was right—and had contacts that opened doors to money.

He specialized in "threat management," which meant recovering items that owners could not report as stolen—letters to a mistress, photos of a secret lover, videos or text messages that compromised men and women too powerful to tolerate blackmail.

Contract murder was the more lucrative next step.

Ford knew it was true.

"The outside probes started thirty-two minutes ago," the Brazilian said when he returned. He put a bottle of water on a table of oiled teak and sat with a glass of wine. "Who was it, sport?"

Ford opened the bottle. "This is where I'm supposed to play dumb or turn it around and ask you." He drank, then shrugged. "Okay. You ever hear of a guy named Winslow Shepherd? A mathematics professor. An Aussie. He goes under the banner of 'activist,' but he's more of a third-rate revolutionary. He got off for bombing a post office years ago because he's better connected than most. Three high school kids were killed."

After a slow shake of the head, Vargas said, "I know the type. What did you do to piss him off? Write a paper endorsing whale hunting or killing seals, or something like that? That might attract a group with enough money and know-how to help him."

"What about the name Julian Solo?"

Vargas, a man not easily impressed, dropped the shields for an instant. "I hope you're guessing."

"I'm not."

"In that case, the Pacific coast of Panama is nice this time of year. That would be my choice—as long as you go the opposite direction. But the shotgun approach—

taking the whole marina off-grid—it makes no sense for a man with his resources. What's the connection?"

"Shepherd is Julian's father. He and I had a . . . falling-out recently."

The Brazilian didn't miss much. "On your *lecture* tour, I assume. Your choice of words—to a commercial pilot anyway—tells me the math professor is no longer a problem. Now the son wants to even the score."

"Not exactly," Ford said. Mack was standing in the office door, ready to search for a boat that probably didn't exist. "I'll be back in a couple of hours. Or stop by the lab tonight—if you're interested."

"A falling-out with the father of a cyberbillionaire," Vargas mused. He sipped his wine. "Guess that explains the drones."

Drones—plural. It stopped Ford in his tracks. "How many have you seen?"

The Brazilian proved his interest by replying, "Counting the two last night?"

When they rounded Lighthouse Point into the Gulf, which was choppy but not too bad, Ford didn't need to check the radar before saying, "There must be forty boats out there. They don't need us. Besides"—he indicated the water, which was marl green—"no one in their right mind would dive this close to shore. Offshore, the viz might be so-so, but not here."

Mack was somewhere inside his head but snapped out of it when he saw the flotilla, plus a Coast Guard chopper approaching from the north. "They don't think it was a prank. My god, word spreads fast. Don't get me wrong—I hope nobody was hurt—but it's not a bad thing for business, if you know what I mean."

Ford was more concerned about the pair of UAVs he'd hidden in the mangroves under a pile of tin sheet roofing. He was eager to turn around, but it wasn't his call. "What do you want to do?"

Mack's response: *Huh?* then shook his head, still not entirely there but enough to hold a conversation. "What I think is, we ought to come back with a barrel of chum and catch that sonuvabitch. To hell with people and their *sharks were here before we were* bullshit. Kill it or drive it off, I don't care. Or, if you're right, if it was some bastard playing a joke, well . . ."

He left that to Ford's imagination. The older man's attention shifted to the beach, where hotels, none over two stories, were lined up beyond a fringe of sea oats and palms. "The place I'm buying is just a couple miles up. I haven't seen it from the water. How about we take a look? By then, if we haven't heard something different on the VHF, we'll turn around."

They ran along the beach past Sanibel Moorings, a bunch of other places, then turned in not far beyond Casa Ybel, where umbrellas bunched like wildflowers. Ford's impatience was mollified by women in two-piece suits, sunning themselves. Mack rambled on about the Grin N Bare It cottages, which they couldn't see from the water, but the narrow access path was there, lined with coconuts.

Mack talked about it being a good investment; a communal lifeboat for themselves and people they trusted.

On and on like that. Easy enough to tune out until the man was several sentences into a different subject, the last fragment startling: ". . . a couple of surfers washed ashore. One, just his torso, the other missing a leg."

Ford was suddenly interested. "Where was this?"

"I just told you, when I was a kid."

"From a shark attack, you mean."

"I was there—my folks ran a little beach takeaway. A carryout, you'd call it. Burgers and snacks and chips—French fries. You know the sort of place. A woman started screaming. By the time I got there, I had to jockey my way through a crowd. I'll never forget it. Some bloke's innards hanging out. At first, I thought it was a pig with a bunch of jellyfish floating around the rib cage. A white pointer had gotten them both. Great whites, you call them."

Ford said, "You're from western New Zealand. I forget the name of the town. Hard to pronounce anyway."

Mack only nodded. "My point is, folks there didn't sit around wringing their hands about what to do. Over the next few days, fishermen brought in three of those bastards. Strung 'em up like the killers they are and took pictures. After that, no more dead surfers and no more nervous tourists. Selling burgers and snass got back to normal."

"You've never told that story before," Ford said, "or someone would've passed it on. How old were you?"

Mack was a large man with a gravelly laugh. "There're a lot of stories I haven't told folks around here."

Something about the way he said it put Ford on alert. "Are you from near Auckland or the South Island?"

"It was a different lifetime," Mack replied, either evading or he didn't hear. He checked on the distant flotilla, which had moved a mile or two closer to Fort Myers Beach. "Hope they find the poor bastards . . . or I hope you're right. Guess we ought to be getting back, Doc. You ready?"

11

TOMLINSON'S SHOWER WAS A BAG SUSPENDED from the mast of his sailboat, *No Más*, a 38-foot Morgan bleached to bone by the tropics. Not just any bag, a catheter bag he associated with a painful incident that involved a urinary blockage and a parasitic fish.

"Would you believe a fish once swam up my dick?"

This was an opening line he could not use with just any woman, but, with the right one, it was guaranteed fun. His explanation, which made the impossible plausible, usually sealed the deal. A candiru, a South American catfish only a few millimeters long, sought refuge in the urinary tracts of certain animals, including men, if one was dumb enough to piss while up to his belly in a candiru habitat.

Painful. But wasn't pain the keystone of enlightenment?

He put on shorts, no underwear, a long-sleeved pullover, tied his hair back with a red wind scarf, and rowed ashore rather than use the engine. Didn't want to drown out the silence of stars and water on this perfect winter's eve.

Ahead was the marina: palm trees draped in Christmas lights, boats decorated, the docks weighted with shadow people carrying drinks amid snippets of laughter. Yeah . . . a whiff of good ganja, too. This was a promising step into the marina's Twenty-six Days of Christmas.

Tonight was Day 14, a Monday. Secret Santa names would be picked from a hat. For snacks: smoked mullet, mango chutney; fried gator tail for hors d'oeuvres.

Water amplified sound. He rowed and eavesdropped between each stroke. His ears were calibrated by experience to filter out men's voices because he preferred what women had to say. True, it was a method of gauging age and availability, but his affection for women transcended base need despite the fact his base needs were legendary. He liked women as people. Really, he did. Eons of subjugation and general male assholishness had made females more sensitive and perceptive. They possessed heightened paranormal powers, if they chose to tap into them.

The female mind was fascinating. And if a woman's mind was also in a lusty mood, then her breasts and warm thighs were a welcome bonus—all shapes, all sizes, it didn't matter as long as their hearts were in the right place.

Tomlinson loved women. Well . . . except for the Chinese dragon lady he'd married and that had lasted only long enough to conceive a daughter. Which is why, by choice, he lived alone on a boat with a forward V-berth big enough for three, even though it had slept as many as five.

Last night, with the veterinarian, one woman had been more than enough.

Gonna get chilly tonight, he thought. *Sure hope Ava doesn't start beating herself over the head with guilt. What'll I do if she cancels?*

He cupped a hand to test a whiff of his own breath. He tugged his hair straight and straightened the red bandana he often wore pirate-style. A man never wanted to count on good fortune, but to dismiss hope invited negative karma and only twice in his life had negative karma gotten him laid, so the less said or thought about that, the better.

I bet I look pretty good, he thought. *Next trip to town, I'll buy a couple more bandanas, different colors.*

Women's laughter, a youthful bell chime amid a familiar chorus, demanded his attention. Tomlinson spun around so fast, he dropped an oar. Moored along A dock, between the Brazilian's yacht and a houseboat patched with duct tape, was a stodgy old Chris-Craft brightened by Japanese lanterns and several busty silhouettes. *Tiger Lilly* was painted on the stern. The owners, Rhonda and JoAnn, were aboard with guests—all female, thus far, and at least two of them new to the marina.

Marta Estéban was there, too.

On the other hand, he thought, *I totally respect Ava's concerns about morality. If she doesn't show, I'll just have to muddle through.*

He recovered the oar and continued to eavesdrop while he rowed. There were many familiar voices, but only two popular topics: computer crashes and a great white shark that had supposedly attacked a boat.

This was of interest. Before and after his own Mac-Book had crashed, he had done research on both subjects for his pal Ford. He had information to share.

Separating the marina from the lab was a stretch of mangrove murkiness. The biologist was up there in a lighted window. He wore a lab apron and gloves for some reason, still hard at work. Seeing his pal, combined with the research he'd done, sapped some of the joy from his holiday mood.

Shit-oh-dear. What to do?

Work before pleasure, he decided.

Tomlinson spun an oar and aimed the dinghy at Ford's house.

Tomlinson's research was on a 32-gig memory card, which the biologist accepted but said, "Tell me the important stuff. The last time I used one of these, it wiped out my computer and backups. In a way, it's a relief not to have the damn thing available, but I'm off the grid for now."

"No firewalls? Oh hell"—Tomlinson snapped his fingers—"I forgot who we're dealing with. Julian, the Black Knight of the Internet. There's a rumor he's hiding out in an embassy in South America, but it's bullshit. I called an old buddy of mine. Remember Ken Kern?"

"Vaguely. He's a scientist of some type. You both attended Harvard."

"Ken was big in the movement, a founder of Students for a Democratic Society—SDS. Back then, he had hair to the middle of his back; a very hip guy who wore a silver infinity necklace along with the Star of David and smoked nothing but unfiltereds. Cigarettes, I'm talking about. A purist, you know? Now he's bald and has a Sigmund Freud goatee. He's senior geneticist at Mass Labs—but still a purist."

At the mention of "geneticist," Ford walked to the screen door. "Did you happen to see the dog out there?"

"Probably swimming, but stay with me for a sec. Ken and Winslow Shepherd were tight until eight years ago."

Ford moved to the south window. "What happened?"

"The U.S. had a national election. Maybe you heard about it."

The biologist didn't bother to respond.

"Actually, this was during the campaign. Ken and Shepherd were part of a candidate's think tank. I'm not going to say what office, but it was national. They were policy types, low-profile geniuses, who chipped in whenever they were needed. The fact they'd both been arrested for blowing shit up and inciting riots required what politicos call a cushioning wall, so it's not like they hung with the candidate—but they did. Quite a few times, in fact."

Ford focused in. "You're telling me they had access to the White House?"

Tomlinson stared for a moment. Inside his head, at the core, was a master entity, a serious, sober being who seldom appeared but who appeared now. "I'm telling you why I'm here. Why I'm narcing out a man who did what he did for all the right reasons but who couldn't handle the power."

"Shepherd or the candidate?"

Tomlinson kept going. "My convictions about this world haven't changed. Same with Ken. He bugged out—or was kicked down the stairs. He wasn't clear about that. Mostly, he spoke generally about Shepherd and some others in the movement. Julian included. Now that they've got power—real power—some have drifted over to the dark side. They use any means available to destroy governments that make war."

Tomlinson twisted a lock of hair and chewed on it. "Ken says they're funding what he considers to be terrorists. They've aligned with someone—Chinese, maybe—to dismantle the whole sick scaffolding."

"Scaffolding of *this* government," Ford said.

"Anyone who gets in the way, they replace or publicly discredit or serve them up to guys with knives. I told him, 'Hey, at least they can't touch you now.' Know what he said? He said, 'I wish that was true, but I won't be bullied.' A good man, Ken Kern."

"I'm sorry to put either one of you in this position." Ford took off his lab apron and sat. "What about finding Shepherd and Julian?"

Tomlinson checked the pocket of his shorts, then the other pocket, and took out a piece of paper. "He gave me the number of another acquaintance. There are people still inside the movement who hate what's going on. China isn't a communal society, it's a freakin' military dictatorship. Ever think you'd see the day?" He unfolded the paper and extended his arm. "I cashed in a whole bunch of favors for this, Doc. Before you take a look, I want you to promise something."

"You have an address?"

"It's the name of a plastic surgery clinic, but not until you promise."

"I can't."

"You haven't even heard what I want."

"I already know. A promise Shepherd won't be killed and I can't do that. There's too much at stake. Plastic surgery, yeah, that makes sense if he wants to disappear."

"Dude . . . you're not even going to peek at the address? It's right *here*. You don't think it bothers me he killed those three kids?"

"How about this," Ford said. "If I get in a tight spot, you give me another shot. Same with what you know about Julian. Until then, let's not change the rules. They've worked for us so far."

"But you asked me, man."

"Yeah, and I don't know what disappoints me most. Me asking or you narcing out your pals. Why do you call it narcing when narcotics aren't involved? Why not 'providing evidence' or . . . No, that's too formal. And 'squealing' went out with Prohibition."

Ford was trying to lighten the mood. Tomlinson had to smile when the man showed his human side. "Good ol' Doc," he said and stuffed the paper in his pocket.

End of subject.

They returned to the reality of the moment. "I saw you through the window, coming in. You were wearing gloves. Why the hell?"

"You ever hear of something called a Faraday cage? Come on, I'll show you."

Ford started toward the door, Tomlinson saying, "A cage—*perfect*—we'll need one. I have a whole new theory about that great white shark. Megalodon—a true prehistoric giant—I'm not the only one who thinks they're still out there."

The biologist only laughed at that.

At tonight's party, Dr. Ava Lindstrom, from Sarasota, felt out of place among people who, while gracious enough, were a tight little group unto themselves. More like a family than friends, even though their ages and backgrounds varied.

Tomlinson had offered to meet her around six, but still no sign of the man, and it was almost seven. A small part of her hoped he wouldn't show. He didn't scare her, but his lifestyle did. Chaos and chemical indulgence had nearly destroyed her as a teen, and a nagging voice still warned that passion was dangerous, and pleasure was the enemy of success.

On the other hand, she'd had a hell of a good time last night. Where was that stringy scarecrow man?

Wearing jeans, boots, and a red collared blouse, she helped herself to an NA beer from a tub filled with ice and roamed for a while. The only person she recognized was Figuerito, a small, fit guy with muscles, who, instead of mingling, was playing with the dog near a boat ramp far removed from the others.

A Cuban, she remembered, who didn't speak English. He'd been in the U.S. only for a month or two.

She strolled closer and watched him hurl something heavy toward the bay—a coconut, it looked like. After what seemed several seconds, the coconut made a hollow thunk when it hit water. The dog charged after it.

Over and over, they did this. Still no Tomlinson, so she tried out her high school Spanish.

"Hello. My name is Ava. Your dog is rapid."

Figuerito stopped, turned, and stared. Arm cocked, he held a coconut like a football. *"¿Rápido?"*

"Sí, very rapid. He is also intelligent," the woman responded.

The Cuban laughed at that. "This dog is a dumbass and a pain in my head. I hope there is an alligator out there who eats him." He crow-hopped and threw the coconut from what he imagined to be centerfield to an invisible cutoff man. "No matter how many times I do this, the dumb bastard keeps coming back."

To Ava's ears, the man's Spanish blurred, he talked so fast, but she did catch a few words. *"Sí*. The dog had pain. The dog has no pain now. What is your name?"

"Fig-u-RI-tow," he said phonetically, while the woman strained to see the retriever, out there in the night, swimming his ass off. "I'm glad you speak Cuban," he added. "I have no one to talk to but that goddamn dog. He follows me everywhere and stinks like fish. I was told an alligator sometimes lives under the mangroves. If the alligator eats him, I would appreciate it if you don't bring him back to life again. On the other hand"—he looked at her and shrugged—"I have only myself to blame."

The doctor woman didn't understand any of that. Figuerito could tell, but she was tall and blond, slim in her cowboy jeans, with a stretchy white band in her hair. And very nice *chichis*, which he remembered from yesterday when she'd waded out in her wet blouse. Her *chichis* were the size of firm avocado pears and he loved avocadoes.

The dog returned with slobber dripping from the coconut. The woman didn't mind. She knelt and stroked his head, cooing, "Good Pablo, nice Pablo, what a smart dog you are, Pablo."

"Pablo?"

"Sí." She continued to coo while the dog's tongue slapped at her face.

"That can't be. If he was Pablo, he would understand when I tell him to get the hell away and leave me alone. Doc never said anything about him being a Spanish dog."

Smiling, the woman looked up and translated, "Peter, yes, that's his name in English," then continued her fawning. "Pablo, so intelligent . . . Pablo such a good, good boy."

Figuerito stared. *Mother of God,* he thought, *nice* chichis, *but the woman's a babbling idiot*—he'd met his share while incarcerated at Havana's Prison for the Insane, which was next to a baseball field, not far from José Martí International.

But that was okay. In a country where even babbling women were beautiful and rich, anything was possible for a man who was strong and willing to work hard. "That's my motorcycle," he said and pointed to the parking lot, where a 1957 Harley-Davidson with red fenders and lots of chrome was parked.

"Motorcycle," the woman repeated in Spanish. "Is very nice."

With his hands, he pantomimed twisting the throttle and made revving sounds. "Would you like to go for a ride?"

The invitation required more gesturing, and the woman, who was six inches taller, appeared interested until she peered over his head and saw Tomlinson in the distance.

"Maybe later," she said in English. "Anyone who loves dogs, I already trust."

Something Mack enjoyed about these parties was that no one played that god-awful Christmas music that hammered the skull when you were shopping or in a car. He'd paid good money for the outdoor speakers spaced around the docks—although a couple of them were fuzzy with age, and the sound quality generally sucked. Even so, he had a proprietary interest in choosing who was in charge of the song list.

Tonight it was Hannah—*Captain* Hannah—who lived aboard a 30-foot Hinckley-type cruiser, but across the bay at the Fisherman's Co-op, not at the marina. She was a willowy hard case with deep South Florida roots, but, for a change, tonight she had eschewed country twang in favor of Caribbean drums, but also mixed in the occasional opera classic.

"I hope she doesn't play *Madame Butterfly*," Rhonda said, fanning charcoal smoke from her face. "It always makes me cry. The part where she puts the dagger to her chest, oh my god, I want to grab her and say, 'Are you nuts?'"

Rhonda had orbited slowly, subtly closer to the grill, until she was at Mack's side. Across the water on A dock, her longtime partner, JoAnn, was holding court aboard *Tiger Lilly*, where lights and plastic mistletoe were strung bow to stern. Rhonda watched her heavyset friend for a while, then asked, "Think she knows?"

Rather than answer that for the thousandth time, Mack stuck to music. "I saw *Madame Butterfly* in English once. I wanted to cry, too, but for different reasons. The main baritone in the opera, I didn't realize he was an American sailor. He's the one she should've—" Mack realized what he was about to suggest, so made a sudden tack. "Hang on to these."

He handed her the tongs and got another bag of alligator meat from the cooler. The fillets had been pounded flat until they were fibrous and white and tender.

Rhonda, still watching JoAnn, said, "She's suspicious about you buying the beach cottages, too."

"Let her think what she wants." Mack reclaimed the tongs, turned the fillets, which were nearly done, and made room for more. "What we should be grilling is shark—but I admit that having Hello, Dolly! back is good for business."

"That's a terrible thing to say." Rhonda's attention returned to the man beside her. "Besides, I heard it was a gag some radio DJ pulled. That's what the Coast Guard thinks. It was on local news about an hour ago. They're still investigating, but that's what one of their spokesmen told a reporter."

"The reporter didn't hear the guy's voice when he was attacked," Mack countered. "I did. I had a parley with the fishing guides. We're going to go out there and kill that bloody bastard. But on the q.t. Greenies on this island would get their panties all in a tither if a shark was killed, but don't give a damn if it kills three or four people."

"You don't really believe that."

No, he didn't, but it was better than talking about JoAnn, who, after a while, Rhonda got back to anyway, saying, "I keep telling her you're buying the cottages for everyone."

Mack called hello to Ford and Tomlinson as they cruised past with a nice-looking blonde sandwiched between them. It was an opportunity to change the subject. "She's a veterinarian," he said. "Remember the woman from yesterday who helped rescue Doc's crazy dog?"

"Why don't you want to talk about this?"

"What am I supposed to say? I'm buying the beach property, sure, so folks will have a place to go if the feds kick us out. But you and I both know it is so we'll have more private time together."

He felt okay about that until Rhonda melted him with her wistful look and asked, "Is that true, Mack?"

No, that wasn't true either . . . Well, it was sort of true. Hell . . . Mack didn't know what the truth was anymore. He had lied his way across three continents and four decades before settling on this island to start a new life. The success he'd achieved as a businessman was unexpected, but nothing else had changed. He was still a dodgy, sneaking bastard.

"Of course it's true," Mack replied and squared himself for a lightning bolt or whatever the hell came next.

"Uh-oh . . . she's waving for me to come over," Rhonda said, then looked him in the eye. "Mack? I don't care about the age difference, and I don't care if it's right or wrong. You are the kindest, most decent man I've ever met." She traced the small of his back with an unseen finger as she passed behind him.

The gator fillets were burning. *Damn*. Mack scorched a hand when he reached to turn them. "Bloody goddamn bastards!"

His head swiveled to see if anyone had heard. It was unlikely with an operatic banshee wailing from outdoor speakers that had cost him fifty bucks apiece. He slammed the grill closed and marched past the bait tanks, up a shell path to the office. Captain Hannah was inside, swaying to the music while she sorted through CDs. A pretty, big-boned woman with raven hair.

"Do me a favor and don't play *Madame Butterfly*," he told her.

"What?"

"You heard me," Mack said because she had.

The woman didn't like that one bit. "If you're worried I'll blow out those old speakers, don't. The noise they make when there's too much bass puts my teeth on edge."

"There's nothing wrong with those speakers," Mack countered, "but that's not the reason. I'm going to do the drawing early. To me, all opera sounds like *Madame Butterfly*." He offered a weak smile. "That's all I meant."

Hannah was too smart to believe him, and didn't care for his tone. She played along, but with an edge. "In that case, Mr. Elf, you're going to need a bucket or something for the list of names." She placed a jar filled with little squares of paper in front of him. "Here're the names, now go find your own bucket. Oh . . . since I did all the work"—under the counter was a pointy green hat—"do *me* a favor and wear this."

It was the rare person who could back down Mack. Capt. Hannah was one of them.

He took the hat and did as he was told.

Ford and the veterinarian were discussing the dog and canine genetics when Mack exited the office, wearing an elf hat and smoking a cigar. Trailing behind was Hannah. Ford's eyes were on her, not Mack, as Mack dumped a jar of names into a bucket, made a few announcements, then said, "Everybody, line up. And remember the rules—no trading names, no gifts over twenty bucks, and if you pick your own damn name, you have to, by god, admit it."

By then, Ava was thinking Ford wasn't such a bad guy after all. If she had to choose, she might have skipped last night with Tomlinson and gotten to know the biologist better. Her current relationship—a long-term affair with her business partner, a married man—was going no-where, and sex was the ultimate game changer. It was the way her mind worked now. Survival mode, Ava thought of it, a way of taking stock before moving ahead with purpose. A year on the streets huffing meth as a teen, a broken pelvis, plus six weeks of rehab, had gradually channeled her toward men who were the safe, straight types. With Ford, she felt safer than usual. Strictly instinct, but too late to change what had happened, so she kept it light, saying, "I love the people here. Does everyone always get along so well?"

The man's response was positive, even generous, but also careful in an odd way.

"Maybe I'm naïve," she said. "I probably am. I haven't lived a very exciting life." She offered a few details—heavily edited—then said, "Or maybe it's the time of year. I'd like to think there's at least one small place in this world where . . ." She let the sentence trail off. Hovering overhead, beneath the stars, was what looked like a toy flying saucer. It was there, then gone.

Ford asked, "Something wrong?"

"I don't know. I think I saw another one of those radio-operated planes." She watched the man's expression change and thought, *Yes . . . with him I am safe.*

They moved to a more secluded spot with a better view of the sky.

"Flying those things has to be an expensive hobby," she said, "but I guess people on the island can afford it." Which the man didn't seem to hear until she added, "Uh-oh . . . where'd the dog go?"

Damn it, that's when Tomlinson appeared, but it was nice the way Ford's hands felt when he turned her toward the guy in the elf hat who was smoking a cigar. "Get in line," he said. "Don't worry, your name's already in the jar."

Even when the biologist reappeared much later, his hand on the hip of a striking raven-haired woman, Ava felt okay about it. This was the way things should be. No need to sneak or pretend, or slip away to a hotel. They cared for each other—anyone could see that.

The same was true when Tomlinson introduced her to the ladies aboard *Tiger Lilly*, then a dozen others, including a psychiatrist, a football coach, a delightful Cuban woman and her daughters, and a handsome Brazilian named Vargas Diemer, who invited her aboard his yacht.

That's where she was, sitting next to Vargas but drinking bottled water, when she looked down at the shimmering lights, where people milled, and decided, *They don't need to hide who they are. Here, it's okay.*

12

THE FARADAY CAGE THE BIOLOGIST BUILT WAS
not as Tomlinson had envisioned. It was more like a tent
made of metal screens, with a floor and roof of tin, hidden in the mangroves not far from the lab.

"In the eighteen hundreds," Ford explained, "a guy
named Faraday proved that electromagnetic waves flow
around conductive surfaces, not through them. That's
why people inside a car are seldom struck by lightning.
Which was no big deal back then, but now, where there's
no place on Earth not bombarded by radio waves,
shielded rooms are used by just about every high-tech

industry there is. I was familiar with the concept but didn't understand the physics—or how easy it is to make something that works."

Until then, Tomlinson had been disappointed. It was unlike his pal to build a skid row–looking jumble of junk that formed a little room for the two battered drones. He'd pictured glistening bars of aluminum, with flotation tanks and a window wide enough for a man's shoulders but too small for the snout of a meat-eating monster who had a taste for vegetarians.

The bit about conductive shielding, though, opened a new door in his head. "I want one. Hell, I want one I can *wear*." It was squishy, here in the mangroves, and so dense only a spattering of blue sky sprinkled through on this balmy sixteenth day of Christmas. He fanned mosquitoes away and inspected the cage walls. "It's mostly plain old window screening."

Ford replied, "Aluminum; eighth-inch mesh. The screens have to be metal."

"Hmm. You'd think radio waves would zoom right through the mesh, but, yeah, the concept is starting to gel. Metal, even metal screening, has its own electrical charge. That's a given. An outside charge, static or non-static, would follow the cage's flow instead of piercing the electron field—the path of least resistance."

Ford said, "Copper's better, from what I've read, but this works okay as long as I get it sealed right. Here . . . let's do a check."

He'd brought a pair of handheld VHF radios, which boaters often carried. He switched them on, reduced squelch until they roared with static, then handed one over. The other he placed inside the mesh cage. When he sealed the hatch, the radio went silent.

"Try transmitting."

Tomlinson said, "Check. Check. Check," and popped the mic key several times, then did a few other tests. "I'll be go to hell. That thing's deader than my first bottle of mezcal and I'm only a couple yards away." He scanned an opening in the branches. "Any drones since the other night?"

"Jeth said he might have seen one, but not over this area. That was yesterday when I was in Tampa."

"I wondered where you were. What's in Tampa?"

"Ybor City," the biologist replied. "We flew up in the seaplane. The Maule. It's an incredible little bush plane."

What Ford meant was *Don't ask*.

Tomlinson never knew what to believe. His pal often claimed to be someplace within driving distance when, in fact, he might have popped down to Peru or the Land of Fumbuck, Can't Say. Better to deal with the man on a real-time basis. "What about all the high-tech stuff up there in space? Or maybe satellite technology is no better than what Julian's been flying around. Hell, I don't even try and keep track anymore."

"I'm not sure about that either." Ford retrieved the radio and sealed the cage. "I've stopped assuming it's Julian. It probably is, but turns out there are some other possibilities."

Tomlinson thought, *Maybe he did go to Tampa*. There was a military base there, U.S. Special Operations; spooks up the yin-yang, from Busch Gardens to Clearwater Beach. He let that go, too. "*Someone's* watching us—and when I say 'us,' I mean the whole damn marina. This morning, I mentioned that to Ava—sort of slipped it into the conversation between coffee and my Wheaties—and the poor girl got foggy-eyed, thinking I was talking about the Big Guy. You know, God. A personal faith-based moment, just the two of us. Like all wounded women, she's attracted to spiritual men."

Ford's attention was on the drones. "We've got to decide whether to dive the Blue Hole this afternoon or in the morning. If it's this afternoon, we might as well carry these back to the lab and load them in the boat." After a moment, he turned. "What do you mean *wounded*?"

"Ava. You didn't pick up on that?"

"Just the opposite. She strikes me as competent and smart; seems to know where she's headed. I'm supposed to call her about the dog."

"I'm crazy about the girl, don't get me wrong, but there're things in her head she keeps covered with a tarp."

"Crazy in love, huh?" Ford's expression read *Bullshit*.

"In a brotherly way. She's a tad naïve, too. I had to rescue her from that snake Vargas the other night. Poor girl's in recovery from something—pills, my guess—and he was trying to feed her a martini."

"When was this?"

"Monday, Secret Santa night. The same day you spent about an hour on Vargas's boat—I saw you two talking on the flybridge. Ava went aboard not long after you left. That surprised me, man. Not just her; you, too, even talking to that guy. Unless you were telling him to keep his paws off Hannah—you know he's got the hots for her."

"That's when she told you she's a recovering addict?"

"No need." Tomlinson tapped his temple. "It's right here under the tarp where she hides things. I knew right off. The other night on my boat, she got high smoking dried basil and mint, then got very, very shaky when I told her it wasn't the real thing. Scared, you know, but also relieved. Addiction's a short trip down, but a long, long way up if you have to make that climb twice."

Ford thought, *You would know,* but chose to study a patch of blue sky and a slow-moving cloud. "The wind will lay down by tonight, so I say we dive tomorrow."

"That's something we need to talk about. When you said 'cage,' I figured you meant *shark cage.* Personally, I think Hello, Dolly! is long gone."

"I'd bet on it," Ford said, "but people prefer drama to facts. The shark was a hoax. You know that."

"I'm talking about something else. If it's not a great white out there, then it's something bigger. That's my theory anyway." His eyes came to a rest on the skid row contraption of wire and tin. "Conductive shield," he murmured. "Don't you wish we could round up all the wounded ladies and keep them in a safe place?"

Ford, walking away, said, "I wouldn't trust either one of us with the key."

His computer didn't work when he connected all the cords, but fifteen minutes later the thing kicked on by itself as if powered by a generator. Not just the computer—the entire system, including an old HP printer that clanked and clattered even though there was nothing in the queue.

Ford sat and watched the screen come alive; light reflected from his glasses. From somewhere, somehow, the system was commandeered with robotic precision. Passwords flashed at lightning speed. Folders opened in a volcanic spew, soon a thousand deep and growing, all this while the old printer tattered like a toy machine gun.

Before he could react—yanking the power cord was his only option—the chaos ceased, replaced by violet beads on the darkening screen.

Julian did it again, he thought, then reasoned, "Why the hell would he bother? They took everything three days ago." Said this out loud.

Exactly. But better to leave the plug in and recover what he could.

"Even if it's compromised," he added.

He rode the chair's casters to the lab station, where there was a yellow legal pad. He had started a list of folders he'd lost; just the important stuff, but there were already nine pages filled with his neat geometrical block print. "This will take days—and no way I can remember everything. So better to wait. Maybe the boy genius overlooked something."

A voice startled him. "Talking to yourself. I do that a lot."

It was a male voice, not fully mature. It seemed to come from the ceiling, but Ford looked first to the door.

"I used to see this shrink—talk about an asshole—and he said talking to yourself is typical of OCD types who live and work alone. Know what I told him? I told him, 'Who else is smart enough to keep up?' This was before the bastard had me sent to a counseling retreat that was actually an asylum for losers."

A mild Aussie accent was punctuated by laughter. Ford's eyes sought a speaker hidden in the room, then glided toward the computer screen.

"In his notes, the shrink called me a silly, destructive narcissist with malignant yadda yadda yadda. Whatever. Maybe you've heard their standard drivel. The man was nothing but a lying puppeteer, which I'd already figured out, and not very bright. He had no idea I'd been harvesting his computer notes since our first session. A month later, police found videos of naked boys on his hard drive and arrested the idiot—about the worst thing that can happen to a man in West Australia. Guess who felt silly then?"

More laughter, and there, staring out from the screen, was Julian Solo, who clapped his hands when Ford made eye contact. "I know, I know, your system doesn't have a built-in camera. Well, Mr. Biologist, it does now."

Julian, with blond, curly locks, wore a black turtleneck in a room with a black backdrop. His face and hair glowed like porcelain.

"I don't call Ph.D.s doctor for the same reason I don't call tin soldiers by their rank. You can be Marion or Ford—or Clarence, for all I care. I doubt if we'll ever speak again."

He squinted at something in the lab. "I used to have an aquarium, even did the scuba thing and caught my own tropicals. What kind of fish are those?"

Ford had seen photos of the man, but to catalog Julian's mannerisms he had to reach back in memory. Years ago, he'd met a truly poisonous fourteen-year-old who'd driven a sister to suicide and was methodically dismantling the mother. Double the kid's age, change the hair color, add sixty points to the little freak's IQ, and it was Julian.

A malignant narcissist. The diagnosis fit.

"Which tank do you mean?" Ford asked. "I have a dozen aquaria in this room."

"*Aquaria*, huh? Nice, the proper plural—as if I give a bugger all. I grew out of hobbies. Most children do. Now the world's my hobby." He pointed a clicker. Ford's computer screen split to show an aquarium on the far wall. It held immature snook and redfish, along with a requisite permit from the state, posted outside the glass. "That's the one. I can zoom in—or just clean those Coke bottles of yours."

Hyperactive; alert to weaknesses, plus a relentless shepherding of his victims. Julian and the adolescent freak had a lot in common.

"Why are we doing this?" Ford asked. "You're a computer whiz. I get it."

"Do you have a hearing problem, too? What kind of fish? A simple question. Never mind—what's that sticker on the glass?"

The camera zoomed in to read the state permit, while Ford said, "I'm going to pull the plug and get back to work."

Julian's eager face filled the screen. "Do! See what happens."

What a strange threat. Did the kid—that's the way

Ford thought of Julian now—did the kid mean the computer would work without power? Or was it a dare to end the conversation?

"Let's stop the sparring," Ford said. "The guy you sent, a guy in a suit, he said you're looking for a missing drone. I don't know anything about it."

"*Two* drones," Julian corrected.

"He told me one, but okay. He—Watts, that was his name—he also gave me a memory stick with a message. Stupidly, I opened it."

"Oh, don't feel too badly, Mr. Biologist. I knew you would. How? Because I've graphed all the characteristics of your type."

KAT had said something similar with the same contempt.

Ignore it. That's what he should have done. Instead, he began a careful retaliation. "You're an intimidating guy, Julian. Can I call you that?"

"Flattery," the kid said.

"I'm trying to be open here."

"Cards-on-the-table stuff—a real Yank attitude. I won't say I haven't been called intimidating before, but what does—"

Ford interrupted, "The story about taking down your psychiatrist, that's spooky. The way you set him up. Christ, but also pretty funny."

Laughter. *"Exactly."*

"Was that in Perth?"

"Fremantle, but let's get back to—"

"Your father was a math professor in Perth; brilliant, from what I've read."

Julian's face began to color. "I don't claim him as a father. If you hadn't bungled the job, he wouldn't be alive."

"Winslow Shepherd. Then I'm right."

"You're right that you bungled the job. A woman was on the balcony that night—KAT, you called her. Poor thing's skull was crushed. Shattered femurs, hands, the whole list. But she still managed to live fifteen minutes before she bled out. I hacked the coroner's computer, so there are plenty of photos. I'll have an album made up for your scrapbook."

Ford said, "Give it to your father. He can add them to the pictures of the three teenagers he killed."

"You're witty, too." Julian smiled. "Denying responsibility—that's something else typical of your type."

"She wouldn't have fallen if your father hadn't grabbed her. Then he used her like a cushion. That's about as cowardly as it gets."

"*Really.* I know you're trying to piss me off, but I find the details interesting. It's exactly the sort of thing poor old Winslow would have done. Is that the way it really happened?"

"You'd have to ask your father," Ford said, intentionally using the word *father* again.

Julian flinched. The word was getting to him. "Do you really want to play this game? Somewhere in that room of yours is a printer. If you'd taken time to look, you'd see the rap sheet I uploaded. Not all of it, just fifteen pages because some dumbass forgot to fill their paper tray. Are you always so sloppy, Clarence?"

Clarence, a nickname that resonated contempt.

Ford overcame the urge to look at the printer. "I was explaining why your psychiatrist story spooked me. It has to do with your father. What I can't help wondering is—"

"Stick to your criminal record," Julian said. "How would you like to be extradited to Mexico for murder? Or Vietnam? Or Colombia? You are one very busy little tin soldier, Clarence." He scooted closer to the camera. "I found dirt your own government doesn't have. Truly vicious shit that would turn the stomachs of your mates at that little marina."

Julian paused to savor what came next. "Poor KAT, she died a horrible death. An attractive woman only thirty-two years old. How would you like your friends to know what you really are?"

Ford, staring into the screen, said, "Tell them."

Julian didn't expect that. "Tough guy, huh? I plan to if I don't get those drones. My shrink would've gotten a woody after a few sessions with you. All the bloody details—how you stalked those poor third-world types and snapped their necks and dragged off their bodies, or put a bullet in their brains. Real serial killer adventure stories. I'll include photos for your friends."

"Send them," Ford said, then backed off a little. "What was Winslow's reaction when you told him about the psychiatrist?"

"You really liked that story."

"I bet your father did, too. What I'm wondering is, how much did he help? You were still in school then. You would have needed help hacking the shrink's computer to upload—"

"No, *Winslow* would have needed help. Why do you insist on—"

"I'm explaining why the story is intimidating," Ford said. "You've got an IQ off the chart, so it's tough for someone like me to comprehend. A kid your age—what, you were in your late teens?—taking down a doctor without your father's help. That's pretty hard to—"

"I was fourteen years old," Julian interrupted. He said it in a way that warned *See who you're dealing with?* "What's even funnier, I planted a camera in the dude's office. I wish you'd seen the look on his face when the cops kicked in his door."

Ford had been waiting for this opening. "No, you don't, Julian."

"Why? You're the one who said it was funny."

"Funny in a different way," Ford said. "Because, if I were a cop in western Australia, I would have tracked down the patient most likely to be a pedophile before arresting the shrink. That's you, Julian. Who else would have had child porn to plant in the guy's hard drive? Your father had nothing to do with it. You said so yourself. That's why I asked."

Julian's porcelain face brightened. He battled for composure, then lost it. *"Motherfucker,"* he said. "No one talks to me that way."

The screen went dark.

Ford sat there expecting the computer to reinitiate contact. It had to happen. The drones were a big deal, and Julian's father was a bigger deal. The kid either wanted Winslow Shepherd dead or Shepherd had enough leverage to demand revenge on the man who had dropped him eight stories onto Mexican tile.

On the printer was the incomplete dossier—a rap sheet, the kid had called it. He leafed through a few pages, then burned it all in the woodstove.

If Julian believed he could blackmail him into submission, Julian was wrong.

Ford went out the door, through the mangroves to the marina, hoping to find Vargas Diemer.

13

VARGAS WAS ON THE PHONE SPEAKING WITH HIS agent in Portuguese when he saw the biologist pass the bait tanks and turn toward A dock.

"Speak of the devil," he said in English, "here he comes now."

The agent switched languages. "What devil is this?"

"I'm not convinced he is," Vargas replied and watched until the biologist disappeared from the porthole glass. "Let's get back to money. There's something special about those drones, or they wouldn't have requested me.

For a couple toy planes they could replace for a quarter a mil? Come on. There's more to it."

"The client made discreet inquiries," the agent replied, "and that's the price the client named. My job is to pass it along."

"Did you confirm Julian Solo is involved?"

"I can't and I won't. I took the liberty of saying you might know where the drones are. Nothing else was discussed. Is that true? You do know?"

"Soon, very soon. But Julian doesn't come up with a lot more money, screw him. I'm working an angle of my own."

"What is this *screw them*?" the agent asked. "Please— it's better if we speak Portuguese."

They did while Vargas carried the phone outside to the aft balcony with its view of the marina. The biologist had stopped to speak to the old women who owned *Tiger Lilly*. At night, sometimes, the incense they burned was disgusting, but they brought the Brazilian homemade cookies or pies, which was nice. From a houseboat, the little Cuban girl, Sabina, joined in the conversation. She was a fireball, that girl; smart and funny, who could make even Vargas laugh.

Vargas liked this little marina. It's why he had stayed so long. Everyone here pleasant and harmless.

Almost everyone.

He watched the biologist turn. They made eye contact. Vargas held up the phone and flashed five fingers twice, meaning *Give me ten minutes*. At the same instant, Mack summoned Ford to the office with a wave. Standing nearby was the dwarf Cuban, who was mentally retarded in an entertaining way, and had a beautiful antique Harley-Davidson.

Vargas continued speaking to his agent while his mind drifted. He wanted that motorcycle. It would be easy enough to trick the Cuban into selling it—and he might one day—but the deal would require an abrupt departure from the marina, and he wasn't ready to leave.

Not just yet.

He enjoyed the people here—it was the closest thing to home since childhood. But there was another reason he prolonged his stay: a local girl, Hannah Smith. Hannah wasn't his type, normally. She was tall and countrified, with a rough manner when offended, but, oh my god, what a body. Vargas had gotten a glimpse recently when he'd surprised her in the shower.

A glimpse was enough.

This was more than a week ago when Ford was in Mexico, as Vargas had confirmed. Hannah, after a rare second glass of champagne, had allowed him to kiss her, and undo the top two buttons of her blouse, before pulling away. But then gave him further encouragement by saying, "I should hop in the shower before I head home."

Vargas took that as an invitation. His mistake had ended their evening, and nearly bloodied his nose when he opened the shower door. But he'd seen enough.

Oh my god.

He wasn't leaving until he had bedded Hannah Smith.

Now the blond veterinarian was on his list, too.

Vargas was still on the phone fifteen minutes later

when the biologist exited the office and crossed the deck toward A dock. "I have to go," he told his agent. "If the money's right, we have a deal. If not, I'll do the job on spec and take my chances."

He pocketed the phone, took the stairs to the main salon, and was lounging in a deck chair when the biologist appeared, saying, "Why do I think you were talking about me?"

Ford didn't trust anyone with details about Mexico, not even friends in Tampa, but he shared some of it with the Brazilian. The bizarre exchange with Julian via computer would have made no sense if he hadn't.

"You're certain it was him?"

This was not the first time they had discussed the boy genius.

"Even if I was, I know better than to believe everything I see on anything electronic. A computer-generated hologram—a projected likeness—would look and sound just like him. The technology's there, so I accept it as a possibility, but—"

"Disney World," the Brazilian said. "I've seen them. Holograms; they're convincing, but you wouldn't confuse one with a real person. Too shimmery . . . no, *translucent* is the word."

"On an LED screen, I might. It has more to do with this guy's behavior. I got him on the subject of his father, and walked him into a fairly harmless trap. A conversational trap meant to back him off a little. I didn't expect him to shut down totally before he told me what he wanted. A hologram wouldn't react like that. He threw a tantrum like a spoiled fourteen-year-old."

A champagne bucket of ice and drinks was on the table that separated their chairs. Ford opened a Corona. As he did, he looked through sliding doors into the yacht's salon where there was a laptop open on a desk. "Is that thing on?" He pointed.

"Always. I didn't tell you about my security shutdown system? It's safe."

After thinking about that for a moment, Ford got back to Julian. "Whatever he wants from me has to do with his father. If it was just the UAVs, he'd let some flunky handle it. Unless . . ." He looked at the Brazilian. "Any ideas?"

Vargas had a very specific idea but replied, "Is this hypothetical or have you made up your mind about contract work? That's where the money is, my friend."

They had talked about that the same night they had discussed Julian. Hiring private professionals to handle overseas security—or a particularly dirty job—was cheaper and safer, politically speaking, than putting a nation's own military at risk.

Small, privatized armies will control the future, according to the Brazilian.

Maybe so. Ford had friends, experienced operators, who were finally, *finally*, being paid what they were worth by top contract agencies such as Triple Canopy, Aegis, and Blackwater, which operated under several names.

Ford replied, "Maybe down the road, but I've changed my mind on this one. Julian is trying to blackmail me, so I have to walk away."

Vargas didn't like the way this was going. "When you say 'walk away,' you mean . . . ?"

"I'll either turn the drones over to people I trust or"—the biologist straightened his glasses—"I haven't decided yet, but I'm not going to bargain with whoever's behind this. Julian, I'm pretty sure. That's the same as admitting I'm guilty of whatever he thinks he's got on me."

"Admirable," the Brazilian said. "A more practical man would put profit ahead of ethics. Experience tells me there might be millions in this if we play it right. You're a noble man, Dr. Ford."

Ford, chuckling, said, "Kiss my ass. He's not getting those drones back. I figure they contain some kind of new technology that hasn't been patented, so he can't risk them being reverse engineered. Either that or it's pirated military technology he's not supposed to have. No one, even Julian, wants to screw with the big-time military powers."

"Military," Vargas said as if surprised. "I guess that's possible—if you've got a good imagination."

"He's hacked enough of their systems. That's not imaginary. And he's got the money . . . probably enough backdoor contacts by now to steal the actual hardware. Or just the plans, that would be enough."

"Don't you think it's more likely he's trying to protect his own little inventions?"

Ford affected a smile. "Until now, I wasn't convinced it was military. Tell me something—do you have proof, or are you guessing?"

The Brazilian's expression transitioned from *Who? Me?* to *Okay . . . I admit it.* "Mostly, it's a guess that's supported by what a source told me . . . but only because I asked." He gestured to his phone on the table. "We just hung up."

"You figured it out for yourself, but you're still in the confirmation process. Smart. How solid is your source?"

"Oh . . . I don't know him well, but his credentials are good. Think about it. Julian's been on the run for more than a year, yet three or four major intelligence agencies haven't managed to find him. Do you actually believe that?"

Ford, looking at the Brazilian, sipped his beer and waited.

"Me neither. It only makes sense if they don't *want* to find him. They can't risk giving him a public platform— and that's what jail and a team of international attorneys would do. I'd bet that one or all three of those UAVs contain something big, something black ops military. A guidance system maybe, or a new weapon the international community would pretend to abhor, but, in fact, wants for its own arsenal."

"*Two* drones," Ford corrected and reached to massage his shoulder. The marina fuel pumps were to his left, where a 21-foot Maverick flats skiff was just pulling in. He'd sold the boat a while back to Hannah, who was at the helm. Her fly-fishing clients—two burly men—sat forward. She glanced over at the Brazilian's yacht, did a double take, then frowned and turned away.

"I wonder what I did to piss her off now," Ford mused.

Vargas, suddenly uneasy, got to his feet and began putting things away. "I've got an agent who handles these matters. I haven't spoken to him for a while, but it wouldn't hurt to throw out some numbers and see if Julian bites. Doc—"

"Yeah?" The biologist was watching Hannah glide around the boat while she secured lines.

"What would you say to a million dollars, clean?"

"She knows I'm looking, that's what galls me." Ford started to say something else, then realized what he'd just heard. "How much?"

"I'll ask for four million, but settle for three-point-five, and we'll split it. You can buy a lot of good deeds down the road by telling your ethics to go to hell for a week. That's one-point-seven-five mil apiece."

Ford turned to the salon doors, which were open, the salon all dark wood and brass inside, where the laptop looked as misplaced as a sextant in an Apple store.

The Brazilian interpreted silence as indecision. "Good. We can at least discuss it. Why not show me the . . . *items* so, when I speak with my agent, I'll have some hard intel to prove I'm serious?"

"Show you the drones, you mean," Ford said. He thought about that, but not for long. "We'll take my truck."

When they pulled onto Mack's new property, the Brazilian, after reading the Grin N Bare It cottages sign, said, "If this is where they're hidden, I'd wager they're gone by now."

"I want to check something." Ford got out and walked to the concrete clubhouse, where the double doors were open, garbage bags stacked outside. Inside, on the cool linoleum floor, lay the retriever. Figueroa was working on what looked like an intercom conduit, but didn't hear the truck arrive because the radio was so damn loud. Cuban salsa.

Ford found the volume, and made it tolerable, before saying, "I've come to get my dog. Who else is here?"

"Take the bastard, thanks be to God. I am so sick of being followed. Even when I stop to piss, he is next to me, which I hate because of what he does."

The dog's ears perked at the sound of snapping fingers, but he got up slowly at Ford's command: "Come."

With a broom, the little Cuban swatted at the dog. "Move your ass, you dirty beast."

"Don't do that," Ford said, "never hit him," as he canceled the command with a hand signal. "I'll let him rest here for a while."

He went to the door. Parked in the shade of a palm was a white compact, probably a rental. Tomlinson's bicycle with *Key West* stickers and a Fausto's basket leaned against cottage number 3. The door there was closed. "Who's he with? I know him too well to believe he's in there working."

"Some might call it work," the Cuban replied, "but, in Cuba, we call it making hot oil. He's with the gringa doctor, the blonde with the nice *chichis*. Do you like avocado pears? I get hungry when I think of her. Other women, it's mangoes."

Ford, shaking his head, took out his cell while Figueroa explained, "I didn't peek."

"I didn't say you did."

"I would've if I was taller, but the windows are too high. Certain sounds tell me things, which is why I turned the music up. All I can think about is food." He pointed to the wall conduit while Ford dialed. "Mack wants to put in flat screen TVs and a large stereo system. I might live here."

Tomlinson answered on the fourth ring, saying, "I'm a little tied up right now, so unless my boat's on fire—"

Ford cut him off. "What's the address of that property you bought?"

"The farm? It doesn't have an address. Well . . . not one I can remember. In a couple of hours, I can—"

"If you look out the window, you'll see me. Would you rather I knock on the door?"

Tomlinson provided directions, then added, "You'll love the place, but try not to step on the vegetables. The garden's near an old rain cistern—you'll see it. Thing's twice the size of the swimming pool here, palms all around for shade. If I ever get it pumped out and cleaned, we'll have a skinny-dipping party."

This last part, Ford realized, was said for the benefit of Ava, the enigmatic veterinarian. He was mildly disappointed, but also fascinated by the unpredictability of women who, aside from decisions regarding men, were otherwise rational in their behavior.

In the truck, he told the Brazilian, "The place we're going's only about five minutes from here."

Fifteen minutes later, just before the Blind Pass Bridge, they turned right onto a shell drive that was more like a fire lane; rough-cut and rutted beneath coconut palms. Ford noticed Vargas slip a hand into the white shirt he wore unbuttoned with the shirttails out, a black crewneck beneath.

"You can leave your gun in the truck," Ford said. "The only thing to worry about around here is maybe poison ivy and a snake or two."

Vargas settled back, but didn't move his hand. "I hate those things. In Brazil, we have an island where it's illegal to go ashore, there are so many poison snakes. Tens of thousands, I've heard."

"*Venomous* snakes," Ford corrected. "In the Amazon?"

"Off São Paulo. You'd need a boat or floatplane. Scientists say there are five hundred snakes per hectare. They hang from trees like vines—golden-headed vipers, among the deadliest in the world. If you're bitten, the flesh melts from your bones." Vargas said the name in Portuguese, then translated: "Island of Nightmares. Small, this island, only forty hectares or so."

Ford did the conversion in his head. "Approximately a hundred acres. Tomlinson calls this place the farm even though it's less than four. He doesn't know, by the way."

"Doesn't know I'm with you? Or that you hid the drones here?"

"I don't want him involved," Ford replied.

Ahead was the palm oasis as described, a lip of pitted concrete visible among wild coffee plants and pink blossoms of frangipani.

"I don't see any buildings," Vargas said.

Ford put the truck in park. "Let's have a look."

It was true the cistern was the size of a backyard pool and made of old-timey shell concrete that still held water to the brim. The surface was green with duckweed about five feet deep, when Ford used a limb to check. Until then, he wasn't sure how to play it, but the size and depth of the cistern made for a workable story.

"I took a chance stashing them underwater, because their telemetry systems are solar-powered. See how the surface is covered? That green stuff is made up of free-floating plants, millions of them. Sunlight can't make it through. Without power, the drones can't be tracked."

Vargas was unconvinced—mystified, in fact—that an intelligent man would make so many reckless assumptions. He moved closer to the cistern. "Something smells rotten here . . . like rotten eggs. Is it the water?"

Ford made eye contact to acknowledge the subtext. "Sulfur water, old-timers call it. Actually, hydrogen sulfide causes the odor. That alone makes this a good place, don't you think?" As he spoke, he held up his cell phone and switched off.

Vargas understood. "Personally, I think it's a terrible choice—no houses around, no security at all. But it's up to you," which had an honest ring if someone was listening. He switched off his phone, allowed thirty seconds, then asked, "Are you sure?"

Ford shrugged and waited until they were in the truck to say, "Now I'll show you the drones."

He did.

Like many women, Hannah was prone to blame herself for the misconduct of men who, if she had risked rudeness earlier, might not have behaved like drunks or simpleton fools later in the day.

Vargas Diemer was no simpleton, and he certainly wasn't drunk the night he'd tried to force his way into the shower. Even so, she felt badly enough about what had happened to divert her attention from her clients and the fish they weren't catching during the last hour of their charter.

"Captain Hannah? Water's clear enough, wouldn't we see snook if they're around?"

It jolted her into the present. "Yes, sir, we would. That's why I was about to pull the stake and pole you past those mangroves. See that little point? The bottom drops off; sort of a swale. You can relax until we're closer, but keep your eyes peeled."

Hannah hopped up on the poling platform. Two itty-bitty snook later, she turned her skiff toward Dinkin's Bay, isolated from her clients by engine noise. She punished herself by recalling small things she could have done to prevent the evening with Vargas from spinning out of control. If she had interjected a warning, or worn a different blouse, or refused a second glass of champagne—myriad opportunities to spare the Brazilian a bloody nose.

My lord, she had smacked him a good one. Her knuckles still hurt.

What Marion Ford would have pointed out was that victims wrongly blame themselves. The man was fair that way. Even as her former lover, he would have been fair.

Sitting at the wheel, Hannah imagined how their exchange would go if she told him about it. How his expression would change when he heard certain details—not everything, of course. She wasn't fool enough to mention Vargas's hands on her breasts, the way her breathing had stopped while he'd freed the top buttons of her blouse. It was a dizzying moment of suspense beyond the understanding of a man—well, beyond Marion's understanding anyway.

She had put a stop to it though, by god, and felt blameless about what happened next . . . blameless until she recalled the slightly tipsy words she'd used to close the evening.

If it's okay, I'll use the guest shower and change clothes before heading home.

No . . . that was an edited version. What she'd said was *Think I'll hop in the shower first,* then something about changing clothes because she traveled by boat. No wonder the Brazilian had heard her words as an invitation.

Oh my lord.

She had to get this matter straightened out.

Hannah tapped the throttle and crossed the shoals off Green Point, doing forty-plus.

What she feared more than guilt was hurting a person she cared about. There was a possibility Marion had heard a more damning version of the story while talking with the Brazilian. She couldn't allow such gossip to go unchallenged.

Damn that Vargas, with his exotic looks and accent. He was fun and elegant but too smooth to be trusted. No telling what kind of lies he had told about that night, which is why she would never allow herself to be alone with the man again.

Well . . . probably.

That decision could wait. The decision about speaking to the biologist could not. Their romantic relationship was over. She knew it. Ford knew it. But she valued the man's respect, and only the truth could guarantee whatever future their friendship held.

Yes, by lord, she had to take action.

Hannah secured the skiff, said good-bye to her clients, and walked to the lab, where she rang the bell—a formality befitting life's zigzag changes.

"Marion," she said when her ex-lover appeared. "I've got something important to say and you're not going to like it."

14

WHEN HANNAH LEFT, FORD WATCHED UNTIL SHE was safely in her boat and gone, then went for his second run of the day. He carried a towel, a small flashlight, and forty bucks in his socks. On Wednesdays during season, the pool bar at West Wind stayed open until seven, an hour after sunset.

He felt pretty good, albeit perplexed by the conflicts of conscience endured by women, particularly strong women, but seldom by scalp hunters like the Brazilian.

Ford probed a few times for anger hiding inside his lizard brain and decided, *None. Well . . . no more than usual.*

It was the sort of lie he often told himself. Self-control required self-deceit.

When he got to the beach, he picked up the pace for another mile, then turned through sea oats to the West Wind, where pool water steamed, it was so warm. A swim and two beers sustained him on the jog home.

His positive attitude vanished when he entered the lab. Julian had paid another robotic visit. On the computer screen was a crime scene photo of KAT. Full color; a woman's face deflated by impact, one dull eye open, a hand thrust out on bloody brown Mexican tile. The photographer had used a flash. Where shadows of palms and a slouching cop pooled, a gathering of incisor teeth glistened.

Ford stared for a while, hoping this was another digital trick. KAT's articulate bone structure had become a gruesome jigsaw puzzle—a misplaced nose, jaws askew like broken scissors. Her skin had imploded into a shattered space that had once been a woman, alive, beautiful.

Near her hips on the tile, like animal tracks, were three bloody palm prints. KAT had done some crawling before she died.

He took a resolute breath and switched off the computer. *She tried to kill me,* he told himself.

No, she would have given orders to have him killed. That, at least, was true. At his best, and worst, he was an objective man, and accuracy always trumped rationalization.

Atop the printer was a thin stack of paper. Only because he'd loaded the damn thing was it less of a surprise. There were more photos of KAT. Hoping Winslow Shepherd might be included—or to prove his own detachment—he leafed through them one by one until he got to what he realized were KAT's autopsy photos, stolen from the coroner's hard drive. Dozens of them, through every stage of the process.

Enough.

It was a balmy December eve, but Ford used a photo to start a fire in the woodstove anyway. When he thrust the last clutch in, one photo drifted up with the flames and KAT's dead eyes, minus the top of her skull, stared out at him while her face melted.

Ford slammed the stove door, yet KAT's image remained.

That's when it hit him, the truth of what he had done, yet his reaction was to stand calmly and think it through.

Julian had been correct about assassinations in foreign lands. He'd accurately referenced techniques that had been used: choke holds and broken necks, and the rare bullet. But the victims weren't victims. They were active combatants; always strong and capable, and always men.

Until now.

KAT would have had me killed, he reminded himself.

That was accurate as well.

There was something else: a missing truth he had shared with Julian of all people. On the balcony, if Shepherd hadn't been such a damn coward, if he hadn't grabbed KAT as a shield, neither of them would have fallen. Ford had tested the rail with his own weight. When the bolts he'd loosened gave way, it would have scared the hell out of them. That was the plan: scare them into talking.

Afterward, depending on what was said, he *might* have taken them for a boat ride. He *might* have used two bullets.

But Shepherd had panicked. The railing could not support the weight of two people, so KAT had suffered longer than necessary.

Exercise was Ford's way of jettisoning stress, but that source was tapped out. The next-best option was to lose himself in work, so he returned to the lab, plucked a lab apron off the hook—and only then realized the photo of KAT was still frozen on the computer screen.

He averted his eyes, wondering, *Didn't I switch off the power? Yes . . . damn right. Unless . . . I'm imagining . . .*

He yanked the plug from the wall, yet KAT's face continued to chide him from the screen. Impossible. What was happening?

In that micro-moment of uncertainty, Ford experienced his first and only glimpse into the mind-set of those who are dragged by fear into insanity.

Then the uncertainty was gone. The glowing screen was another trick. It was Julian's way of proving his dominance over cyberspace and all who relied on it.

Well, dependence was easily severed. The computer was bulky, years out of date. He scooped it from the desk and let the screen door slam behind him. Deck lights were off. Moonlight glazed the mangroves and tinted the shallows where he dropped the computer over the railing. Satisfying, the splash the damn thing made.

He stood there with a pleased expression, even though he'd have to wade in and dispose of the wreckage properly come morning.

"Doc—it's Ava. Ava Lindstrom. Are you okay?"

Outside the gate, hand on the bell lanyard, stood the vet from Sarasota. She'd brought the dog. "I tried calling, but . . . Maybe I chose a bad time."

"Couldn't be better," Ford said.

He invented a lie about the computer while he followed the woman and the dog up the stairs.

Talk about a life in opposition: ten minutes ago, he'd been leafing through autopsy photos of a woman he'd killed before escaping through the jungles of Belize. Now he was thumbing through Ava's doctoral dissertation, saying, "I can make tea, if you'd like. It's a little warm for a fire, but tea, something herbal, might be nice. Or a blanket?"

They were in what qualified as a sitting room because there were two chairs, a reading lamp near the shortwave radio, and shelves of books. The bedroom, separated only by a curtain, was to the left. The galley, with a sink and propane stove, was a wider space but part of the same room.

"I'll make it myself, if that's okay," she said. "I like futzing around in a strange kitchen. How people eat says a lot about who they are."

"A vet and a social scientist," Ford said not as a joke, but she laughed anyway; a pleasant sound on a night so still, he could hear dew dripping from the eves and faraway snatches of music.

She got up, straightened her blouse, made a funnel with her hands, and pulled her hair back. Ford watched her walk to the galley, noted the slim lines and curvatures, and got a glimpse of her lower back when she reached to open a cupboard. No tattoo, thank god—but why should he care? This wasn't a social call.

He returned to the dissertation, which was titled *Behavioral and Phenotypic Diversity in* Canis familiaris *When Genetically Engineered*.

Interesting.

As he read, the dog got up, went halfway to the galley, then did an about-face and plopped down on his feet. Not near them, *on* them.

"Geezus," he said. "Do you mind?"

The dog banged his head on the floor, already asleep.

Ava was too busy filling the kettle to notice. An innocent question seemed a good way to draw her attention. "How was the party?"

"You don't need to make small talk with me, Doc," she said from the sink. "Go ahead and read."

He did, and was surprised when he got to the third paragraph of the abstract:

Dogs, as we know them, are the product of centuries of reckless genetic experiments resulting in structural maladies and diseases that are "breed" specific. This will be discussed in the body of this work.

For fifteen thousand years, man has aspired to create the "perfect" dog. Ironically, now that we possess the genetic technology to create a better, if not perfect, dog, we must first wade through millennia of man-made mistakes.

Ford gave a low whistle. "This is impressive. Is that your main interest—research—or was it opening a clinic?"

Her reply was undecipherable over the whistling tea-kettle, so Ford let it go until she returned, carrying two steaming mugs.

"It was quiet," she said, which threw him until he realized she was answering his question about the party. "I think people are a little too hungover from the fifteenth day of Christmas to really enjoy the sixteenth. Is it always like this? Hard to imagine they've got ten more days of having too much fun."

"I'm surprised they let you escape," Ford said. The mug was hot—mint and chamomile tea, which he wasn't wild about, but said, "Smells good. How many people were there?"

She sat opposite him in an upholstered chair he'd bought at the Goodwill on Palm Ridge and centered her tea on a footstool. "If you're asking where Tomlinson is, he was with those two nice women on that funny old boat. Them and three girls from a local college. I forget the name. He didn't seem to notice when I left."

Ford turned a page and said, "Ah."

"Ah yourself. I didn't stalk off because I was jealous. Tomlinson and I are friends. That's the extent of it—well, except for three nights ago. Sometimes, not often, I do something so out of character, it shocks even me. But that's okay. I'm trying to learn to go easier on myself." The woman had a good smile; sat there, watching, to see how he handled that.

"Dogs have thirty-nine pairs of chromosomes," Ford replied. "That's more than primates, as I recollect. I've got his folder in the lab, the DNA results are there," speaking about the dog, who was tangled in his feet again. "They link him to at least five different breeds, but mostly Chesapeake. Hang on, I'll find it."

"Not until we get something straight. Let me ask you something."

Ford sat back, thinking, *Now what?*

"Why didn't you offer me a beer instead of tea? I'll tell you why. This afternoon, at that beach place the owner is buying, Tomlinson and I had a long talk. We were in one of the cottages; I saw you drive up and whatever you think was going on wasn't. Anyway, he somehow knew I . . . well, that I had some problems as a kid. Who doesn't? But that was a long time ago, so, as I told him, that doesn't mean I'm fragile or damaged goods, or can or can't choose what I want to drink—or smoke, for that matter. It's something I wanted you to know."

"There's only one thing I can say," he replied. "Do you want a beer?"

"No, but you do. So stop pretending you're enjoying that damn tea, dump it in the sink, and come back with what you actually want. And bring the DNA results, while you're at it. Oh—something else."

He was moving by then. "Yeah?"

"I don't believe your story about dropping the computer. Why'd you really throw it in the water?"

"If this is one those total honesty conversations, no offense, Ava, but we don't know each other well enough."

"I was just asking."

"Okay. Well, I got pissed off. Someone hacked into my system and I was tired of it. He's an Internet pro who's way out of my league, so I took the layman's approach. That's all I'm going to tell you."

Ava's expression read *Intriguing*, but she said, "Fair enough," and sipped her tea.

After that, things were more comfortable. They spent an hour going through the data and talked about the previous owner, a geneticist from Atlanta who'd used test tubes and breeding stock to raise retrievers. The woman vet saying, "He got a lot of things right, if you like a dog who can't bark, who's loyal; who would drown trying to retrieve a car if it went into the water but, otherwise, isn't very bright. Not bright in the way some shepherds and collies, a few other breeds, are. But much smarter than, say, an Afghan. Have you ever met an Afghan?"

Ford asked, "Loyal to someone he thinks saved his life? That's another oddity, his behavior after he nearly drowned. Let's try something."

He stood, tapped his left thigh, and said, "*Heel.*"

The dog vaulted from sleep to his side, braced him into the galley, turned in step, then performed the other basics while Ava watched—*Back . . . Down . . . Up . . . Sit . . .* then a two-minute *Stay*. Ears perked; yellow eyes gleamed until he heard the release command—*Okay*—and was soon asleep again by the chair.

Ford said, "I don't believe in the mouse-and-lion story, but the way he bonded with Figueroa, I've got to wonder."

"Not so odd," Ava said. "What do you mean *mouse-and-lion?*"

"The kid's story; maybe it was an elephant. A mouse

pulls a thorn from the foot of whatever it was—a lion, I'm pretty sure—and the lion is instantly loyal."

He explained how he and Tomlinson had found the dog starving in the Everglades, the decomposed head of a Burmese python, its teeth buried in the dog's neck.

"I made notes about the scars," Ava said. "I had no idea he'd survived something like that." She was hunkered down, elbows on knees, totally into it. "You saved Pete, then Figueroa saved him. I get it. So maybe that explains some of his behavior."

Ford didn't bother to comment on the name. He'd slipped off his boat shoes, bare feet now on the sleeping dog's ribs. "If it does, the only reason he's here is because you put him on a leash. But where's the leash?"

"I didn't. That's what I meant. What you don't know is that Figueroa hit Pete with a broom not half an hour ago. He followed me, I didn't make him come."

"I warned Figgy about that."

"He didn't hit him hard."

"That little bastard." Ford started to get up.

"Don't get mad. It was more of a soft whack on the butt. Not that I approve." The woman started to explain she'd reprimanded the Cuban, but her Spanish was poor. Then she suddenly went silent and her face paled.

Ford followed her gaze to the galley and the windows over the sink. "What's wrong?"

"I . . . I thought I saw someone . . . *something*." After a moment, still staring, she added, "Probably a bird or . . . just a reflection."

Ford gauged the change in her voice, her sudden paleness and a slackening of facial muscularity. All signaled fear. He switched off the lamp next to the reading chair and got up. "I think I'll get that beer. Want anything?"

"Is there someone else in the house?"

"Just us. What did you see?"

"Nothing—probably just a weird reflection. *Really*. It was there and gone," she said, but her voice was tight.

No doubt now. Ava was afraid.

He went into the galley, switched off the wall light, and stood at the windows, which were dark but for moonlight and the marina's glow beyond the mangroves. After a quiet minute, he turned. "Whatever you saw, the way this house is built—it's just a wooden platform on stilts—we would have felt the vibration if someone was walking around out there."

He remembered something else. "And the dog would have made a weird grunting sound—almost a growl. Turn on the light and see for yourself. I'll bet he's still asleep."

Ava remained seated, a huddled silhouette, so he found the wall switch and saw that she wasn't crying, exactly, but upset. "My god," she said. "What's wrong with me?" She sniffed as if it were nothing. "Just give me a minute."

He placed a hand on her shoulder. "What did you see?"

She managed to reply, "You wouldn't understand," then withdrew into a troubled silence.

Ford waited, never sure what to do in these situations, while he looked from window to window. Unlikely that a woman who had triumphed over the rigors of vet school was also a spooky neurotic prone to hallucinations.

He believed that until she finally said, "It's happened

before. Just now in the window, I saw the man who nearly killed me a long time ago."

"*Killed* you?"

"Close enough—like a flashback. That's the way it's described. I've been off the meds so long, I didn't think it would ever happen again. Doc"—she patted his hand— "can we keep this between ourselves?"

"How many years ago?"

"Him? Fifteen, almost sixteen. Did you hear me? I want to be able to come back to this place without dragging my past with me. Understand?"

Tomlinson's better equipped to handle this—that's what he was thinking, but said, "It will never leave the room. Do you want to talk about it?"

"Weird it would happen tonight," Ava said. She gave another optimistic sniff. "His face was so different this time. All bandaged up like he'd been in an accident—probably wishful thinking on my part, huh?" Mild laughter.

Ford's focus sharpened. "His *face* was bandaged. Are you saying he did or didn't resemble the man who—"

"No, that guy who attacked me was huge, an animal. The last time a flashback hit me like this was years ago. But it was always him, not some face wrapped like a mummy. That's an improvement, at least."

Ford looked at the retriever who, aside from an occasional tail thump, was asleep, then looked to the screen door, the lab and an empty computer desk beyond.

"I don't think you're imagining things," he said.

"But you said—"

He got up. "Don't worry, you're safe. And there's nothing wrong with your mind."

Ava's expression read *What in the world are you talking about?*

"I should have thought of this when you came in. Would you mind turning off your cell phone? And what about a laptop or any other electronics in your purse?"

She had an iPad and was switching that off, too, as he slid past the bedroom curtain to a window that confirmed he was right. Hurrying toward the gate, closer to the mangroves than the house, was a man with gauze or a hood for a head and something in his hand—a knife, maybe.

At least, it *appeared* to be a knife.

The moon wasn't bright and the man was gone by the time Ford switched on the dock lights. Either way, the situation required caution. Hidden atop the wardrobe was a twenty-round magazine. It snapped cleanly into the Sig P226 kept beneath the mattress.

"*Stay,*" Ford said to the dog, not Ava, and went out the door after what might be one of Julian's tricks, or the terrorist David Cashmere.

Máximo, as he was known to ISIS operatives.

15

BECAUSE ON THE PHONE HIS PAL HAD SAID, "GET your butt over here," Tomlinson bid adieu to the ladies on *Tiger Lilly* and jogged to the lab, where he found Ford searching the mangroves with a flashlight.

"Ava's in the house," he said. "Stay with her or take her to your boat, or something."

"What's going on, man?"

"Oh—and turn off your cell phone." Ford dropped down from the boardwalk, poked around in the trees looking for something, then came out, saying, "I saw a guy out here. She did, too, but the house didn't vibrate like it does when someone's on the deck, and the dog didn't growl. No footprints either, even in this muck. What's that tell you?"

Tomlinson felt for the joint behind his ear, asking, "Is that a gun in your back pocket?"

"What we saw could have been a projected image," Ford explained. "A hologram, maybe, but flatter, like an old movie on a screen. I find that hard to believe, so stay here for a sec and watch to see if you see any anything flying around."

"Stay with Pete, you mean. Ava told me how you came up with the name, and I totally approve."

The biologist said, "I won't be long," and took off through the mangroves toward the marina. A few minutes later, he returned via the parking lot.

"No footprints, nothing," he said, "but I still think it was a man. Either way, they're trying to spook me into leading them to the drones. It's a gambit: scare a person, he'll go directly to whatever it is that needs protecting. What I think is, we should load my boat and dive the Blue Hole tonight. Or"—he thought about it for a moment—"maybe tomorrow night. Leave a couple hours after sunset. It depends. There's someone I need to talk to."

No one could yank the blinders off a mellow Yuletide buzz like his pal the biologist, but this was a genuinely crazed proposal. "Check me if I'm wrong," Tomlinson replied, "but if it's dark—and it *is* dark—how will we know the hole is blue, or even if it's a hole, until the sun's up"—he eyed his very cool Bathys Hawaii watch—"which is exactly in eight to ten hours."

The instant those words were out of his mouth, he regretted it because he knew what was coming.

"How stoned are you?" Ford asked.

Tomlinson hated that question.

"On the Budweiser scale? I'd say about a four. That's how many Clydesdales it would take to drag my ass out there to a hundred feet of water, where we can't see diddly-squat unless that shark waits to shit me out after breakfast. *Hermano*, tell me you're not serious."

Asking Marion Ford if he was serious was comparable to asking a bear if it enjoyed the woods. There was not an ounce of levity when the man responded, "I need to have a word with Vargas. You're going to look after Ava, right?"

"Love to," Tomlinson said, but in an airy way that warned his pal he was pissed and about to get serious. "There're a couple things I'd like to clear up first. No, I'll summarize: drop the cloak-and-dagger bullshit and tell me what's going on. Usually, you avoid that Brazilian like the plague. Now you want to consult with him. And you're chasing around after goddamn holograms?"

Ford stared for a moment. "It's more than just Vargas. What's your problem?"

It was rare for the biologist to draw upon his limited sensory powers, but when he did, he was often dead-on. "I stopped at the farm an hour ago," Tomlinson said. "Now I know why you asked for the address. Would you mind explaining why you drained the cistern?"

"What?"

His pal was genuinely surprised, which surprised Tomlinson. "Yeah . . . all the water's gone. I don't know how many hundreds of gallons, but it would've taken a hell of a big pump. On the bottom, mud and limbs, some raccoon bones. They left that crap and piped the water toward my garden, which flooded my chili peppers and didn't do my basil any good either."

"We need to talk," Ford said and started to add something but was interrupted by a clattering noise coming from his house. Ava was outside on the upper deck, watching them. "That's my printer," he said. "*Shit*." But soon refocused. "You're right. I owe you an explanation, plus I need your help. But, for now, keep an eye on Ava, okay?"

Tomlinson felt better after that; a little pissy, true, but maintained his warrior attitude regarding parties and his duty to women.

He escorted Ava to the marina. On the way, he did some mild probing to see if she was in a drop-the-soap mood, and it was okay when she told him, "That was a onetime thing, sweetie. But we can still hang out."

They did after he'd smoked a jay, beautifully rolled, all sprinkled with crystals from his kef box. His Bic made the joint glitter like a tiara.

Mostly, they kibitzed with JoAnn and Rhonda, aboard *Tiger Lilly*, and a few other gentle souls who were oblivious to the strange goings-on down the shoreline at Doc's place. Lights popped off and on beneath the stilthouse; mangroves flared, at one point, with what appeared to be welding sparks. Or . . . was the biologist experimenting with some hellish new tactical device designed to foil the devil's work?

It wouldn't be the first time.

The doobie crystals were doing their magic. Tomlinson's consciousness opened to every sinister detail and all of the irony implied. Gradually, a key truth was made known to him: in this quiet little marina, where nothing was out of the ordinary, there was no such thing as odd behavior.

Evidence flowed over him, but *only* him. At one point, Mack strolled past carrying the little Cuban girl, Sabina, who was asleep, and remarked, "Sometimes, I miss the old days. There was more, I don't know . . . *excitement*, don't you think?"

Excitement? Dear Geezus, clearly the portly old Kiwi didn't notice the laser beam stabbing at the stars above Ford's house. Too late to point and say, "Tell that to Darth Vader," plus it was bad form to narc out a buddy.

By then, the laser was back in its sheath, replaced by the rumble of twin giant outboards, then more mysterious lights from the biologist's mad laboratory.

No one noticed. Not one freakin' word did they say.

There were moments when Tomlinson had to hunker within his head and ask a poignant question: When, exactly, had his life spun out of control?

No . . . control was an ancillary issue. The question was: when had his life been swept into the orbit of Dinkin's Bay, a potent gravitational system that tolerated all but whiners and the mundane yet still cracked wise about his "hippie-dippie" spirituality?

The hypocrisy irritated the hell out of him. Nothing, including three stints in an insane asylum with shock treatments for lunch, had prepared him for the unrealities of this island enclave.

But . . . on the other hand, Dinkin's Bay was a fun little place, and he could have done a lot worse.

Ava leaned a shoulder against him. "What do you think of him?"

The Brazilian approached from the direction of the mangroves, looking starched but carefree in appearance, like an ad for rayon slacks.

"Are you asking as a woman or for my professional opinion?"

The poor girl was still jittery from whatever had happened at the lab. "Both. I don't know, he seems interesting, but men are usually better judges when it comes to men."

"Got a pheromone wallop, did you?" Tomlinson gave that some thought. "My initial reaction is to say Doc wouldn't hang with a guy who's a poisonous scalp hunter and asshole. After review, however, I'll edit that down a bit. Vargas is a dangerous, egocentric prick. Stay away at all costs."

The woman asked, "Really?" as if more interested than before.

Amazing.

"I hate to say it, Ava, but you'd fit right in here."

"Really?" This was said with the same perky naïveté. "I think so, too."

As a Ph.D. and a Rienzi Zen master, he was obligated to give the woman's delusions a quick once-over. "Tell me something. Folks here don't strike you as . . . oh, say, as fucked-up and crazy as a gaggle of loons? No need to rush to judgment. Let your thoughts settle and percolate a bit."

Ava took that entirely wrong as well. "You're hilarious," she said, then beheld the docks, where the drunken minions included blue-collar rednecks, rich righties, and socialite pinkos, who voted the straight ticket but hedged on taxes. "You're right," she said finally. "I've never met nicer people anywhere."

Okeydokey.

Clearly, the woman's behavior required monitoring.

Tomlinson stayed at her side until she finally tired, which was around eleven, then hopped on his bike and followed her rental car two miles to her condo and safely inside. When he returned, the good news was, the lights in Ford's lab were off.

Thank the Good Lord. It meant the biologist had suffered a tight sphincter lapse and changed his plans. They wouldn't dive the Captiva Blue Hole until they could actually see the goddamn shark before it ate them.

The best news was this: he could get some sleep.

Nope. Not so fast. As he closed the parking lot gate, Ford appeared, with Pete trotting along at his side.

"I want to show you something," the biologist said. Then had to ask that same tiresome damn question: "How stoned are you?"

On the dissecting table was NOAA's big-picture nautical chart of Florida, Cuba, and the Caribbean. Ford had used a draftsman's compass to create circles that radiated out from Sanibel Island.

"If Julian sets foot on American soil, he'll be arrested. Well . . . could be. Same with his father, who, presumably, is still in a hospital somewhere. Is your offer still good to see the address?"

"It was some ritzy cosmetic surgery and rehab place in Mexico. Sure. I've got no loyalties to those two."

"If you're right, it means they're working with someone," Ford said. "No way do I believe they're launching drones from more than three hundred miles away. What do you think?"

He had already explained he'd used the cistern to test the Brazilian, and also as a ploy for whoever might be eavesdropping from some satellite high in the sky.

Clearly, someone was.

"I think twenty miles is a stretch," Tomlinson replied. "More like ten. Depends on the technology and the operator."

"Risk sneaking his personal drones into Florida?" Ford could accept that but didn't like it. "He could bribe someone in the Bahamas or Cuba to let him do anything. Even Julian doesn't want to screw with U.S. Customs agents."

He touched a finger below Cuba, where the chart ended. "For someone on the run, the easiest countries to buy passports and a new identity are the island nations way down in the Caribbean. Dominica or Saint Kitts. Antigua, you can buy what they call a Golden Passport for a quarter million. Antigua's closer, but still a thousand miles."

"You're hung up on the land-based thing," Tomlinson said. "Think about it—if you were a billionaire in trouble with the law, you're not going to let yourself be cornered on some third-world island where the cops can be bribed."

"He's operating from a boat?" Ford had considered that, but hadn't factored in the *money's no object* part. "I see what you're saying. Not just any boat—an ocean-going, transatlantic type equipped with all his electronic toys. Julian could be somewhere in the Gulf right now—"

"Think even bigger," Tomlinson said, "and richer." He hunkered over the chart and decided he needed a beer but came back with a Diet Coke instead. This signaled he was serious, so Ford placed a legal pad on the table, grabbed a folder of documents fresh from the printer, and left his friend alone to work it through.

On the legal pad were four circles. Each contained a name: Julian, Winslow, KAT, Cashmere. Those circles were joined by lines that branched to a dozen smaller circles, some of which contained question marks, others that bore names such as Freeport, Bahamas; Havana; and Playa del Carmen, Mexico. Beneath several were dates and sometimes key words such as *Double agent . . . Psychotic . . . Chinese funding?*

After a glance, Tomlinson said to Ford, who was going out the door, "Jesus Christ, I'm glad you didn't spring this on me out of the blue. How many hours before the Chicoms drop a nuke on Dinkin's Bay?"

The biologist laughed, but not much. "It gets worse," he said and gestured with the folder. "I'll show you when I get back."

The screen door banged closed. Tomlinson sat in the silence of aquarium aerators while the tide tugged at pilings beneath the floor. He rolled his shoulders, then concentrated on his breathing. All part of a sensory warm-up ceremony. He was, after all, a pro at this sort of thing.

It was true.

Years ago, he'd dodged military service by qualifying for a bureaucratic clusterfest that attempted to harness the sensory powers of mankind. Remote viewing, the suits in uniforms called it, because terms such as *ESP*, *astral projection*, and *psychometry* were just too damn freaky for suits to grasp—even though the Russians had proven such powers exist.

Stargate, the program was called. Each morning, at zero eight hundred, they had met in a dun-colored building that matched the dreary Maryland sky.

God, how Tomlinson hated dancing to military time. Which is why he'd flubbed enough tests, and pissed off enough stars-and-bars, to be booted out on his joyful ass.

The power to sense human vibes out there in the geosphere, however, had only grown stronger over the years.

He pulled the legal pad close enough to touch his nose to it, then danced his fingertips over the chaos of circles that Ford perceived as an orderly diagram. Slowly, slowly, the chaos reassembled in his brain as an unfolding landscape. The landscape was littered with tangents, albeit important to events, but had nothing to do with the shit storm surrounding his pal.

One by one, using a pencil, he x'd out superfluous influences.

Chinese funding. *Out.*

Double agent. *Out.*

Havana . . . Freeport and seven other notations. *Out.*

When the complicated diagram had been reduced to two primary circles, Tomlinson added a third circle and wrote *Marion Ford*.

It was just like the biologist to leave himself out of the bigger picture.

That picture was gaining resolution in Tomlinson's mind.

He pushed the legal pad away and concentrated on the nautical chart. When his consciousness was ready, he closed his eyes and floated his fingers over the chart as if touching a Ouija board.

He opened them to see his index finger doodling a circle. The circle encompassed an area in the Gulf of Mexico between the Yucatán and Sanibel Island.

For twenty minutes, his mind drifted among a landscape of open sea.

His cell rang—Ava Lindstrom calling. It gave him a chill seeing her name because he knew something terrible had just happened.

After watching his friend through the laboratory window for a moment, Ford carried the folder down the steps, through the mangroves to the marina, where Christmas decorations still blazed but only a few shadow people were awake.

It was midnight.

The dog followed him to the docks, where he'd hoped to speak with Vargas. Too late. The Brazilian's yacht was two miles away, just exiting Dinkin's Bay, its running lights a trident of red, white, and green. There was always the VHF, or a cell call, but the business Ford wanted to discuss was too personal. And dangerous.

In the ice maker, he found one of Mack's Steinlager

beers, and carried the folder to the picnic table. The printer had recently kicked out 150-some pages, compliments of Julian Solo. What they contained were the tawdry secrets of everyone associated with the marina. The contents had been hacked from nameless computer banks, and some government sources, but mostly from personal laptops owned by people Ford knew and cared about. The information, which included photos and videos, had been parsed, categorized, and, when required, cross-linked with authenticating data such as screenshots.

Atop it all was a list of demands and Julian's unsigned note. The note ended *Clarence. Who feels silly now?*

Not silly. Sick. Ford had witnessed nausea caused by anxiety but had never experienced it. He pressed the icy bottle to his forehead, then opened the folder.

All the major players associated with Dinkin's Bay were there. None were the people they pretended to be, according to Julian and his scavenging robots.

Ford told the dog, "Go swim," then did what he had to do. Leafing through those pages was the saddest form of voyeurism. No juicy gossip tidbits here. Instead, arrest reports, bankruptcies, medical files, venereal diseases, and photos so graphic that he crushed the photos one by one before they came into focus.

On the picnic table, a pile began to accumulate. He filled a bucket with water and it became a makeshift shredder.

Julian couldn't improvise paper clips, so he'd used formatting and varied typefaces to separate individual files. Names were in boldface italics.

Graeme M. MacKinlay, who owned the marina, was not Mack's real name. He was not from New Zealand. He was from Tasmania, an island off Australia, where he was wanted for assault, grand theft, and running an illegal carnival show.

A carnival? *Geezus.*

Ford skipped the next few pages, which contained more damning evidence against Mack and what might have been a recent medical report.

JoAnn Smallwood. His lifted his head from the page and found *Tiger Lilly* moored next to Coach Mike West-hoff's boat. The lights were off in the old Chris-Craft; a dozy darkness emanated from the cabin.

"Go to hell," Ford told Julian and moved JoAnn's dossier to the bottom of the pile without opening it. He did the same with Rhonda Lister, his cousin Ransom Gatrell, and several other names he knew too well to sully them or their families by risking a look.

Ava Lindstrom.

Why the hell include a woman who was only visiting the island?

Because she'd been in his house, Ford realized. That spooked him. Julian's note had included a threat: *I'll make an example of someone close to you.* Meshed with Tomlinson's claim about addiction and what little Ava had told him about her past, he sensed trouble, so he went through the first few pages. As a teen, Ava had been arrested for possession of drugs, petty theft—several times—and also prostitution.

That was the biggie. All court records had been ex-punged but were still available, obviously, to a master hacker. After that, aside from stints in rehab, there were no damning details to add about the woman.

Ava fought her way out, Ford thought. *She stayed strong—good for her.*

Three more photos went into the bucket.

Jeth Nicholes and the other fishing guides were there, as well as their wives. All good people. He wanted to maintain that conviction, so he kept going and was soon near the end of the stack.

Capt. Hannah Smith.

The name stopped him. It was because of Julian's threat. But what the hell could he have found on a woman who was as devoted to her religious precepts as she was to her friends, her family, and her own ideals of behavior?

Beneath Hannah's cover page were only three . . . no, four pages. His fingers hesitated there. He got up, checked on the dog, checked to confirm the Brazilian's yacht had disappeared from the channel, then returned to the folder.

With a thumb, he strummed those four pages . . . and saw the corner of a photo. He plucked the photo out and crushed it. But he saw enough to recognize Hannah's wet hair and knew it had been snapped while she was showering.

There was no way she would have posed for such a shot. A camera had been hidden somewhere in the ceiling vent of the shower on Vargas Diemer's yacht.

Ford slammed the folder closed and looked toward the opening into Dinkin's Bay. "You son of a bitch," he said.

He called the dog and was dealing with the bucket when he decided he'd better make sure he was right before chasing the Brazilian down and choking him to death.

Another look at the soggy photo proved nothing. Shot from above, it could have been any shower, anywhere. No date stamp. Even so, Vargas was the likely voyeur.

Ford slapped the dog to heel and jogged toward his house. At the very least, he would call Hannah to make sure the file hadn't been uploaded to her own laptop as well.

That possibility scared him more than any threat Julian had made: his friends would be destroyed if Ford didn't cooperate.

Okay. Julian had won. For now.

Ford knew it was true when Tomlinson came running out of the mangroves, saying, "Man, why didn't you answer your damn phone? We gotta go. Ava found something on her computer—I don't know what, but she tried to kill herself."

On her computer . . .

Ford didn't hear much else until they were in the truck, where Tomlinson explained, "She was hysterical, so I'm not sure about anything, except she took an overdose of something and woke up·in the bathroom, bleeding. A slit wrist, I think."

Later, sitting in the HealthPark ER off Summerlin Road, Ford said to Tomlinson, who was reading through the folder, "I'll kill him."

"I'll help you," the Zen Buddhist master replied. "And I know how."

16

UNWINDING AFTER TWENTY-FOUR HOURS OF SERI-
ous spiritual trauma required ceremony.

It was two a.m.

Tomlinson was alone on his sailboat. He lit a candle, mumbled a prayer, and sat in full lotus position, staring at the flame. Twice a day, every day, he meditated unless on a Key West tear, although lately Pensacola had become a fave—the best oysters, and prettier women.

Steady on. Now was not the time to allow his focus to drift. Concentrate, breathe, cling to no thoughts.

Soon the candle flame displaced all else.

Meditation had saved his sanity. This was a *No BS* truth he never ever joked about and another reason he felt guilty about the pretty veterinarian. He had sensed her problems but had been too damn stoned to zoom in and realize she was still in trouble.

Meditation might have helped her.

Poor Ava. She'd had no idea what awaited when she stumbled onto Dinkin's Bay. Not that the marina possessed a destructive karma. Just the opposite—it was a place of light and positive ions, but occasionally that light dimmed. Destiny often played a role.

Last night had been one of those nights.

Dr. Ava Lindstrom would live, but she would never return to the marina. Tomlinson had dealt with enough drug people to know how scars were dealt with. She would withdraw into her shell for a while, then pretend to be the person she wanted to project: an accomplished professional, generally happy, always dependable. She would gravitate closer to one or two good friends, who would encourage her to move her clinic from Sarasota to somewhere else—out of state, most likely.

She had no choice. Julian Solo had copied Ava's file to her entire list of clients.

On the bright side—and there was always a bright side—she was, thus far, the only victim. He and Ford had spent the day packing for a trip and nosing around. Mack and Rhonda and the others at Dinkin's Bay were unaware of what awaited if certain demands weren't met.

Julian wanted the drones. His father, Winslow Shepherd, wanted the biologist dead. Well . . . he wanted to meet Ford on an eighth-floor balcony in Mexico. The rest was obvious.

Bizarre.

This was Tomlinson's interpretation of a cryptic, unsigned note. Julian owed his father a favor, apparently, or the pair had renegotiated the rights to a patent or a software finesse.

Who knew? It was all related to some prior event that had seriously pissed off the math professor.

Ford had remained mum on specifics, but you didn't have to be a Weatherman to read between the lines.

Tomlinson had *been* a Weatherman. That tidbit, no doubt, had been included in the information sent by Julian. He was guessing, because his own file was missing when he opened the folder.

Ford had sloughed that off, too, saying, "Only children and the truly wicked are immune from slander."

Like Ava, Marion Ford had no choice. He was going to Mexico.

Not good. From the instant of their first meeting, Tomlinson knew the biologist would die in a country not his own and from a bullet or blow from an unseen enemy. It was an insight he'd never shared. Same with the prescient conviction that his own death would be by drowning. This alone suggested their vulnerable asses were better off in a bar or a woman's bed come sunrise.

No way, José. The biologist was a dutiful man.

One or both of them would die or . . . they *wouldn't*. Karma could be a beauteous circle or a bitch with fangs, but *destiny* was not carved in stone.

When he was done meditating, he blew out the candle and opened a slim volume he had read many times: *The Anarchist's Cookbook*. The recipes included how to improvise small bombs, and poisons, and other mayhem designed to chip away at the political scaffolding of an industrial giant.

Ironic.

Around three, he dozed off.

Then came four a.m. A raucous knocking launched him, cat-like, to the ceiling. Worse, it interrupted a mildly kinky sex dream, which was typical after a stressful day.

Sweet Jesus—suddenly, he was tangled on the floor. He threw off the sheet, got up, and hollered, "Who's out there?"

A stupid question, but he flicked on the aft cockpit lights anyway and went up the steps.

"I've got coffee in a thermos and your dive gear's packed," the biologist said, then winced and looked away. "Christ—get some pants on."

Back down the steps in a fog, but still lucid enough to inquire, "What time is it?"

"It'll be light in three hours," Ford replied. "I want to be done by then."

What Tomlinson didn't understand, and didn't ask when he stepped down into the biologist's high-tech, rubberized inflatable monster boat, was *Why the hell was the dog aboard?*

Pete's yellow eyes glared at him from the seat to the left of the wheel. The copilot's seat. *His* seat, under normal circumstances.

They freed the lines and got under way, Ford saying, "If you have a cell phone, leave it on. For now."

"Where's yours?" Tomlinson asked. The biologist always locked his cell in a waterproof case on the console.

"I loaned it to someone" was the cryptic reply.

Okay.

It was dark, only a partial moon with stars to brighten the heavy dew and the shimmering presence of the marina. Tomlinson slid past the console, barefoot, and took a seat on the cooler. Forward, under the bow canopy, were vague, washtub-sized shapes covered with a tarp.

The drones.

They idled clear of the basin; then the sudden torque of twin 250 Mercs pinned Tomlinson's hair back. After that, no more talking—not him, while Ford made a couple of inaudible calls on the VHF.

It was chilly this December morn. Tomlinson wore a jacket of red, blue, white, and yellow rags, tied long ago by Seminole women in the Glades. It was a gift from Chief Buffalo Tiger. He'd brought it along for good juju but now pulled it around him for warmth and settled back for the ride. If it wasn't for the dog, he would have curled up among the drones, but Pete had switched places and was asleep. So he slipped around the console to the copilot's seat and made himself familiar with the controls. Lots of toggle switches and glowing screens to learn about, so he asked questions as needed.

Stay on your toes was the mantra for today.

At Lighthouse Point, they skimmed along the beach past the Tarpon Bay access. There were lights on in one of the Grin N Bare It cottages. Tomlinson glanced at Ford, who nodded and said, "Mack," loud enough to imply the rest. Meaning Rhonda was probably there, too.

Then the monster boat banked due west toward an orange quarter moon. After a slight correction north, the biologist switched off all electronics but for running lights. Half an hour later, he killed those, too, and they rode in the rhythmic silence of a winter moon, engines, and stars.

Tomlinson, the celestial navigator, had those fiery star markers embedded in his soul. He stroked his hair and feasted on the winter sky. A few degrees south of the elliptic were Aldebaran and Tau; Betelgeuse framed Orion, a constellation of ancient silver angles. In the west, near the low, setting moon, was Capella. Polaris anchored the universe to the northern pole.

The human fist when extended covers about ten degrees of outer space or one's inner compass. A thumb adds two degrees.

He employed both. They were on a heading of 275 degrees, give or take, on a rhumb line to Mexico, if they had the fuel. Yucatán, and the jungles of Quintana Roo were only 380 miles southwest. A dozen times, he'd made that crossing under sail.

Not tonight, but it was doable, considering who was at the wheel. You could criticize the biologist's lack of imagination and his other nerdy flaws, but, by god, he could drive a boat. With electronics off—no autopilot, no chart plotter, no lights, nothing—he steered an unwavering course. The fact that a night vision monocular was strapped to his eye—an unsettling cyclopean visage—did not lessen the feat.

"It'll be dead-flat calm come sunrise," Ford said. "That's good. Want some coffee? It's in a thermos under your seat."

Café con leche, Cubano-style. Not enough sugar, of course, but pretty good for a guy who cooked as if doing chemistry experiments. He poured and passed a plastic cup around.

"Too much sugar," the biologist commented.

Tomlinson flipped him the bird and continued to root through the cooler. There was a newly cut stalk of dwarf Orinoco bananas, bags of dried fruit, a block of cheese, hot sauce from Colombia, some other stuff, and down on the bottom, under the ice, a six-pack of Genesee Bock Beer.

"Breakfast!" Smiling, he came up holding a bottle.

"Not before I dive," Ford said, "but go ahead, if you want. You'll stand safety watch with your gear ready. There's no need for both of us to go in the water."

"Seriously . . . I'm not diving?"

Ford didn't hear the relief in his pal's voice. "I want to make this quick. If you're right about Julian living on a ship of some type, we need you topside. Are you okay with that?"

Damn straight, Tomlinson was okay with that.

After a few incredible bananas and swallows of Bock beer, his metabolism shifted from neutral into a functioning gear. He began to take stock of where they were. It meant calibrating a fist with the halo glow in the east and readying himself when Doc said, "To find this place, I've got to use the electronics, but only for a minute or two, then I'll power off for a while. It won't give you much time to learn how the system works."

That was okay, too. Tomlinson didn't need electronics. They were both concerned they were being tracked by satellite or being followed by drones or a boat . . . or something bigger that Ford had failed to consider. But why add worry to the man's full plate?

Ford pulled off the night vision monocular and handed it over. "Keep watch for a while. My eyes need time to adjust before I switch on the sonar."

Through the lens, a billion stars became an infinity of pearls. Satellites appeared and dragged a glowing grid across the void. The moon, half full, shimmered above the western horizon.

No sign of boats afloat or things that fly, so Tomlinson studied the electronics suite when it came to life. According to the GPS, they were 31.89 miles from Sanibel Lighthouse in eighty feet of water.

This was important. They had left the territorial waters of the United States—the twelve-mile limit—far behind. The U.S. exclusive economic zone, however, extended two hundred nautical miles from the Florida peninsula. Maritime law was something he and Ford had discussed because of what might or might not happen if Julian's people showed up.

A bank of glowing LED screens offered more data. The chart plotter indicated it would be 2.2 miles before they should begin a serious search for the Captiva Blue Hole. The bottom was hard sand. On sonar, it showed as a flowing scroll of red. Fish—there weren't many—appeared as series of sideways V shapes. Once, however, a school of bait was so tightly grouped, it scrolled beneath as one giant living mass.

"How do you know it's not just one big damn fish?" Tomlinson asked.

"Stop worrying about that shark," Ford replied and

dropped the boat off plane. "Get the marker ready. I've been out here a couple of times and it's not easy to find." Then raised his voice to tell the dog, "*Stay*."

Pete was a regular little soldier, depending on who gave the orders. Tomlinson had to give the stubborn hulk his due.

Like plowing a field, back and forth they went, while the screens fed information. The Blue Hole wasn't an address you could punch into a GPS even though they had the numbers. It was a hole in the Earth, not large, and shielded from sonar by a limestone ledge that covered all but a crevice.

Even with the monster boat's high-tech equipage, it took a while.

"You ready?" the biologist called over the engine noise.

Tomlinson held an orange buoy connected to two hundred feet of line and a ten-pound weight. When told, he dumped it over the side. In the glare of a spotlight, the buoy fluttered while the line deployed, then drifted still.

They anchored, drifted back. On the sonar screen, a scrolling red bottom was suddenly breached by a chasm of deepest blue.

There it was: the opening to an archaic spring ninety feet below.

Tomlinson dropped two safety lines, with Cyalume sticks attached incrementally. The sticks throbbed like fireflies until they vanished into the depths. Ford focused on getting the drones ready, then his dive gear, which, for some reason, included a metal ammo box.

"What's in there?"

"Plastic explosives," the biologist replied. "Don't touch."

It was an hour before first light—five-fifty a.m. on the seventeenth day of Christmas.

17

AT FIFTY FEET, FORD'S BUOYANCY COMPENSATOR vest began to compress. The more it compressed, the faster he descended from starlight into blackness. He popped some air to slow his descent and illuminated a little dive computer. The green-and-yellow tank strapped to his back contained nitrox gas, a mix of oxygen and nitrogen. Nitrox extended his bottom time. At one hundred feet, he had twenty minutes. Any longer, he would have to make a decompression stop.

Ford set the alarm for sixteen minutes, to err on the

side of safety, and continued to descend fins first. Diving solo was dangerous enough.

Clamped to his mask were twin LED lights, one over each ear. When his depth gauge read seventy feet, he activated the lights and panned full circle. A school of amberjack glittered like gold at the edge of visibility. Barracuda drifted as motionless as rungs, and a single hammerhead shark—not big, a skinny eight-footer—trailed the jacks.

Below his fins was a moonscape of sand, rubble, and sea fans. The drones were already there, a few yards apart, attached to the rope that guided him down. Each was harnessed to a cement block, a Cyalume stick, and an air bag. The bags could be inflated by pulling a string or with a regulator.

If the wrong people tried to bring them to the surface, it would be the last thing they ever did.

Under electrical tape, molded to both fuselages, was a glob of C-4 plastic explosives. Not much. In Tampa, the man he trusted had provided one standard block in a Mylar wrapper. The stuff had the texture of modeling clay and weighed about a pound.

Half of the block was still aboard the boat.

Ford had already inserted detonator cords, tipped with crimping sleeves—hopefully, not long enough to be seen with a remote underwater camera. In his vest pocket were four tiny detonators. Two were pressure-sensitive. They would be set to go off as the air bags neared the surface. He didn't want to damage the ancient spring, just get his message across. The other two detonators were electronic and synced to the same ultra-high-frequency signal. They could be activated from a boat or even a low-flying plane.

First, though, he had to find the crevice.

His dive computer had no GPS—satellite signals can't penetrate more than a few feet of saltwater. But he had an electronic compass that pointed him to a spot he estimated was twenty yards away. Dragging the drones, he set off down a tunnel of light not much wider than his shoulders. Rubble and sea fans transitioned to an area of sand so fine, it blossomed around him in a cloud. Bad for visibility, but a sign he was heading in the right direction.

Blue holes in the Gulf were conduits to inland lakes, rivers, and aquifers. For eons, freshwater had percolated through this sand and, over time, had ground it to powder. Another indicator was a reduction in buoyancy—objects sank faster in freshwater. There was also a chilly thermocline change.

The crevice couldn't be far.

He stopped and checked his gauges: only twelve minutes of safe bottom time remained. He filled a small vial with water for testing, then continued on, pulling the drones along the bottom. It was a clumsy process that produced a sandstorm. Sand boiled around his mask and caused his own flashlights to blind him—the equivalent of driving through a snowstorm at night.

He switched off one light, changed the angle of the other, but still couldn't see worth a damn. So he killed the second light, too, and proceeded blindly with the compass as his only guide.

This darkness was a void without borders. Sound and touch, taste and temperature, became reference points.

Large fish, when frightened, explode to flight with a crackle of muscle density. He heard several big fish spook off. Grouper, most likely. This suggested there were rock hiding places ahead.

He removed the regulator and tasted the water. It had a sulfuric bite and wasn't salty. In the 1500s, Spanish ships had stopped at blue holes in the Gulf to replenish their water supply. Underground rivers had gushed like fountains in those days. This was no longer true. Five centuries of dredging, building, and diking had damaged Florida's aquifers, but a trickle of freshwater still flowed here.

Something else he heard: sonar pings and whistling—a pod of dolphins or porpoise, he guessed—moving rapidly toward him. There was nothing unsettling about that.

I want to dive this place when I can see, Ford thought, then consulted the glowing gauges attached to his BC vest. Depth: 92′. Bottom time: 9 minutes 45 seconds and ticking. According to the compass, he'd stayed on track, so he had to be within a few yards of his destination.

He dragged the drones closer, reached to turn on a light—and that's when a wall of water hit him with the impact of a passing truck. The current tumbled him forward, then down into the denser gravity of a freshwater space without bottom. But there were ledges. His tank clanked off rocks; limestone abraded a knee and his right arm. Two bursts of gas into his BC slowed his fall. A third burst stopped it. He hung there suspended, disoriented, until he switched on the flashlights.

He was in a cave of sorts. Below his fins, a column of water angled into an earthen gloom. Above was a limestone awning that opened out into night . . . but two glowing Cyalume sticks told him the drones were up there on the lip of the crevice.

The Captiva Blue Hole. He'd found it. But what the hell had caused a jet-stream current so sudden and powerful, it had knocked him down?

He thought about the pod of dolphins he'd heard pinging. Maybe they'd come flying past in silence and one had rammed him. Or . . . the collective force of their wake had done it.

Nothing like that had ever happened before.

Ford gathered his composure by consulting gauges. Depth: 105´. Bottom time: 7 minutes 20 seconds and ticking. The glowing numerals of his watch—a Graham Chronofighter—told him it was six-forty a.m. Only a few minutes until first light.

There was still a lot to do.

He kicked his way to the lip of the crevice. Just inside the ledge was a concave area large enough to hide the drones from any diver not using a telemetry guidance system.

Perfect.

Visibility was good now that the sandstorm had abated. Using a crimper, he joined two detonators to each drone and secured them with tie wraps. In the world of explosives, introducing electric current provides a spooky moment. That's what he was doing, activating power switches, when he heard a rhythmic thump-thump-thump from ninety feet above, which startled the hell out of him at first.

When he heard it again, though, the thumping assumed

a Morse code pattern: *thump . . . thump . . . thump . . . thump-thump-thump.* Over and over, in groups of three.

Geezus. Was Tomlinson sending him an SOS by beating on the hull of the boat?

More likely, the Zen hipster had gotten bored and was dancing, stomping the deck, to tunes by the Stones, or the Troggs doing "Wild Thing."

Wild thing . . . thunk-thunk-thunk . . . you make my heart sing.

That seemed to fit, but it didn't matter. Bottom time: 2 minutes 30 seconds.

Ford went back to work. When the detonators had been activated, he set the switches to 0.00, which was one atmosphere of pressure, then armed all four. God help the diver who failed to hit the *Deactivated* button before surfacing.

It was different with the remote detonators. Punch in a three-digit code. *Boom!*

Tomlinson was sitting at the console, monitoring the radar screen and anything else of interest. The biologist had been down about ten minutes when another massive school of fish registered on the sonar. At the same instant, the boat jolted as if slapped by a wake, then listed and rolled on unseen waves.

"What the hell!"

He jumped to his feet and grabbed a flashlight. His first thought was that Ford had done an emergency ascent and crashed into the hull. He probed an area near the stern and was relieved to see nitrox bubbles pooling near the safety line. Ford had been in the same spot for several minutes.

Unless . . . unless he'd had to jettison his tank for some reason. It was possible.

Tomlinson circled the boat, alert for movement on the surface, which was oily calm. To the west, the Gulf was waxen. The moon was melting into an orange sea. In the east, the first pale rind of daylight had appeared. Nearby, a school of dolphins or porpoises plumed a single silver geyser toward the fading stars. That's all he saw. No sign of his friend.

Ford had told him not to turn on the underwater lights, but he did anyway. Two dazzling banks of LEDs floated them in a lucent pool that faded to black twenty feet below. Nothing down there but crabs adrift and the tiny glowing insect eyes of shrimp.

He was moving toward the bow when the retriever put its front paws on the portside gunnel and made a grunting noise while he stared at the moon.

Tomlinson started to say, "Piss in that box—" but stopped when he saw what the dog saw. "Jesus Christ," he muttered and stepped back.

Speeding toward them out of the moon was a tall, black vertical object that cleaved the surface and displaced a wall of orange water. It was a football field away but closing fast.

A periscope, he thought, because that's what he'd anticipated: Julian in some kind of super-yacht or his own private submarine. "Think bigger and richer," he'd told Ford.

"Get down, Pete," he hollered, but the damn dog was vibrating, similar to a growl, and didn't budge.

Seventy yards, then fifty—the thing kept coming, on a collision course, and was soon close enough for Tomlinson to realize it wasn't a periscope. It was a dorsal fin.

"Shit-oh-dear. It's *her*."

Dolly. The great white shark that had surfaced in the area more than three weeks ago. She was eighteen feet long and weighed more than a ton, according to news stories, but looked bigger now, much bigger, in moonlight, and had to be doing twenty knots.

A gun. Ford always had a gun hidden somewhere. Tomlinson lunged for the console and spent a frantic few seconds searching, but couldn't stop himself from taking another look. He stood, turned, and Dolly was there, her six-foot dorsal at eye level, a waterfall streaming from her back.

Tomlinson hollered, "Hold on," to the retriever and prepared for impact . . . but there was no impact, just a mountainous rush of water that tilted the boat sideways. It took a moment to understand. The shark had sounded.

He rushed to the starboard gunnel and looked over in time to see a massive shadow that angled downward. The dog saw it, too, and leaped over the side, swam in a confused circle, then dived headfirst in pursuit but only managed six or seven feet before it surfaced. All of this visible in the underwater lights.

"Doc's down there, you idiot. Get your ass in the boat. We've got to warn him."

The dog continued doing what it was doing while Tomlinson wondered, *Warn him how?*

A screen in the electronics suite drew his attention: sonar showed a massive blue blob at fifty feet . . . then sixty. The shark was diving. He stood fixated and watched, yet also noticed a new blip on the radar screen. A boat—or a low-flying plane—was approaching from several miles away, also on a collision course.

That snapped him out of it. "You can't make this shit up," he yelled and rushed to the stern.

Near the boarding ladder, his dive gear was ready, laid out in an orderly fashion. He grabbed the BC vest, then realized there wasn't enough time. Doc was due to surface soon—in three minutes, according to the bezel of his watch.

There was only one option: Morse code.

He stomped the deck with a series of SOS warnings while yelling to the dog, "Get your crazy butt in the boat."

Then he checked the horizon for a boat or low-flying plane, wondering, *What next?*

When Ford looked up into the glare of lights and saw a massive fish coming at him, he ducked into the crevice and watched it rocket past. A series of low-frequency whistles pierced his rib cage while a jet-stream wake banged him against limestone.

This explained what had happened earlier.

He waited. The animal made another pass, this time slow enough for his flashlights to provide a better look. The white saddle patch near its dorsal was as distinctive as the animal's size—almost twenty feet long and at least two tons.

It was an amazing encounter, but the delay had extended his time on the bottom. A short decompression stop was protocol—probably unnecessary, but he did it anyway; clung to the safety line at thirty-three feet, where the boat's underwater LEDs provided a dome of visibility. He floated suspended in space for two minutes and regretted not having a camera when the creature swam past again.

Wait . . . he did have a camera, but he'd never used the damn thing. It was built into his cell phone–sized dive computer. When the creature made a fourth pass, he fired off a dozen shots. Some looked pretty good. After another two minutes, he kicked to the surface, where he was surprised to see his dog in the water and that Tomlinson was not dancing, just frantic.

"In the boat, man, get in the damn boat," he yelled. "Holy shit, the *size* of that thing—but don't panic. Panic, man, your splashing might attract her. But"—he cupped his hands to be heard—"I might be wrong!"

Ford, smiling, played dumb. "Wrong about what?"

"Hurry up."

"Was it a shark?"

"Huh?"

"What did you see?"

"Jesus-f'ing-Christ, just move your ass, Doc. *Please?*"

It was morning twilight, the sun not yet up, but a corona of bronze rimmed the east. Ford submerged and did a slow three-sixty, seeing demarcations of blue funnel into black, a few barracuda on the periphery, a sparkling cloud of bait. Then got a scare himself when something grabbed his dive vest from behind and pulled him to the surface.

It was the dog. The retriever had retrieved its owner.

"Get away," he said, while Tomlinson yelled dire warnings if he didn't get his butt in gear.

Ford thought, *I should savor this.* It was because he knew something Tomlinson did not: this might be the last time he saw his friend—or the dog, for that matter. So he kicked past the safety line, then took his sweet damn time at the transom while he boosted the dog aboard. Next, he handed up a sack of gear, his scuba rig, but remained in the water while he asked, "Did you see a shark? The only shark I saw was a hammerhead and it wasn't big enough to worry about."

Hilarious, Tomlinson's reaction. "What part of get your ass in the boat don't you understand? I mean it. *Now.* A thing that size can bite your legs off in one pass. Here . . ." Tomlinson extended his hand.

Ford ignored it; instead, belly flopped over the inflated collar into the boat. He grabbed a towel, sat there, with fins, the mask on his forehead, wearing a shorty wet suit. "It couldn't have gone any smoother down there." He looked east. "Sun's just coming up. We're right on time."

Tomlinson's expression: *Have you lost your mind?* "You didn't see it? That thing had to have blotted out the sky. Hell . . . I could see from up here. She swam right past you at least twice and you just hung there like soap-on-a-rope. No, dope-on-a-rope. And don't get me started on that idiot dog."

"You're kidding. Just now?"

Tomlinson tugged at his hair. "It was a freakin' great white shark, man. Not a hammerhead. Biggest I've ever . . . Like, we're talking longer than this boat. Almost as wide. You don't get it? It was *Dolly*, the one that's been hanging around eating boats and shit." He draped a hand over the T-top and stood on one leg like a stork while he searched the surface. "She cruised past like a submarine. That's what I thought it was at first—Julian in a high-tech Captain Nemomobile. You know, really truckin' like it was going to ram us."

"A *submarine*?" Ford had to smile.

"Hey, *hermano*, anything's possible if you've got the dou-re-mi. But then I saw her dorsal fin and she went under. Like Hello, Dolly! smelled food, something tasty on the bottom. Smelled *you*, in other words. Man, I didn't know whether to shit or wind my wristwatch, so I resorted to my old Boy Scout training. You didn't hear my SOS?"

Impossible to play dumb after that. When Ford laughed, it was usually an inward chuckle, but this time he opened up, which nearly turned into a laughing jag. Between breaths, he spoke in fragments. "The look on your face when you . . . Oh my god. What a circus—the dog swimming in circles and you're up here stomping grapes. That's what it looked like; then . . . *a submarine*? Oh Geezus, this is too good . . ."

Tomlinson showed his impatience by storing dive gear and checking Pete's water bucket, then banged a locker closed and waited for the biologist to regain his normal countenance, which was a blend of tolerance and mild skepticism.

Ford croaked out a few more gems before he finally calmed and said, "It wasn't a shark, it was a killer whale. You didn't hear the thing spout when it breached?"

"Whale? Man, I know the difference between . . ." Tomlinson paused to think. "The spouting, yeah, I thought it was a school of porpoise. I didn't know there were killer whales in the Gulf. Not here anyway."

"He's a transient," Ford said. "A male, probably, traveling alone. At first, I figured it was a false killer or a pilot whale, but then he cruised past close enough . . . Geezus, what a wake he threw." He popped the dive computer free of its case. "Have a look."

Tomlinson flipped through a couple of decent shots while Ford talked about what had happened down there in the dark, then said, "You know that video circulating around of the supposed great white? The blurry one. I was fairly certain from the rear edge of the dorsal, but I thought the same thing—no killer whales here—so I checked some of the journals. Only a small population lives in the Gulf, fewer than five hundred, spread between Texas and Mexico, and a few seen off Key West. They're transients, as opposed to a resident population—a subspecies of killer whale that doesn't breed with outsiders. Some believe that anyway. The dorsal fins are slightly different, and they're more solitary."

Ford got up, took a look around, then nodded at the little dive computer. "That's my Christmas present to Fast Eddie. I drew his name, and those photos are better than anything else I can think of. There's his proof it's safe to dive. Mack will like them, too. You know, good for business; charter a boat and look for . . ." He lost the thread; went to the electronics suite and focused on the radar screen. Then turned east, shielding his eyes. "That's Dan Futch in our new Maule," he said and pointed to a speck on the horizon. "Don't get pissed off, okay? There's something I didn't tell you. I would've, but kept waiting for you to ask why I brought the dog."

Tomlinson thought, *He doesn't plan on returning,* but replied, "So I'll have company when I drive this monster-ass boat back to Sanibel. No need for me to ask—you forget my paranormal powers."

That was always good for a smile, but this time it got a rare hoot of laughter. "You didn't know I was leaving from here. Admit it."

"Next stop, Mexico," Tomlinson said. "Don't worry. I know better than to ask questions. But there is one little thing I want to talk about."

While Ford listened, he placed his passport on the console, then made a pile that included his billfold, keys to his truck, the metal ammo box, and an oversized envelope. When they were done discussing what Tomlinson wanted to discuss, he tapped the pile. "I want you to hang on to this stuff—until I get back, of course. The person I loaned my phone to will drop it at the lab in a day or two. And this"—he opened the ammo box—"we need to go over a few details now."

A seaplane, blue on white with white pontoons, buzzed them, then circled south and turned to land.

"Sure," Tomlinson replied. "Anything you say. The only *no* in my vocabulary begins with a *k*."

18

FORD'S MAULE AMPHIBIOUS AIRCRAFT WAS A
small four-seater designed to land damn near anywhere
and equipped to make long hauls. Fully fueled, its four-
cylinder turbo could cruise at 160 knots for more than six
hundred nautical miles.

Crossing the Gulf of Mexico with a tailwind was a
two-hour hop that Dan Futch, a veteran pilot, had made
before—often clandestinely. That meant flying low,
sometimes only a hundred feet off the water, so they took
turns at the yoke to mitigate eyestrain. On a morning this
calm, the Earth's curvature blended with the sea's waxen

borders, so the altimeter played a role. To converse, they wore headphone transceivers and discussed all sorts of things, including how much fun Dan would have tonight alone in the luxury suite Ford had reserved beachfront, Playa del Carmen.

Thirty miles out, they raised the Yucatán Peninsula. Cumulus clouds marked shoals and jungle beaches, then an isolated bay south of Tulum where, more than a week ago, Ford had created a base camp. The resort was a few miles to the west, a strand of white beach and white buildings amid forest green. There was no parasail aloft today.

They descended almost to the water and decreased speed, Dan saying, "You don't want me to do a flyover. Right?"

Ford shook his head. "Just a touch-and-go in case somebody sees us come in. Once we're down, dump me and take off. You know, like you're practicing landings. We'll hook up tomorrow."

No more questions from the pilot.

At tree level, he threaded a narrow opening into the Bay of Ascension and banked to port as Ford gave directions, then pointed to a ribbon of blue that guaranteed safe water. Pontoons made contact; the little Maule bucked and reared through a silver plume. They were down but still moving fast in a plane that was now a boat.

Ford had his gear ready in a buoyant, watertight bag. He opened the door but kept his headphones on. "See that rise where the tree line changes?"

Futch used the pedals to turn and reduced speed. A minute later, he hollered out the door, "You're good to go, man. See you tomorrow." He waited until his passenger had rolled free of the pontoons, then punched the throttle and went airborne again.

Ford watched from the water while he battled to get one fin, then the other, over his jungle boots. The Maule exited the opening at mangrove level, then banked north as if headed for Playa del Carmen.

When the plane was gone, Ford swam toward a hillock of palm trees, then into a winding creek where the Maya had quarried limestone.

This trip, he carried no satellite phone, no electronics of any kind. Too dangerous. Nor could he buy a boat. He couldn't risk being recognized.

Winslow Shepherd was waiting for him nearby—or soon would be—at an unfinished condo that had eight floors. Their "meeting" was scheduled for five-thirty, a little before sunset.

Julian's note had included this and other details, but nothing about his father's condition. Presumably, Shepherd would be on crutches or in a wheelchair and he would have bodyguards as attendants—one of them David Abdel Cashmere.

This was an inference. The math professor, via Julian, had offered Ford two choices: step off the balcony on his own or allow himself to be pushed off.

Either way, poor old Winslow wants your head.

This was a line from Julian's note.

The note had included other directives as well.

What Ford had brought was the jungle hammock and

a couple of MREs for food. He strung the hammock in the shade and climbed in to escape the bugs. While trying to get comfortable, he found the page from Tomlinson's manuscript he'd left there more than a week ago. Nothing else to read, so he had a look. This time, the first paragraph grabbed his attention.

My inner voice tells me I have no worth beyond the kindness I show strangers. It claims I make clown faces, and have no power to escape the puppeteer's strings . . .

Puppeteer . . . It was an odd word, a word seldom used in this age of electronic manipulation. But so what? Tomlinson was a master of the esoteric. Yet the word resonated and bounced around in Ford's memory, looking for a match.

Puppeteer . . . ?

He was by the water, eating cold lasagna, when it finally came to him. Julian had used the word to describe his father. No . . . his psychiatrist, the one he'd framed for pedophilia.

Ford tried to recall the exact usage. Something about Julian's shrink being a lying puppeteer and not particularly smart, so he'd cut the strings by planting photos on the shrink's computer. Maybe Julian hadn't used the phrase *cutting the strings*, but that was the result.

It was an interesting coincidence, but only as a mind game.

He had a lot to do before his appointment.

It was a four-mile swim and slog to the resort without

a boat, but only a few hundred yards to the place where he'd hidden the standup paddleboard—if it was still there.

It was. He sloshed the board clean with water, hopped up, and paddled back to camp.

In a place like this, the best disguise was to look like a tourist who couldn't tolerate the sun. An hour later, he paddled past the resort with a towel draped over his head and wearing a ball cap to hold the towel in place. Strapped to the front of the board was his gear bag, which might have contained a picnic lunch.

It did not.

The building where he was to meet Shepherd was a concrete shell a mile up the beach. A bulldozer and construction junk were scattered around a bare five-acre lot, far removed from the resort's plush landscaping and cameras. There was no beach here, just rocks and mud, until they trucked in sand. No people either, not even workers, which suggested the company had run out of money. It wasn't unusual in third-world boom areas.

He paddled past the building into an area shielded from slow ocean rollers by a stretch of coral, some of it exposed by the falling tide. Among propeller scars and junk, a purple rivulet threaded the shoals into a miniature cenote about the size of the Captiva Blue Hole. The water was deep and clear, but the surface was a slow whirlpool of Styrofoam and garbage that had been snared by the current as well as a host of mindless moon jellies and one massive Portuguese man-of-war.

Ford drifted over the hole, then paddled toward a field of coconut palms that adjoined the construction acreage.

It was an old copra plantation. The trees were eighty

feet tall, neatly spaced, each capped with an umbrella of feathery green. On the ground, split coconuts had been laid out on racks to dry. There was a fire pit, too, for extracting oil, but it didn't look like it had been used for a while. He waded ashore, hid the board among the trees, and carried his bag toward the concrete shell that might or might not one day be a condominium.

The eighth floor was an unfinished clone of Winslow Shepherd's building at the resort. There were two suites. Both faced the sea. No doors or windows or balcony railings, just bare concrete walls and a concrete stairway with rebar protruding like bone.

From the foyer, Ford looked down—a seventy-foot drop to a floor littered with junk. The stairway was an ascending series of switchbacks. Banisters had been installed on the lower three, metal balusters on the fourth, but that's all.

He wondered, *How the hell can a man on crutches, or in a wheelchair, make it up those stairs?*

In the elevator well was the answer. Far below was a steel platform attached to cables and, presumably, a power source. It made sense. Workmen had to move materials somehow, the heavy stuff—what was left of it anyway. On the bottom floor he'd seen only a stack of drywall and a stack of something else under a tarp, but he hadn't bothered to look.

He would.

First, though, he went out onto the balcony of the suite closest to the copra plantation. Below, dump trucks had piled a mountain of sand that would be used to create the beach. The retired math professor would not choose sand as a landing spot for a man he wanted to watch die.

No, the adjoining suite would be Shepherd's choice for tonight's event. Preparations hadn't started, but a Honda generator, floor lamps, an Igloo awaiting ice, and a stack of folding chairs told him this was the place.

Shepherd or Julian, or both, had invited guests.

No rail on the eighth-floor balcony here either. Ford went to the edge and looked down on the remains of a concrete seawall that bristled with barnacles. He stepped back, took a breath, then peered over once again. For a queasy instant, KAT's body was sprawled there; her face, from the photos, bloody, contorted, teeth displaced. He imagined weightlessness, falling, the shattering impact, and how it would feel to survive for a few minutes and try to crawl away.

That was enough. He was done with it. If he went off that balcony, it would not be because he went peacefully.

Outsmarting Julian required preparation. He did a careful search of the balcony's deck and walls. Holes for some of the fixtures and the railing had been drilled. They might be useful, depending on what was under the tarp on the bottom floor.

Each wall was buttressed by an outside beam connected at roof level. What he needed was a place to hide a weapon that couldn't be easily found. Was there space enough above the beams? To find out, he turned his back to the rocks below, slid his heels to the precipice, and wedged a shoulder against the wall. Then had to stand on tiptoes, reach around, and explore with his fingers.

Geezus. There had to be a better place.

There wasn't.

Finally, he looked for hidden cameras. There were none.

Good.

What Ford had known from the start was this: the personal secrets of his friends at Dinkin's Bay would not die with him. Only Julian Solo's death could guarantee that. The man was a malevolent narcissist, by the diagnosis of his own psychiatrist. Disease made him predictable. Julian did only what pleased him, or increased his power over others, and what Julian wanted, truly wanted, was to *see for himself* what happened on this balcony tonight.

Ford was counting on it. If he was wrong, he was better off jumping now.

It was two-fifteen p.m. Not much time left to prepare. He went down the stairs in a hurry to see if there was anything useful under the tarp. Too fast for someone with tactical training and who was aware that small mistakes get people killed. As he leaped to skip the last step, his ankle was snared by a trip wire. It sprawled him onto the concrete below, where he rolled and then looked up.

David Cashmere was there, a knife in his hand and already wearing his executioner's hood.

19

TOMLINSON WATCHED THE SEAPLANE TAKE OFF and bank west, its fuselage blue and white in the wash of a rising sun. It wasn't quite seven-thirty; nothing left to do here, all alone thirty miles from land, yet he lingered.

Julian Solo was out here, too, he believed. Maybe not close but somewhere. His powers of distant viewing were a tad rusty, and never a hundred percent accurate, but pretty damn good when he kicked his sentient radar into overdrive.

"Stop moving around," he told the dog. "I'm trying to get into the zone."

Another Bock breakfast beer seemed to help. He carried it to the bow and let his nose become a dowsing rod like old-time spiritualists had used to find water. A quarter turn to the north . . . a turn to the west, then a correctional turn to the southwest, put him on a sensory beam that felt about right. But there were no ships out there on the horizon when he opened his eyes.

"That doesn't mean diddly-squat," he told the dog. "Line of sight from sea level is only a couple of miles. Less then twelve, even for one of those big oceangoing mothers that like to run down sailboats when they get the chance."

He went to the electronics suite and switched on the radar. The little seaplane was a blip, flying crazy low, and already twenty miles away. To the northeast, a couple of fast-moving vessels were off Boca Grande, and several more to the east. But nothing to the southwest—not within twenty-four miles, the radar's max range.

Hmm . . .

"I've been wrong before," he said, "but I'm not wrong this time. It's a sort of fizzy feeling I get where the brain stem connects to my medulla. Trust me, Julian will be here, but later. Around sunset, give or take. Or tomorrow night. He's an international criminal. They're like cockroaches. They hate the light."

A little after nine, Tomlinson dropped an orange marker buoy. Fifteen minutes later, he hauled anchor and cruised around for a while looking for the killer whale, then pointed the boat toward Sanibel. When cell reception was good enough, he called Ava and left a message. He tried again after he'd cleared the causeway but had to be satisfied with her lukewarm text response:

Feeling better, will call in few days.

Woodring Point was only a couple of miles ahead, then the entrance into Dinkin's Bay.

Play it fast and cool, he reminded himself. *Don't use the channel; run the flats straight to the lab.*

He didn't want to have to answer the question, "Where's Doc?"

No need to worry about questions. Half the Dinkin's Bay population was clustered around a truck labeled TAMPA BAY FREIGHT, when he arrived, and a box the size of a refrigerator. By the time he got the boat moored, and the dog fed, and fish in a dozen aquariums, too, the box had been opened, but Mack, Figgy, Rhonda, and several others were still outside the marina office, ogling what the box had contained.

"An outdoor sound system," Mack grinned. "I guess I don't have to put up with any more bitching from you music expert types—not that the speakers we have aren't perfectly fine."

Tomlinson, a music aficionado, said, "I feel like kissing you right on the lips. How much did this set you back?"

That got a laugh from everyone except Figgy, who didn't understand a word but knew fine-looking outdoor speakers when he saw them. There were six, plus an amplifier that came to his chest and a bunch of other shiny-looking gear.

Rhonda trotted up and gave Tomlinson a hug. "Thanks, sweetie. That's from all of us. You are the kindest, most generous man I've ever met . . ." She glanced at Mack. "Well, one of the two most generous men."

Tomlinson had no idea what she was talking about but offered a goofy shrug, saying, "I'm just happy to be in the top ten. What do we have here?"

He moved to examine the commercial-sized outdoor speakers, a megawatt amplifier, and a complicated-looking input bank, all labeled *PRX600 Professional* in chrome.

"I used to work as a roadie for the band America, and a very sweet gig it was. They had a system similar to this. I forget the manufacturer. Erin and the guys probably chose the very best from several, but you know how merchandising works. *PRX* could be the generic label for all sorts of brands."

"Thank god," Rhonda said. "We have no idea how to hook it up. Can you do it or should we call a professional?"

"You're talking to a professional," Tomlinson assured her. "Once you get a feel for how electrons flow; sound and proper amplification, it's sort of like riding a bicycle. I'll have her done by tomorrow afternoon, no prob."

Mack drifted off for a moment as if he had a better idea. "Tell you what, with Jeth or Fast Eddie helping, I might set it and give it a practice run before tonight's party."

That was okay with Tomlinson. He took one of the boxes and read the small print on the back. " 'Mingxuan Audio, Made in China.' Never heard of it, but I can tell just from the components it's professional-grade. Seriously, Mack, this had to cost you ten or twelve grand."

More laughter.

Tomlinson looked up. "Am I missing something here?"

"You can drop the act," Rhonda said. "We know."

"Of course you do. Uhh . . . know what?"

"Come on," Mack said. "Who else would leave old sun-bleached hundred-dollar bills as Christmas gifts? From the moment Marta's little girl came running up to show me, I knew you were the mystery Santa. We all figured it out, so you can stop pretending. But this"—he patted one of the speakers—"was totally unexpected."

Tomlinson stood, not concerned but interested. "It wasn't me."

"Sur-r-r-re it wasn't."

"I love the whole Kris Kringle thing, but, seriously. I didn't order this, and I haven't been giving away hundred-dollar bills. Who was the box addressed to?"

Mack stared at him a moment, then checked the invoice in his hand. "General delivery, Dinkin's Bay Marina, all shipping charges paid. And there was a card around here someplace."

Rhonda had it. "All it says is 'Silent Nights Suck' and it's signed 'Mystery Santa.' Not an actual signature; it's typed. The 'Silent Night' part, too. Here, look for yourself." She handed Tomlinson the card; a corny one, with Santa dancing around a sombrero while Rudolph played the steel drums.

"A sombrero—weird," he said. "And the rest is just tacky and plain damn rude."

Mack responded, "That's another reason we thought it was you," then grew thoughtful, looking at all the expensive electronics. "You think at least ten thousand?"

"More like eight to twelve, that's ballpark for a low-end pro system, but this stuff looks like the real McCoy. Could be twenty grand." Tomlinson moved to the amplifier. "Did it come with directions or a schematic or something? I can figure it out, but I want to do it right the first time—if you don't have it up and running by the time I get back."

Mack was still puzzled. "Who in the hell would give the marina twenty grand's worth of sound equipment? It had to be someone with money to burn." He glanced toward the docks, where the Brazilian's slip was vacant, but dismissed the idea. "On this island, it could be anyone, I suppose. Be nice even to the assholes, that's what I always say, because you never know who they might mention in their will." After a beat, he asked again, "Are you sure it wasn't you?"

"As sure as God makes little green apples." Tomlinson got up, steadied himself, and got his bearings. "Store this stuff someplace and I'll get to work on it tomorrow. Or maybe tonight, we'll see. Doc had me up at dark-damn-thirty this morning and I need a nap." Then he answered what someone was bound to ask by saying, "We hooked up with some sort of research vessel this morning and I've got to pick him up around sunset."

A partial truth was the best he could do.

By noon, Tomlinson was asleep in the hammock outside the biologist's lab but woke up, sweating, at two in the hellish heat of a nightmare. Discordant elements spun on a collision course in his head. Hooded jihadists, sharks the size of Megalodons, a boiling ball of fire, and Ava's slack, unconscious face.

Paranormal powers told him Ava was in trouble again, so he called.

His paranormal powers were wrong. She answered; didn't sound like the confident professional she was before but was doing fairly well. Next, he tried JoAnn and Rhonda aboard *Tiger Lilly*. Perhaps that sicko, Julian, had leaked more personal files.

No . . . everything was hunky-dory there, too. JoAnn, who was in charge of tonight's music list, had just heard about the new sound system. She was excited about trying an unusual mix of Gregorian chants, operatic sopranos, and Buffett's lesser-known classics. Normally, Tomlinson would have dived headfirst into this debate, but not now.

Dreams did not create themselves. Something was wrong somewhere. As he knew, but seldom took the trouble to explain, his sensory abilities weren't a "power" that had an off-on switch, nor could they be aimed like a rifle. They were a conduit to waves of energy accessed by opening the receptors. Claircognizance, some called it, which he thought of as "breathing awareness."

All the other hokey terms—*astral projection*, *ESP*, *clairvoyance*, *psychometry*—could be defined the same way.

On the other hand . . . psychometry *was* different, in that it required a physical conduit. Human beings emitted an energy signature, each unique. This energy seeped into objects they touched, or wore or used, particularly if the item was a valued possession.

Near the hammock, on the wall outside the laboratory, Ford's favorite fishing rods were stored vertically in a rack. Tomlinson selected a 9-weight Sage fly rod with a golden Seamaster reel. The rod was made of graphite, a good conductor. He carried it outside to the deck and went through the dowsing process. Facing west, his breathing slowed. He opened his mind to distant images and allowed them to flow uncensored.

Palm trees . . . a concrete vault . . . No . . . an abandoned gray building . . . Water of turquoise flowed over black water . . . Steel drums, donkeys . . . Santa Claus dancing in a sombrero.

Shit-oh-dear.

Tomlinson opened his eyes. That damn Christmas card had thrown him off the scent. On the bright side, he'd gotten a whiff of the biologist's vibe and had sensed no danger awaiting.

Was that possible?

No freakin' way, José.

He tried again.

This time, the gray building was displaced by a vibe of strongest loathing. Images assumed the likeness of his nightmare: a shark the size of Megalodon, a swirling cauldron of fire, a Jihadist's scream . . . Then Julian Solo, his pearlescent face, overpowered all else.

Several minutes later, Tomlinson opened his eyes.

He was certain now of what he must do.

Two hours before sunset, he was thirty miles offshore in Ford's monster boat, anchored over the Captiva Blue Hole, where he expected a true monster to appear.

If not tonight, by morning.

20

WHEN FORD CAME RUNNING DOWN THE STEPS, hit the trip wire, and fell, his bad shoulder absorbed most of the impact. The pain was bearable, but he needed time to recover, so he said to the man in the executioner's hood, "Winslow won't like it if you kill me now. You'll piss Julian off, too. Is that what you want? And think about their guests—there are at least six chairs stacked up there."

He got to his feet as David Cashmere approached but eyed the floor. Possible weapons included a chunk of two-by-four and a coil of wire.

Christ. On the eighth floor, his bag was filled with all

sorts of options. He'd left the 9mm Sig Sauer pistol up there, too. It was on the ledge where nobody in their right mind would risk searching.

"It's . . . *you*," Cashmere said. His surprise was genuine. "I didn't think you'd have the balls to show."

Ford edged closer to the wire, saying, "Mexico's nice. Why wouldn't I?"

"To save your ass. Man . . . I can't believe this—the last person I expected to find snooping around. But like I told the others, you'd be dead by tomorrow anyway."

What the hell did that mean?

The failed actor ripped off the hood, then some gauze bandages and tape, yelling, "Look what you did to my face, you filthy pig. *Look at me!* This is nothing compared to what I'll do to you." He spun the ruby-handled knife— a martial arts showman—and glared.

The wooden stake had torn away flesh and muscle below Cashmere's left eye. A third blow had plowed a hairless furrow down the side of his head. Sutures bristled from the wounds. His skin was stained red by Betadine, and muscle damage caused him to speak from the side of his mouth. An old-time TV gangster—that was the effect.

Ford went into hostage mode by using names to make it personal. "David, calm down. Why don't you call Julian right now and get him over here. Or Shepherd? I stopped by to see what I'm getting into. You would've done the same. I'm meeting them here tonight. You do *know* about the meeting."

Cashmere came toward him, his chin leading the way. "Shut up, bitch, and do what I tell you. You haven't taken a really good look yet. See this? *See my face?*"

Ford peered for a moment. "It could have been worse. A lot worse . . . really," he said and slid closer to the coil of wire. "I did a sloppy job, I admit it. On the other hand, if I didn't have a reason to apologize, you'd be dead. Would you rather I'd killed you, David? So drop it. Where's Julian?"

"Enough about goddamn Julian, think about the mess you made of my face." He tilted his chin to pose, so furious his voice shook. Then spun the knife so its scimitar blade was poised overhead. "What I want you to do is get on your belly—get on your goddamn belly!—so I can wire your hands. How do you think women look at me now? Like I'm a freak, a goddamn Frankenstein. I was handsome, you sick asshole. Handsome—all the ladies said so—but not after what you did."

Ford held his hands palms out and backed away. "Take it easy. David . . . listen to me. I'm not going to get on my belly. Winslow Shepherd wants me here at five-thirty and that's what I'm going to do. What are you going to tell him if—" A crazy glow in Cashmere's eyes demanded a different approach. "But the important thing is, women don't care about a few scars. What you're worried about is how you'll look on camera. Isn't that right? Think about it. In feature films, how many pretty-boy stars make it big? But character actors, men who've earned some scars—"

"Shut your mouth," Cashmere said, but was interested enough to lower the knife a little. "I'm not falling for your bullshit again. That parachute, or whatever they called it, drug me out into the goddamn ocean. There were sharks; I nearly drowned. All because you lied, told me not to unbuckle that damn harness." He paused and touched a finger to his face and scoffed. "The movie business—as if you know a goddamn thing."

Ford thought, *He's imagining himself on the screen.* "I'm not going to apologize for letting the rope go. I botched the job, yeah, but I'm not going to apologize for anything else. It's business, part of what we do. No one knows that better than you."

A lot depended on how Máximo handled that.

"I never let anyone drown," Cashmere countered, which told Ford he might have some breathing room— but then the man's phone beeped with a text message, which he read, then looked up with a *You lying bastard* expression.

Ford thought, *Uh-oh.*

"Where's your cell phone?" Cashmere demanded. He didn't wait for a response. "Empty your pockets. Remember when you told me to empty my pockets?"

"I didn't bring a phone," Ford said but did as told; turned around and did his back pockets, too. "What's the problem?"

"The problem is your phone landed at Cancún International an hour ago. Old Man Shepherd's convinced you're in a rental car driving down from Playa del Carmen, almost to Tulum by now. How do you explain that?"

The Delta flight out of Tampa was late, that was the explanation, but Ford said, "I was about to tell you. This morning at Miami International, someone stole my phone. Why else would I be here without one?"

Cashmere stood there while his mind put things together. His eyes found the concrete stairway, followed it to the eighth floor. "You were rigging some kind of trap when I came in, weren't you? Up there, banging on something. I figured it was some poor-ass Mexican thief robbing the place."

"Surprised?" Ford said. "Yeah, I could hear it in your voice. How do you think I felt when I looked up and saw you? There's no trap. Just a stack of chairs and stuff for the meeting; they haven't even been set up yet. Go ahead"—he motioned to the stairs—"see for yourself."

"You expect me to believe someone stole your phone?"

"Have you ever been to Miami? Look, I understand why you're pissed off, but I meant what I said. I'm not in the movie business, but where I live, a lot of Hollywood types hang out. The pretty-boy actors never make it—"

Cashmere, with an odd smile, interrupted. "I know exactly where you live, dumbass." Said it in a way that hinted at something else. "Know what I think? You're full of shit."

Ford said, "Okay, but you're missing an opportunity here. Not that a producer could hire you to work in the States, but there are film companies based in Florida that shoot all over the world. See it from their perspective. You're a real-life bad guy who actually looks like"—Ford sensed this was a sensitive area—"who looks tough enough, has a few scars to prove he's been around. What I did to you was strictly business. Does that mean we can't have a conversation?"

The man's almond eyes dulled momentarily. He turned inward and tried to picture it happening, but his eyes soon sparked and he returned madder than before.

"Full of shit, just like I said. What I think is Old Man Shepherd won't care about tonight if I save him from whatever it is you rigged up there. Especially when he sees how you look after you go off that balcony this afternoon." Using the knife as a prod, he walked closer, saying, "Move or I'll start cutting off pieces."

Something in his tone promised he would start hacking at the first opportunity, so Ford spun and sprinted up the stairs two steps at a time. Cashmere followed, mad enough to forget the trip wire he'd set. Ford hoped it would happen but wasn't sure until he heard a thud, then the clatter of metal hitting concrete.

When he turned, the man was weaponless on the floor below, staring at bone splinters protruding from his right hand. "Oh shit . . . I'm . . . I'm hurt bad," he sputtered, going into shock just like before when the parasail crashed. "Get me to a doctor, man." He held up his shattered hand. "See what you did?"

"You need a surgeon," Ford said, "and fast. From here, it looks like your elbow's broken, too. You could end up a cripple."

"That's what I'm saying, asshole! Come on, help me up. Shit . . . or bleed to death." The man rocked back and forth on his knees, hand elevated, blood streaming down his arm, until he realized the biologist hadn't moved. "Please. I'll make it worth your while."

"I don't see how."

"My elbow," Cashmere moaned, "my whole arm's crooked . . . Shit!" He looked up. "Tonight, you'll see. I'll . . . help you tonight. Really. Or money—you want money? How about twenty thousand cash up front? Another fifty thousand when you get me to a doctor. Come on, man. I didn't mean that stuff about doing the balcony thing now."

"I didn't think you did," Ford lied. "In the boat, I've got a first-aid kit. Then, sure, a doctor—as long as you tell me what you know about tonight."

"A boat?"

"Did you see a car out there, dumbass?"

"Okay, okay, just take me to a hospital. I've got a rental, but get this bleeding stopped first."

Ford got the man on his feet and helped keep the hand elevated, saying, "Calm down, you'll be okay. It's not as bad as it looks."

"I feel like I'm going to vomit."

"A compound fracture. The important thing is, get it cleaned and iced, then some antibiotic spray. Everything we need's in the first-aid kit."

"There's a clinic not far from here. In Tulum. You're not just saying that to make me feel better?"

Ford replied, "I've seen a lot worse," and led the former Chicagoan outside into the copra grove, the two of them soon talking with a false familiarity created by stress. Frightened men in pain are often chatty.

Cashmere had no loyalty to Winslow Shepherd or Julian. He didn't mind revealing what he knew, but shared it between bouts of obsessing about his shattered hand. Julian wasn't in Mexico, he said. This was a setback that might require a change of plans.

Okay. Ford would play it out but had one last question for the Jihadist assassin. "What did you mean when you said I'd be dead by tomorrow?"

"Nothing, man. It was just talk. You know, like to scare you. Whoa"—he stumbled; Ford caught his good arm before he went down—"I feel like I'm gonna faint. How far's your boat?"

The man was evading.

Ford said, "Tell me," and applied pressure to the annular ligament of Cashmere's elbow.

"Hey . . . that *hurts*. Dude, you trying to break this arm, too?"

The actor was acting. The instant his elbow was free, he tried to run, but Ford tripped him and took him to the ground. A footrace could not be risked, so he killed David Abdel Cashmere there, a shady spot, snapped his neck. The only sound was a grunt, then a rattling wheeze, and he hid the body under a bunch of palm fronds.

Ford returned to the condo. Twenty minutes later, he came back with his Vertx gear bag, a tarp, and some other things from the pile he'd found under the tarp inside the building.

Cashmere's phone, room key, wallet, the ruby-handled knife, and executioner's hood went into a waterproof bag, along with the keys to a rental car hidden somewhere. His body went onto the paddleboard, then into the miniature Blue Hole.

In ten feet of water, Ford looped wire to a limestone boulder, gave it a push, and let the boulder's weight drag the Chicagoan deeper. And that's where he would stay, suspended among feeding moon jellies, in the shadow of drifting men-of-war, until they had consumed him or set him free.

But the unexplained threat stuck with Ford as he paddled back to shore.

You would be dead by tomorrow anyway.

Steal a dead man's cell phone, you own his identity for
as long as people believe he is alive. Steal his car, you own
the contents.

Ford was eager to see what Cashmere's rental contained.

It was a Toyota SUV, hidden beside the bulldozer's
bulk. Behind the backseat were three large suitcases and
a steel lockbox. On the passenger's seat was a computer
bag. The floor was a bachelor's heap of clothes, empty
beer bottles, crumpled Marlboro packs, and one *Hollywood Insider*.

Ford thought, *A Jihadist on Christmas vacation.*

He took the Cancún road north toward Tulum and
turned onto a shady tractor lane hidden from the road.
He parked and took inventory.

The computer bag contained an IBM laptop. He
didn't open it—Julian was out there somewhere monitoring everything. More importantly, this computer had
been owned by a high-ranking terrorist operative. It
might contain self-destruct software if a password wasn't
immediately entered. Deliver it to the U.S. Consulate at
Mérida, however, or to Special Operations Command in
Tampa, and experts might harvest information that
would save lives.

The Maximum Assassin's laptop could turn out to be
an intelligence coup.

The suitcases were hard-shell Samsonites, but no problem. Ford removed one, used his knife to jimmy the hinges without breaking the locks, then stepped back.

Cashmere hadn't lied about having money. Inside were twenty vacuum-sealed plastic bags. A bag on the top was open. It contained blocks of U.S. hundred-dollar bills. They were neatly wrapped in stacks of $15,000; eight blocks in this bag alone, and it looked like two blocks were missing.

Ford did the math: just under three million in cash . . . if it wasn't counterfeit.

The bags were rubberized plastic. He pierced one with the knife. The sound was similar to opening vacuum-sealed coffee. Inside were ten blocks of U.S. hundreds that looked and felt like the real deal.

He inspected the outside of the bag. No markings that he could see, but his fingers found an embossed area on one of the corners. The sun was tilting westward but provided sufficient light to make out a tiny Chinese seal—a chop, it was called. *Chop*, as in bang a hammer or hit one's hand on an embossing stamp. The word had been used for thousands of years by the Chinese and had sprouted many meanings.

The tiny symbol told Ford the money was probably counterfeit, and there was no better counterfeiter in the world than the Chinese government.

He opened the other two Samsonites. They were packed with the same sealed bags. So make it nine million in cash.

Ingenious. A double-edged weapon: fund terrorism to fight the Western world while also damaging the U.S.

economy. The cost? Only the price of paper, ink, and production.

Ford kept an unopened bag of cash, closed the suitcases, and was turning his attention to the lockbox, when Cashmere's phone buzzed.

A text message appeared: Lost Clarence's phone 20km south Cancún. Find him.

Clarence—Ford's nickname. He had already skimmed through enough messages on the phone to know the text was from Julian. Julian and his father had been using Cashmere as a go-between to share updates. It had been a busy day for all three. Now Julian was worried because Ford's cell phone had been deactivated somewhere midway between Cancún and the resort, an area near the little village of Tulum.

A reply was required. Ford hadn't had time to read all of the texts, so he did a quick review. Cashmere's writing style was more formal than the way he spoke and all of his texts ended with the abbreviation *SWT* or the word *Inshallah*.

Ford had no idea what SWT stood for, but he added it anyway after typing Shall I detain? Or get rid of C?

Julian's reply: Use your fucking brain.

That put an end to any hope of a dialogue that might reveal Julian's whereabouts.

He pocketed the phone and returned his attention to the lockbox, which was bulky, made of galvanized steel. He couldn't pry the thing open if he'd wanted, but no need. The key to the box was in Cashmere's billfold.

This was not something to unlock in a rush. There might be a trip wire or an alarm. Finally, he opened the lid to find a terrorist's workshop inside. Five components are required for improvising bombs—an explosive charge, a power source, a trigger, a detonator, and something to hold it all together, such as electrical tape. Everything needed was here in multiple variations. Enough to blow up a dozen day care centers—Cashmere's favorite target— or a sizable airport.

Ford checked his watch—less than three hours until sunset. He went through the contents faster than he should have, but *carefully*.

Emulex was the explosive of choice. He thought it was dynamite, at first, because it was packed in red cardboard tubes—two dozen sticks of a composition far more powerful than TNT. There was a tool kit containing detonators, switches, and power sources of all types—from D cord and blasting caps to throwaway cell phones; a couple garage openers, too.

Among the detonators was a tiny microphone on what resembled a blasting cap. Ford lifted it with two delicate fingers and saw that it was labeled *High Decibel Activator*. He wasn't an explosives expert, but he'd been through enough schools to know this was something new.

Sound was a weapon. Prehistoric whales had exploded their prey with high- or low-decibel bombs. Sound could now explode modern prey as well.

The decibel activator caused him to picture the drones lying in the gloom of the Captiva Blue Hole. He fingered the bruise on his shoulder and thought about Julian Solo. Cashmere had claimed Solo wasn't in Mexico. Nothing on his phone suggested otherwise.

So . . . maybe Tomlinson was right. Maybe Julian was

on a luxury yacht somewhere off Sanibel, poised to re-cover his expensive toys. If true, it was time to seriously consider other options.

He started the SUV, locked the doors, and went over it in his head. Julian couldn't be trusted, and his location remained an unknown. Ford couldn't kill a man he couldn't find, so why risk a fall from an eighth-story balcony?

It was different with Winslow Shepherd. Tomlinson had provided Shepherd's address: a ritzy cosmetic sur-gery/rehab clinic near Tulum, midway between the re-sort and Playa del Carmen. It wasn't the right address, but close enough. The actual location had been provided by the chatty Jihadist just before he died. He'd described a beach house, not far from the clinic's gate, with an open view to the sea and a porch on three sides.

This was an important detail. To a camera, an elevated porch might resemble a balcony.

There were other variables to consider. Shepherd would have at least one bodyguard, probably more. His men would recognize Cashmere's SUV, of course, and seize the contents if they found it. Ford couldn't risk putting coun-terfeit money into circulation or the little bomb factory back in operation, so that had to be dealt with in advance.

Another review of Cashmere's phone was required. He found bits of useful information and also a puzzling text message. It was an automated update from a company named Port of Tampa Freight Hauling.

It read Shipment labeled PRX600 Professional has arrived. Awaiting final delivery. Send address via tele-phone or email, which must include an electronic sig-nature. Thanks for your business!

The message had been received two days ago.

The text seemed unrelated to what Ford was dealing with yet posed obvious questions. Why would David Cashmere, an international criminal, ship a package to Tampa, Florida? A package large enough to require a freight company to handle it—a PRX600, whatever the hell that was. The combination of elements set off alarm bells. Terrorist cells had been operating in Florida since before 9/11—two of the hijackers had learned to fly at a field south of Sarasota.

Explosives?

Could be. But, more likely, a Jet Ski with a name like PRX600 Professional.

Ford filed the puzzle away for later. There wasn't much time and he had a lot to do.

He spun the SUV around and returned to the concrete building—the stack of folding chairs he'd seen bothered him. Twenty minutes later, he was driving north toward Tulum on Mexico 307, a narrow macadam two-lane. Not much traffic. A few rental cars or a taxi bound for the resort and the occasional donkey cart loaded with bananas or piled high with yucca.

On an open stretch, he used Cashmere's phone to dial 001, then his own cell number. No service. He tried again a few miles south of Tulum on a gravel road that ran along the sea. Same thing.

Ahead was a sheltered spot to pull off. He parked among a strand of coco palms and spent several more uneasy minutes with his head buried in the terrorist's workshop before he pulled away.

A mile later, the road improved. The scenery became

a tropical postcard of palms and Caribbean blue. When a billboard announced that the clinic—*Clínica Cirugía Estética*—was only a kilometer away, he turned right onto a sandy lane toward the sea. Down a hill and across a creek was the clinic's VIP beach house, where Winslow Shepherd was recuperating.

The chatty Jihadist had given accurate directions.

He turned cross-country and stopped where sea grapes provided cover and an elevated view of the house. It was built on stilts of rainforest timber; a Mayan-style château painted key lime green. A handicapped van was parked outside. No other vehicles, which was a surprise. Steps and a ramp led up to glistening doors and a walk-around porch. The porch overlooked dunes and a beach, where glassy rollers broke.

Ford sat for a while, watching for activity inside the house. None. The same was true of a row of beach cabanas several hundred yards north. Weird. Where was the audience who would use the folding chairs stacked on the concrete balcony? On the other hand, maybe the cabanas were inhabited by patients who, after cosmetic surgery, had to avoid the sun.

His focus softened. His eyes moved to the sea, an expanse of gelatinous turquoise. Strange . . . he'd made that crossing only a few hours ago yet Florida felt so far away. At Dinkin's Bay, the sun would set soon—there was an hour time difference—and Jeth or Figgy, or someone, would be burying bottles of beer in ice while Mack amped up the party music loud. Too loud for the marina's corroded old sound system.

Sound—that word again.

David Cashmere's threat nudged at the memory circuits: *You would be dead by tomorrow anyway.*

Ford was not an emotional man. He didn't believe in intuition or other psychic fiction, yet the sudden feeling of dread he experienced was real. It jarred him.

He sat back, thinking, *Did I miss something?*

It was possible. Julian Solo was a billionaire psycho who also happened to be a genius—just ask the man. Cashmere was no genius, but he enjoyed killing, and he'd recently shipped a large package to Tampa.

Was there a connection?

Sound . . . the word spun around in his memory and finally attached itself to a tiny microphone detonator.

Shit. Ford slapped the steering. The U.S. Special Operations Command was in Tampa, at MacDill, not far from the port. The freight company had received Cashmere's package, but the actual delivery address had been sent by email yesterday. Or today.

He grabbed the cell phone from the passenger seat and dialed 0, hoping to get a local operator. Instead, he got a recording, in Spanish, that suggested he try later. He dialed 001 and the number of a man he trusted. A computer prompted him to enter David Cashmere's overseas code.

No clue.

Just for the hell of it, he tried Tomlinson—a Zen master psychic who might not require the help of satellites and passwords.

The Zen psychic failed to answer a phone that did not ring.

"Technology, my ass," Ford muttered and dialed the

operator several more times while his sense of dread gradually faded and gave way to reality. The reality was this: no one could sneak an explosive into the Special Ops center at MacDill. Security was too damn tight. Particularly if it was a box large enough to require a freight truck to deliver it.

Focus, he told himself. After several slow breaths, he checked his watch, which was on Florida time. Less than an hour before sunset on Sanibel; only four-fifteen p.m. here.

He opened his gear stash, selected what he might need, including the 9mm Sig Sauer pistol, then took a last look before locking the SUV. The vehicle was still a mess, but two of the Samsonite suitcases were gone, as was Cashmere's laptop.

It was a safety precaution. On an assignment, nothing ever went as planned.

The pistol went into a Galco holster inside the back of his pants. His Vertx gear bag—lighter than before—went over his shoulder. Ford hiked through the sand dunes and down the hill to the VIP beach house as if he were expected.

Attitude counted. If the math professor wouldn't cut a deal, or if bodyguards tried to interfere, he would pull the Sig and insist they all return to the concrete balcony.

If they refused or agreed, either way, Julian—wherever he was—would pay a price for destroying the reputations of Ford's friends at Dinkin's Bay.

21

AN HOUR BEFORE SUNSET, TOMLINSON AND THE dog were still anchored over the Captiva Blue Hole when a vessel appeared on radar, twelve miles southwest. He zoomed in—it was big, an oil tanker, or one of those damn oceangoing cruise ships that liked to run down innocent sailboats.

It had happened to him before.

Nothing to worry about, though, because he was aboard Ford's high-tech monster boat, not his floating home, *No Más*. And the vessel, whatever it was, was moving slowly. Yeah . . . a tanker, probably, one of those oil-shitting stinkpots hauling black gold from one billionaire to another.

Billionaire. Julian Solo came into his head. The albino bastard was out there somewhere. An hour of deep meditation and a couple of Steinlagers had convinced him it was true. If it was Julian's super-yacht, he wouldn't make an appearance at that pace until well after dark.

The dog, Pete, who was asleep in the shade of the bow cover, thumped his tail a couple of times when Tomlinson shielded his eyes and looked into the sun. Nothing out there but terns divebombing a school of bait, the horizon a slow procession of waves, Mexico somewhere beyond. As he searched, static on the VHF broke through and he heard Mack hailing, "*No Más . . . No Más . . .* do you copy?" The reception was so degraded by thirty miles of water, he had to guess at the last few words.

Tomlinson took the mic and sat at the console. "Got you, but transmission is broken. Do you read?"

Mack came back, saying, "I'm trying to hook up the new . . . Where the hell are . . ." and the rest was garbled.

They went back and forth like that until Tomlinson figured out Mack was trying to enlist his help connecting the fancy new sound system. There was some question about whether to solder the speakers; another about where the hell was Doc and his boat?

Frustrating. "I'll try your landline," Tomlinson said finally and signed off.

His phone was on the console next to the ammo box and a remote detonator, which Ford had left behind. He folded the schematic he'd been reading and closed the box. There was no cell reception out here, but he opened

his phone anyway and was surprised to see a missed call
from a number he didn't recognize. There was a message
and the message packed a punch. It was Marion Ford,
saying, "Technology, my ass."

The familiar voice caused Pete to look up with his ears
perked, ready for action.

Understandable. Those three words contained a heavy
hit of emotion; dread, anxiety, the whole ugly mix. He
listened to it twice—definitely Ford, yet zero balls on the
phone display. *Weird.* He hit *Redial* several times without
result. It gave him something to do while his eyes wandered to the electronics suite, then did a double take.

Christ! Now there were two vessels to the southwest.
The tanker, or mega-yacht, had halved the distance, and
a much smaller boat was only two miles away and closing,
not fast but steadily.

Tomlinson jumped to his feet and squinted into the sun.
For a moment, he saw it; got a glimpse of the distant boat's
flybridge and a bristling array of antennas. Then it was gone,
lost behind distant waves. The vessel did not reappear.

He blinked and looked again. Seabirds . . . Waxen
waves; a few white breakers. Wind was freshening. In the
sun's copper glare a hundred yards away, a plume of spray
rained upward, then another geyser misted the sky. It was
a school of porpoise. No—off the stern, a huge gray fin
pierced the surface and cast a gliding shadow that
sounded beneath the monster boat's hull.

The killer whale's dorsal looked different in the afternoon light.

"Stay," he told the dog. "I'm not going in after you if
you turn stupid again."

The western horizon lifted and descended. The vessel he'd spotted had vanished. He checked the radar. It was true. Only the big tanker pinged the screen from eight miles away.

Impossible.

Fifteen minutes later, he was still puzzled when the sea began to boil, and a conning tower breached the surface.

"Your radio has been jammed," a booming voice warned. "Prepare to be boarded."

The conning tower levitated above a streaming waterfall. Beneath the falls, a fuselage the size of a private jet bubbled to the surface. The craft resembled a beluga whale with dwarf wings and a four-bladed tail. Camouflage colors of blue, gray, and green created a seamless skin until a hatch opened. A man with porcelain hair appeared and called over, "I'd like to show you around, Dr. Tomlinson."

Julian Solo. Tomlinson had been right the first time— the crazy bastard *did* have a submarine.

Julian's head was oversized, his shoulders narrow. He smelled of electrical conduit and lavender. Tomlinson couldn't look into the man's eyes, which were a dark, vitreous blue, without seeing Ava's bloody wrists. Years of dealing with pissed-off cops, however, had schooled him in the art of pretending to be amiable and attentive.

"How much did this thing set you back?" he asked— another inane question to mask what he was really thinking, which was *I've got to kill this man. But can I do it?*

Hydraulic steps had led them to the flybridge, where the only crewman—Watts was his name—left them while his boss gloated over the spaceship control panel. There was a pressure-compensated radar dome, anti-roll stabilizers, and a Bluetooth-linked redundancy system that, from a distant laptop, could turn this 40-foot vessel into an unmanned drone.

"I stay too busy moving to keep track of expenses," the billionaire replied with a slight Aussie accent. "In Dubai—have you ever been to the Jebel Ali Free Zone there? Man, it is truly awesome. Anyway, Exomos—that's the company's name—they have a showroom there. By appointment only, of course—some of the world's top security people check you out first. Exomos builds luxury submersibles; totally top secret, so people like me don't have to sweat publicity. You ever hear of them?"

Tomlinson looked down at Ford's boat, anchored alongside where the dog, Pete, stared up with blazing yellow eyes. "Wow, you could have one heck of a party on this thing. I had no idea, man."

"About Exomos? In Dubai, you can choose from a dozen models. Actually tour through them—picture small subs on the showroom floor instead of RVs or Lear jets." Solo, dressed like an Apple nerd in a black crewneck, chuckled at that. "Base price for this one—she could sleep ten, but I only wanted two staterooms—the price starts at around twelve mil, U.S. There's a company out of Portland, too. U.S. Submarines. They built my big submersible. This one I like because I can carry it around port to port and drop off anytime I want. More of a recreational thing, really."

Tomlinson looked to the southwest. From the tower, he could see a distant silhouette that was familiar. "You use an oil tanker as a mother ship?"

Solo stared at him. "Don't ask stupid questions. I was telling you about my primary submersible—a Phoenix 1000 is the standard model. She's sixty-five meters, and has an indoor gym and a pool, but"—now he was hoping for a reaction—"everything I own is built for me. No one else. I am nobody's puppet. Get it? Man, I cut the strings."

Geezus. Tomlinson felt momentarily dizzy because he recognized the line he'd written long ago. "Are you saying, uhh . . . or maybe—"

"When I was in school," Julian said, "this prick of a shrink had me institutionalized. Shock treatments, the whole nightmare protocol. Yeah, I could really relate to your book. A lot of the writing was fuzzy-wuzzy mystic crap—hey, we all have to make a buck, right?—but some of it helped pull me through. I admit it. I don't want to give you too much credit, though. I've never met anyone—movie stars, kings, politicians, you name it—they all disappointed me when I finally met them. So let's put it this way"—he smiled—"why do you think you're still alive?"

Solo waited for an answer while Tomlinson thought, *This kid's as crazy as Ming the Merciless.*

"I'll tell you why," the kid billionaire said, "but first we're going to recover those drones your asshole pal stole from me. I know they're here, but the telemetry signal is weak, like it's being blocked by something. So you're going to help me. *Right?*"

Tomlinson played along, saying, "Hey, man, what's yours is yours. They're on the bottom, inside a sort of limestone crevice. That could be the problem."

Watts reappeared in his naval whites, carrying an iPad. "Security is tracking two helicopters, probably Coast Guard. One out of Key West, the other out of Tampa. Do you want to sit out here in the open, Julie, or do you want to dive?" An informal formality was acceptable on this recreational sub.

"Were they scrambled? What's their heading?" Solo's wide, pale face pivoted to the sky.

"There was a distress call a few minutes ago. It's not routine. A vessel seventy miles off Marco Island is taking on water, so that's probably it. Here"—Watts showed him something on the iPad—"this is their projected course. The system will alert us if—"

"Yeah, play it safe. Let's get moving."

"Whoa," Tomlinson said, "I need to hop down and make sure my dog hasn't turned over his water bucket. Or bring him aboard—he's nuts when it comes to retrieving. I'm afraid he'll follow us. Seriously, even underwater, which he—"

"He belongs to your asshole pal," Julian cut in, "not you. Just because I didn't send your rap sheet along with the others doesn't mean I don't know every detail about your life." He turned to Watts and gestured toward Ford's boat. "We're going to sink that piece of junk, so take us down and float the scanners. Then I have a real treat for you, doctor—or can I call you Tomlinson? You understand why I don't use bullshit titles."

"Sink my . . . but *why*?"

"It's not your boat and that's not your dog," Julian replied in a nettling manner that probed for weakness. "Or how about Zen Shyster? I'll never get to know you well enough to call you Tom, let's be honest."

Tomlinson's amiable mask vanished. "Dude, if you read my book, you know all about karma. Hurt that dog, you'll burn for it. Hear me? Burn."

Julian liked that. "Good. You're not the pussy I thought you'd be. Come on . . ." He started toward the steps. "Below, in the salon, I've got a high-def big screen. Thanks to you—well, your book helped a little—I cut the strings. Now I'm finally going to kill the puppeteer. Get it? That lying old man you had so much fun doing drugs with in San Francisco, or wherever it was. I want you to be there when he dies."

Tomlinson said, "Kill your *father*. What's that have to do with Marion Ford? Unless he was somehow involved in . . ." He shifted to a safer approach. "Listen to me. Karma is the wrong way to destroy yourself, if that's what you're trying to do. It's not too late to turn this around."

Julian rolled his eyes while Tomlinson continued, "Take your drones and go home. I don't give a shit where you live. Dude, you don't have to stop the momentum. You understand? Just change the polarity. I can show you how. But killing your own father is just flat out balls-to-the-wall nuts."

"His name is Winslow Shepherd. *Okay*? Please stop with the lectures. This is business. You'll watch it all happen in real time. After I don't know how many millions in lawsuits, poor old Winslow will finally hand over documents that confirm he's been lying all these years and . . ."

Well, the details aren't important. You're worried about a dog? Just wait until you see what happens to your asshole pal—that's Winslow's final payoff before I get what *I* want."

Julian did it. From below the surface, from a football field away, he touched a button on a periscope and exploded Ford's boat with what Watts, the slinky first mate, referred to as a sonic grenade.

Tomlinson felt the percussion but refused to look at the screen until it was over. Inflated Kevlar tubes floated upside down among debris that did not include a swimming dog.

Julian had to ask himself, *Why is this famous Zen master fraud so damn eager, suddenly, to help recover the drones?*

He took Watts aside. "You searched him?"

"Always. I'm surprised you brought him aboard."

"And used the scanner?"

"Look at him," Watts said. "What's to search?"

Their guest was in the salon, where transparent acrylic panels transformed the walls into an open-sea aquarium. The man was barefoot, wearing baggy shorts, a purple tank top, and a red bandana to tie back his hair.

"He's a druggy," Julian said. "I grew up around freaks like him and they're good at hiding their stash. That's why you should have used the scanner. Instead of a stash, he might have something else."

Watts had been with Solo long enough to be afraid, yet still function as his confidant and aide. "Julie, relax. I found it. A little kef box, and a couple of joints in a little leather bag. That's all. Plus, the regular stuff: his phone and wallet—a couple hundred bucks—his driver's license, a few phone numbers on a bar napkin. He's a drunk, too. I can search him again, but I think we ought to get going."

"You're worried about those helos."

Watts tapped the iPad. "So far, they're still on course to the vessel in distress."

Solo looked for himself. "I want a satellite shot of that boat. It could be a decoy, so get the numbers or the registry and run them. Link every piece of data through the field servoid, and put *Evergreen* on alert."

Evergreen was a Panamax tanker built by the Chinese to transit the Canal. Now it was his office and, sometimes, mobile home.

After another look at the iPad, he added, "The FBI couldn't organize a piss-up in a brewery, but the NSA . . ." He let that hang while he thought about it. "Just in case, send a reminder to our friend in D.C. Tell him I own Winslow as of today. If something's going on, have him stop it or the truth about him and Winslow might just leak into cyberland. Tell him—no, hint; make it subtle— that I already have the old man's confession, all legal and notarized, to back it up."

Watts nodded toward their guest, who stood mesmerized by drifting amberjack and a veil of silver herring that parted as the sub descended. "He's not returning with us to—"

"No," Julian said. "The famous Zen mystic was killed when his boat's fuel tank exploded. But we'll save that for later. How much time do I have?"

"Our guy's meeting Winslow at five, Central Standard. They'll be on whatever balcony he chooses by five-thirty—six-thirty, Florida time—and we've already got the satellite linked to—"

"Then I have more than an hour," Julian said and went down three Plexiglas steps to the salon, where there was a lounge area that faced a bulkhead and a bank of widescreen displays that showed camera views forward and aft. Another screen provided a global view of the sub's location on a live feed satellite view of the Earth. Sprinkled across Europe, the Middle East, the Americas, and Asia were hundreds of tiny red LED lights.

"Know what those represent?" he asked Tomlinson.

The skinny man jolted as if he'd been dozing. "Lights . . . ? I don't know. Cities? Doesn't seem like there're enough . . . or . . ." He lost interest and sniffed. "Let's grab those drones, then talk about how the hell I'm getting home, before you give me the tour. Okay?"

"Each light represents a cybercenter I control. Businesses. Name anything you want. Coffeemakers, eBooks, a mail-order bride. A team of mercenaries—anything, man. Prostitutes; hell, a block of fine hashish. Order today, our transport networks will have it at your door tomorrow. I created the software scaffolding for all that shit, now I'm developing drone delivery systems. In other words, *I own it all.*" Julian looked up at the taller man, thinking he would be impressed.

He wasn't. "Dude, I've got a date tonight. The kind that's not inflatable, so do you mind?" Tomlinson wandered away and pressed his nose to the glass as if he preferred the company of fish on the other side.

That would soon happen.

Julian tried again. "I expected you of all people to understand. Take another look at that screen. There are no bullshit outlines of countries—countries don't exist anymore. They're just parking lots with flags. Those lights represent the real power centers. You want social change? You want peace? Fuck the White House, contact Microsoft, or Amazon—or me. *That's* what I've accomplished."

Tomlinson glanced back. "There's a quote from my book you might remember: 'We are only passengers in a brain that's steered by the equivalent of a chimp—unless we banish his ass to the sex closet and aspire to a higher good.' Dude, that's your chimp talking." He stopped and waited while the sub slowed with computer precision; a cloud of silver sand flooded toward them. "We're on the bottom," he said. "Are we using scuba gear?"

Julian grimaced. "You're even dumber than I expected. Come on, show me that ledge—and you'd better not be lying."

So far, the old fraud's reaction to what had happened was a disappointment. There had been no whimper of protest when the boat exploded, and no begging to search for the dead mutt's body.

Zen Shyster—that nickname, at least, irritated the hell out of this worn-out string bean hipster. Julian fed off the pain he inflicted, so he used the nickname again before saying, "You should try reading a few books instead of writing that pabulum you write. Why would I use scuba gear when I've got this?"

They had moved aft through two pressurized doors into a conical space made of clear acrylic, just enough room for two men and a control panel. Drones could be deployed from the compartment, or recovered through an unpressurized closet below the deck.

"If I feel like diving," Julian said, "I flood this area, the hatch slides back, and I'm gone. But I wouldn't bother with a spot that's so damn boring."

The murk had settled to reveal a sandy desert where only sea fans and one giant hermit crab clunked along in its shell hideaway. Beyond, a low limestone crest angled downward into a hole in the desert floor.

A thought popped into Tomlinson's mind. "You said the telemetry signal was weak. If it was weak, how'd you know to look in this area?"

"It would break your heart to know," Julian chuckled while he punched in codes. "A neighbor of yours sold me the GPS numbers. He's due to make a big chunk more money if things go right. Can the ol' Zen Shyster handle that? Now shut up while I send out my recovery mule."

"Someone at my marina?"

"You heard me."

The Brazilian sold us out, Tomlinson thought and watched a drone the diameter of a bowling ball jettison out onto the sand. The ball provided a cog for tank treads that powered the vehicle toward the ledge, while the drone's body sprouted camera eyes and piercing LED lights. A sand cloud traced its progress to the ledge, where the vehicle vanished into the Captiva Blue Hole.

Julian was having fun working buttons and a toggle stick. "Watch the monitor and talk me in," he said. "They

bugger well better be there. One, I don't care about, but
the other one, an amphib, is a Penguin UAV that I re-
tooled and fitted with miniature gelatin amplifiers. You
wouldn't understand, but the technology is proprietary
and I could lose a bundle if it got in the wrong hands.
The military will pay close to fifty mil."

On an iPad display, the mule's LED lights transformed
gray stone to pastels of green and blue. Tomlinson said,
"There's a small chamber to the left as you enter. The
exact depth is . . . Damn, I had it written down somewhere."

"Got 'em," Julian said, and there they were, both
drones beneath a blanket of sand, each attached to an
inflatable bag. "Why did your idiot pal use so much electrical tape? Sloppy bugger . . . but no problem. Watch
this."

The bowling ball deployed claspers that clamped onto
the saucer-looking drone. It tilted, pivoted, and tractored
the larger UAV back to the sub. The floor beneath them
vibrated and made a clanking noise when the vehicle was
stowed in a compartment under the deck. The bowling
ball reappeared, its claspers raised like claws on a scor-
pion. The zeppelin drone came next.

Tomlinson had begun meditative breathing, prepared
for what he was about to do. He touched a hand to the
red bandana on his head as he asked, "Are you going to
pressurize the area under the deck? Or are we surfacing
first?"

Julian was about to answer when Watts rushed in and
said, "Julie, our guy in Mexico has already started."

"*What?*"

"I know, I know—an hour early, but the live feed is coming in through the surface scanners. You'd better hurry because it's happening fast."

In the salon, on the center screen, was Marion Ford on an open porch or balcony, palm trees in the background. The image was crisp but unsteady, and the sound was poor. The lens swung to Winslow Shepherd, who had aged and was in a wheelchair, then back to the biologist, who—my god—had pulled a gun, his arms extended, the gun dwarfed by two big hands. Shepherd was yelling, "I won't do . . ." the last part lost in garble.

Julian slapped the wall. "I want to hear this, goddamn it. We've got to surface."

"We can't because of those helicopters," Watts said, then his expression changed when he looked at his iPad. "Uh-oh . . . I was afraid of this. We've got a real problem here, Julie. Oh . . . shit."

Tomlinson couldn't take his eyes off of the screen, where Ford was now walking toward Shepherd, the gun still aimed at the Australian's chest; the biologist's expression cold, unemotional, totally focused. Tomlinson's fingers moved independently to search for the detonator hidden under his bandana. As he did, he thought, *They're not alone—why doesn't he stop them?*

Meaning the cameraman—whoever it was—shooting the video.

22

FROM THE BEACH HOUSE STAIRS, MINUTES BE-
fore he cornered Winslow Shepherd, Ford looked back
and saw a van banging toward him on the sandy road,
coming fast, windows black in the late-afternoon sunlight.

He thought about hiding until the van took a hard
right. That told him the driver had seen Cashmere's SUV
parked behind the dunes, which would have made no
sense if the van contained Cashmere's people, or bodyguards, or even financial backers.

On the porch he looked through a window, and

ducked under several others, until he got to the side door
and entered through the kitchen. No holiday decorations
here. The place had the vinyl odor of a newly decorated
rental; a big, open space with a vaulted ceiling, all furnish-
ings staged for photos, not people.

For several beats, he stood and listened. A TV was on
somewhere in the house . . . or was it two or more people
talking?

He shifted the gear bag and flicked the safety on the
little Sig Sauer without unholstering the pistol. The
kitchen spilled into a dining area, no walls to separate it
from the great room, where there was a rock fireplace,
built for effect rather than warmth. He stopped and listened but kept an eye on the front door. Whoever was in
the van was busy with Cashmere's SUV.

Good.

Again, he heard voices, then a phone's ringtone, but
he also heard what might have been CNN World News.
No telling if the phone was in the house or on TV. It was
unlikely that Shepherd was here unattended, but he
waited until the voices stopped before he drew the pistol
and went to a window near the front door.

No sign of the van.

He crossed to the seaward side of the house, checking
rooms as he went, then through open sliding doors to a
patio—and there he was. The math professor was in a
wheelchair with his back to Ford, watching the news. His
elegant silver hair was sprayed in place, and he wore a
blue shirt with a starched collar. One leg of his gray business slacks had been slit to make room for a cast that went
from ankle to thigh.

Winslow was already dressed for their meeting on the concrete balcony. This implied a true bloodthirsty eagerness. The man still had an hour to make the twenty-minute ride.

The van, Ford realized, had come as an escort, or to provide a driver for the handicapped van outside. Possibly both.

Maybe Shepherd *was* alone.

He took a quiet step and changed angles. The patio was more of a TV and reading area that accessed the porch through another set of sliding glass doors. The doors were open. Beyond, through breezy coconut fronds, was a panoramic view of the sea. To the left, inside the TV room, was a wooden door—a bathroom, perhaps. To the right were bookshelves.

Ford lowered the pistol and stepped in. What he wanted to say was *Aren't you supposed to be dead?* But said, simply, "Show me your hands, professor. I just want to talk."

Unlike the Chicago jihadist, Shepherd exhibited no surprise, but said almost the same damn thing. "I didn't think you'd have the balls to show up. Brought a gun, did you? That's typical. Your solution to everything, you Yank prick. Are you worried I'll kick you to death with my cast?"

"If it wasn't for those high school kids you killed," Ford replied, "I might ask how your leg's doing. Put your hands behind your head. I want to see what you're sitting on."

"My ass, you idiot."

Ford spun the wheelchair around and bulled Shepherd onto the porch, stopping just short of the railing. Ten feet below was a sandy ridge. "Do you want to go off another balcony? Keep it up."

Shepherd's face reddened, but he submitted to a search. Ford stepped back. "In a few minutes, your people are going to show up in a van—if they don't get greedy. Either way, I've got a proposition, and we don't have much time."

"What the hell is that supposed to—"

Ford cut him off. "I know about the deal you have with your son—or Julian—I don't care what you call him. You're supposed to deliver some documents to David Cashmere after he kills me. Notarized documents. Or after you watch me fall eight stories onto those rocks—I *saw* the place. Julian will be at a computer someplace, enjoying himself while he watches it happen. What you don't know is, once you deliver the papers, Cashmere is supposed to kill *you*. That's the deal they made. That's what Julian really wants to see—Cashmere cut off your head . . . with this."

From the gear bag, Ford produced the ruby-handled knife.

Shepherd backed his wheelchair to create space while his eyes moved to the TV room as if searching for help. "How did you get that?"

"Cashmere won't bother you, if that's what you're worried about. That's some boy you raised, professor. Julian's blackmailing me, but he'll back off if I have something he wants. That's my offer: give me those documents, you'll live. If you don't, I'll find them anyway and kill you myself. I wouldn't mind, after what you did to that woman. Did you even know her name?"

Shepherd's breathing changed. "Liar!" he yelled, then gritted his teeth. "A bloody mongrel liar, that's what you are. *You.* You're the one who killed her. Julian, we've had our problems, but cut my head off? My own son? That's bugger-all bullshit. You should have stayed in Florida—you'd be dead anyway in a couple of days."

He continued to rage while Ford pulled the pistol and started toward him. "What's that mean? A couple of days—tell me."

Shepherd taunted him with laugher. "You won't live long enough to find out."

"Cashmere did something. What? I know he sent a package to Florida, maybe my marina. Tell me what's in it."

"Burn in hell—that's what's going to happen to your friends. Too bad you can't wish them a Merry Christmas."

Explosives, Ford realized. But detonated how? He cocked the hammer and focused the TruGlo sights while Shepherd's face blurred. "A bomb of some type. I get it. Now, the papers—your last chance, Winslow. Where are they?"

From the TV room, a voice called, "Got 'em right here, Marion. Aren't you a little ahead of schedule?"

Ford turned to see a sound suppressor aimed at him from inside the sliding doors, the shooter screened by a curtain. "Toss your weapon over the railing. Nice and easy . . . Or just place it on the deck. If I can't trust you, who can I trust?"

Shepherd bellowed, "It's about bloody damn time!" while Vargas Diemer stepped onto the porch in crisp slacks and a white blazer, wearing surgical gloves. He was taking video with a phone from the point of view of the little pistol leveled at Ford.

"I'll holster it instead," Ford said. He did, adding, "Now you."

Vargas made a clicking sound of disapproval. "Sorry, sport. For me, this is strictly business. Isn't it a bitch if you get emotionally involved? I'm surprised at you, Doc."

Shepherd was yelling, "Do it! Kill him. No . . . give me the gun," which only caused the Brazilian to grimace as if amused. "What do you think, Doc? He doesn't look like much of a marksman to me."

Ford said, "I know what you're doing—sending video to Julian. What kind of deal did *you* make?"

"A good one, I hope. Let's find out." Vargas held the phone at arm's length and filmed himself, saying, "I don't have you on speaker, Julian, so just do what I say. The instant you transfer those funds, my phone will ding—you know how bank alerts work. A Swiss bank, in my case. I've already sent photos of the old man's documents. Check your email, you'll see the attachments, but they can't be opened until my bank sends the alert. When that happens, we're good to go, and you'll watch what happens next, all live."

Thirty seconds later: *Ding.*

Vargas braced the phone against the pistol's suppressor, swung the pistol, and shot the former math professor twice, once in the face, and a second round that pierced the man's temple from a foot away. A gusher of blood and Shepherd's twitching hands provided a video close-up. Vargas held the angle for several seconds, then looked over and said, "Sorry, sport, but I've got to earn my pay."

Before the Brazilian fired, Ford said, "You don't really expect me to go over the railing?"

23

WHEN THE BRAZILIAN, THAT WEASEL, SHOT MAR-
ion Ford off the balcony, Tomlinson was already dazed
from the fast sequence of events that had played out on
widescreen TV.

Winslow saying, *Your friends will burn in hell*, because
of a package that had been sent. Then, *Too bad you can't
wish them Merry Christmas.*

Ford saying, *A bomb of some type*, the rest garbled, but
the sound quality was improving as the submarine as-
cended toward the surface.

Then the close-up of blood spouting from the head of

Winslow Shepherd, his former Harley companion. It was sickening, but worse was watching Vargas shoot his best friend.

The video continued only a few seconds longer when a thunderclap—*Boom!*—shook the lens. Next came a rapid somersaulting shot of sky and sand as if the camera had followed Ford off the balcony. If the phone landed, it had landed facedown. The TV went dark.

Show's over.

As Julian watched, his milky face took on a reddish glow. First, as if speaking to his father during the bloody close-ups, "My god . . . the bastard did it. See what you made me do! I warned you, you pathetic old liar," then, after Ford was shot, yelling, "Where's his body, goddamn it. That was part of our deal. Show me Clarence's goddamn body!"

In response to the thundering sound that ended the video, he said only, "Lightning . . . Do you believe this shit? Just my luck. It must have struck close by."

Now Julian was pacing. "None of it went like I planned. Watts . . . Watts—get that idiot's agent on the screen. I'll put him out of business for this. Cashmere, too—where was that raghead bugger? He was supposed to use his knife. *The knife*—I told him how many times? I wanted to hear Winslow beg, that was the plan. *Crying* for my forgiveness."

Watts, however, was pacing, too, fixated on his iPad. "Julian . . . Julian? *Julie*, you've got to listen to me. I stopped our ascent."

Julian replied, "Can you believe such incompetence from—" then realized what he'd just heard. "You did . . . Without asking me?"

Watts thrust out the iPad and backed away. "Look for yourself. It's the helicopters. We just got satellite confirmation, and the system has triangulated their course. Less than a minute ago, both made sharp turns. One is headed for *Evergreen*, the other is coming toward us, only fifteen miles out. We still have time—"

Julian yanked the iPad away and scowled into the screen. "What's the visibility?"

"From a chopper? We're at thirty feet now, almost periscope depth. They'll see us—or the wreckage up there. On the other hand, if we run too close to the bottom, we'll stir up a shit storm of sand and they'll see that, too."

Tomlinson stood quietly while they bickered. He'd been calming himself with meditative breathing, expecting to die when the sub hit the surface. Pressure-activated detonators on the drones would see to that. Now he had to postpone the inevitable because he'd translated the conversation he'd heard: a package containing a bomb had been delivered to Dinkin's Bay.

It was the new sound system. Had to be.

Merry Christmas, Winslow had said.

Less than an hour ago, Mack had radioed for advice on how to hook up the system. But there might still be time.

He reached under his bandana and removed the detonator. It was a rubberized cube with a flip-up cover. Nothing to it: flick a safety switch, hit power, then use the four numerical buttons to punch in a three-digit code.

The code was 6-4-3; easy to remember. In a baseball score book, it represented a double play. Shortstop to second, to first base.

Ford's idea.

Tomlinson stepped forward and raised his voice to be heard. "Boys . . . Boys . . . I'm not in the best of moods right now—what, with seeing your hired gun shoot my best friend—so shut the hell up and just listen. Okay?"

Watts, then Julian, pivoted, their expressions asking *Are you crazy?*

"We're not going anywhere," Tomlinson told them. "And we're sure as hell not going to surface. What you *will* do is give me a working phone so I can call my marina. It's sort of a family emergency thing—or maybe you planned that, too."

The look Watts flashed his boss promised *I'll handle this.* "I know you're upset," he said, "but shit happens, right? The fact is, we can't let you make a phone call. Like the helicopters we're worried about, calls can be triangulated. Say"—Watts offered a condescending smile—"how about a nice, cold beer? Sound good? Then you can sit there like a good boy while we go about our work."

"How about you stick some plastic explosives up your ass," Tomlinson replied, "because that's what's about to happen." He held the detonator out for them to see. "There's a pressure switch on those drones. They'll blow up if we surface. This is the remote. I can blow us all up from here, too."

He thumbed opened the lid. "Watch closely. This is the power button—see? Yeah . . . a little red flashing light. Now all I have to do is enter a code. Three simple numbers and the plastic explosives go *Boom!*"

"You can't bluff us into giving you a phone," Watts said. He slid past Julian, took the iPad, and began to tap at the display as if unconcerned.

Tomlinson held the detonator higher and extended the index finger of his left hand. "The code is six-four-three. Does that ring a bell? No . . . I suppose not." His finger punched 6 . . . 4 . . . then he waited with his finger poised over the final number.

"He's out of his mind," Julian said to Watts, who had begun to work furiously on the iPad.

Tomlinson flashed his craziest look. "We'll compare paddle scars one day, dude, but right now you're going to give me a phone."

"This can all be worked out," Watts said, which gave him time to enter a few final commands. Then he turned to Julian and said, *"Listen."*

Clank-clank . . . Clank-clank. They all heard metallic sounds coming from under the stern, then the thump of an underwater hatch.

"Now we *have* to surface," Watts said and typed in new commands. "But not for long. We'll dive right away and pick them up later."

Tomlinson's stomach fluttered with a sudden, rapid ascent and he knew what had happened. The drones had been jettisoned. Now the sub was fleeing upward at full speed.

No choice. He had to do it.

True. The sadness that descended upon Tomlinson was the sweetest pain he'd experienced, but he didn't cling or tarry. He entered the final digit—3—and, a millisecond later, he was only semiconscious when a hole in the fuselage sucked him, free and clear, into the deep blue sea.

24

VARGAS EXITED THROUGH THE FRONT DOOR OF the beach house, down the steps to a large white van with a wheelchair lift, and scanned for the source of the explosion. Not a huge report; more like a couple of flash-bangs that shook the floors and caused him to fumble his phone.

Unexpected, but the timing was useful.

Not far away, black smoke boiled from behind sand dunes—Ford had booby-trapped his vehicle, but why? Cries for help and sirens were to be anticipated, but there were none. Instead, he heard distant laughter. On the ridge by the road, children had gathered beneath a slow-twirling cloud of confetti, but it wasn't confetti.

Vargas stowed his briefcase and ventured away from the van. Scattered in the sand were several U.S. hundred-dollar bills. Another drifted toward him. The bill was scorched.

He pocketed a few and returned to the van, amused. Marion Ford was a man who stuck to his routine at the expense of fun, but only a fool would assume the biologist was predictable.

It was a detail to be filed away.

Up a ramp, inside the van, was a dented Kawasaki motorcycle. He had learned from experience that a rental car was a liability if pursued in traffic, or anywhere else, in the third world. Rental cars stood out here. Poverty dominated in an area like Quintana Roo. Until now . . . Vargas glanced at the confetti still spiraling down—several million dollars in green bills, at least. Children and a few giddy mothers were there, dancing with their faces tilted upward. They resembled flowers trying to catch rain.

Ford wasn't the greedy type, but he wasn't a fool. He wouldn't have left that much money unguarded. The bills were either marked or they were counterfeit.

What did it matter? Even if it took only a few weeks for the nearest bank, or the *federalistas*, to figure it out, families here were guaranteed the most extravagant December in history. And those children . . . Well, Vargas knew nothing about children, but he knew people. A few would thrive. Most would fail.

It was the way the world worked.

He slammed the kick-starter, revved the engine, and

bounced cross-country, using the dunes as a screen. A quick look at the blazing SUV told him the robbers had arrived in a black Toyota van.

Julian had said Winslow's bodyguards would be driving a black van. Three, all from the Middle East, even though he saw only two.

Their bodies would not be easy to identify.

In the touristy village of Playa del Carmen, Vargas parked the motorcycle in an alley and left the key in the ignition. Only then did he remove the surgical gloves.

The private airport was a few miles west. He took a cab and cleared Customs by slipping the agent two hundred-dollar bills he'd found in the sand. He'd already filed the FAA's electronic EAPIS forms and a flight plan yesterday morning.

"You are early, señor," the agent said with a slight bow.

The Brazilian was still ahead of schedule. It was five forty-five p.m., not dark, but soon would be.

"Is that a problem?"

"You are the only one here this late, and I would have been ready anyway. Come, I'll show you."

Outside in the fading light, his plane had been washed, waxed, and was waiting on the tarmac. It was a six-seat Cessna Citation, with twin turbofan engines, that, on paper, was owned by a sham LLC in Lauderdale. Cruising speed, 550 mph; max range, 1,200 nautical miles. A fun little jet to fly on short hops, and it was only an hour to Naples, where he'd moored his yacht. There was an area of docks and restaurants there called Tin City. He would arrive in time for a fine dinner and, hopefully, find one of those attractive Naples beach *condesas* to help him celebrate his recent windfall.

It was quite a haul for one day's work, as his bank had confirmed by email. Julian had paid him $1.5 million for the location of the drones, and to orchestrate the murder of his father, Winslow Shepherd.

Events hadn't gone precisely as planned, but they never did. It wasn't his fault the schedule had been moved up, or that a terrorist freak named Cashmere hadn't appeared.

Shooting the biologist, a last-minute bargain, had been billed to Shepherd. Julian, of course, had provided the money—another $500,000.

Total: Two million U.S. dollars, transferred as euros. He had asked for four, but not bad.

Vargas set his watch—a Breitling Aerospace—to Florida time, but he couldn't leave yet. He strolled out on the tarmac. No one around. He noted a blue-and-white Maule not far from his Cessna, the little amphib moored with wheels down.

Twenty minutes later, he was in the private lounge, filling out his preflight checklist, when the agent reappeared. "You asked to be notified, señor, if a taxi arrived. The car is waiting out front."

"How many passengers?"

"The windows are tinted and it's nearly dark, señor. It is a very nice taxi."

The Brazilian nodded at his briefcase in a meaningful way.

The agent said, "Your belongings are safe," and tapped his breast pocket. The folded hundreds were stashed there, yet the bulge suggested a wad of bills had been recently added.

Vargas followed the man through a hall to the office, where glass doors were also tinted, the gated *calle* beyond. Outside was a yellow taxi with black windows. A lighted Virgin Mary statuette provided a hood ornament. A decal reading *Me Paseo Con Dios* covered the upper windshield with translucent blue.

Translation: I Ride With God.

"Yes, the car, very nice," Vargas said and went out the door as the driver cranked the window down and called out in Spanish, "Do you desire a taxi, *patrón*?"

Patrón is a term of respect that means *boss*.

"I'd like to speak with your passenger." Vargas leaned to the window and looked in the backseat. There was no one there. "Where is he? How many people did you bring?"

The driver shrugged the way men do when they have been bribed not to talk.

"I'm an *idiota*," the Brazilian muttered and ran past the agent, through the office and down the hall, where the lounge door had not been closed, as he'd feared. He slowed and looked in. As he did, the door burst inward. The impact stumbled him forward, then two big hands latched on from behind, spun him, and slammed him hard against the wall.

Vargas was looking into the puzzled eyes of the biologist, who said, "I could have broken an ankle, dumbass."

Vargas didn't fight back. "And I could have shot you. It's not like you gave me any advance warning. Get your hands off me. *Now*."

Ford applied a slight pressure to his throat. "Are you sure you missed intentionally?"

Vargas glared and waited.

"I need my phone," Ford said. "Where is it? Or tell me the combination to your briefcase." He released his grip and stepped away. "You didn't hear what Shepherd said about a package delivered to Dinkin's Bay? Explosives; some sort of improvised bomb. That's what pisses me off more than anything. We should have warned them half an hour ago. Instead—"

"I already did," Vargas interrupted while straightening his collar.

"You spoke to Mack?"

"No one answered at the marina, so I called Sanibel police. Doc"—they stood nose to nose—"don't ever touch me again."

Ford allowed the man some room. "How long ago?"

"Just before your surprise appearance at the beach house. I'd been talking with Winslow. Do you understand the risk I was taking? I used a throwaway phone to call Sanibel, but, even so . . ." He looked around for his brief-case. "What did you do with it?"

The case was beside a vinyl chair, an ashtray nearby, snacks and mini-bottles of liquor on the bar behind. Vargas inspected the leather for scratches, opened it, tossed Ford's cell on the chair, and locked it again, his manner aloof.

"What did Sanibel police say?"

"What they always say. They'll look into it."

Ford was tempted to slam him into another wall but said, "Come on, I'm sorry I roughed you up, but it's been a tough day."

"Thanks to me, a profitable day as well," Vargas countered. "Are you sure something else isn't bothering you?"

"Like what?"

"I'll take a wild guess. Hannah, maybe?"

"Only if you did something really stupid," Ford replied.

"Then I'm right."

"You'd better hope you're wrong. Julian got ahold of a photo, a voyeur shot of her in the shower. I happen to know Hannah was aboard your boat one night while I was away. I swear to god, if you—"

Vargas, unconcerned, said, "My computer system was never breached—remember?" He was scanning a weather report on his phone. "Ask Julian who the sick bastard was, but it wasn't me. By the way"—he made eye contact—"the percentages have changed as of this instant. Instead of a sixty-forty split, it's seventy-thirty, with my agent's fee coming off your end. If you don't like it, *live* with it. In this business, it's not smart to accept money you haven't earned."

The Brazilian checked his watch and hefted the briefcase, all packed and ready to go—until he saw Ford trying to use his phone. "I wouldn't do that. The signal will ping the nearest tower. If someone checks, there are three good reasons back in Tulum you don't want to be tied to Mexico. Maybe four. As I left, I noticed you had some car problems. Did you happen to run into a freak named Cashmere?"

Ford motioned to the runway where the Cessna Citation sat, sleek and ready. "You don't think that's evidence enough?"

"The flight plan I filed is perfectly legit. I'm here for two days of Christmas shopping. The Customs agent was kind enough to act as my surrogate buyer while I explored the local sights. No telling what he came back with, but I'm sure the gifts are tasteful. And *legal*. I didn't sneak in under the radar. What about you . . . Doc?"

Ford pocketed his phone for now. "Tell me how it went with Sanibel police."

The Brazilian went out the door onto the tarmac, then looked back. "Are you coming or not? I'll give you a ride—that's up to you—but I'm having dinner in Naples. I want time to clean up after we land."

Vargas didn't say anything about Sanibel again until they were almost to the plane. "The woman I spoke to assumed I was the bomber—or a crank—so I didn't hear all she had to say before I splashed the phone."

"When you called the—"

"Yes, the cops. I told her a package had been sent to the marina, general delivery, and I was certain it contained explosives. Enough to blow up a couple of buildings, but that was a guess— I didn't say it was a guess, of course, or where I got the information. Winslow didn't share many specifics, but he told me enough. He got on the subject by mentioning how lucky I was to have moved my boat because—"

"What was in the package? If it was a simple mail bomb, it would have gone off the moment—"

"I couldn't ask, he'd have been suspicious," Vargas said. "But he finally got around to it and said a music box of some type with a volume-sensitive detonator. A small package, I suppose, wrapped like a Christmas gift—it's another guess I couldn't admit. The woman cop seemed dubious, but I did hear a dispatcher in the background scramble a squad car or two. If there was a problem, I'm sure they've cleared the place by now."

Ford pictured the blasting cap with a mini-microphone attached—that damn ex-Chicagoan. He and Shepherd, both experienced bombers, had joined forces. "If the marina was still standing when the cops got there. Did she say anything else? Or don't you give a damn?"

Vargas remained aloof while he touched an electronic key. Lighting LEDs inside the Cessna flared on. The boarding door opened; steps descended with a hydraulic whine. "You're going to use that phone anyway, aren't you?"

"I can't take a chance Mack and the others don't realize this isn't just a bomb scare. Plus, my pilot pal's not far from here and I have to let him know."

"The explosives are real," the Brazilian said. "The music box was sent with a card signed *Your Mysterious Santa* or something similar. Cute, huh? Only Julian could have provided information that detailed. I didn't mention Julian to the woman cop, of course. Julian Solo, the international criminal? She would have been convinced I'm nuts. But the card, yes. That's what convinced me the explosives were real."

Ford suddenly felt optimistic. "If Tomlinson reads the card, he'll know something's wrong. It was the stupidest mistake they could have made. Julian, with all his high-tech bullshit, never figured it out—the Secret Santa thing. Tomlinson's the one who's been giving those hundred-dollar bills away. I'm sure of it. He'll know it's a setup."

Vargas, from inside the plane, looked down with an odd expression as the boarding steps retracted. "You think so, huh? Doc . . . Tomlinson didn't give those hundred-dollar bills away. It was me," he said, then pulled the hatch closed and sealed it.

Ford was pondering, *An international hit man who plays Secret Santa on his days off?*

Absurd.

The truth would have to wait. He exchanged texts with Dan Futch, and was dialing Tomlinson for the third time when the Brazilian's jet went airborne.

25

TOMLINSON'S KARMIC RIDDLE: THERE ARE FOUR passengers on an airplane. Only one is destined to die in a plane crash. So where are the three missing parachutes?

He had created this modern Zen koan to nudge his students toward enlightenment.

His favorite answer: *What is the sound of four asses puckering?*

A more thoughtful response was *Karma can be a beauteous circle or a bitch with fangs, but Destiny is not carved in stone.*

In a perfect world, he might have been comforted by

this concept when the explosion spewed him through the sub's fuselage into the bowels of a late-afternoon sea.

Instead, his last cognitive thought was *Fuck me, Louie . . . this is gonna hurt.*

After that, the world turned weird and very, very blurry.

Breathing seawater was better than breathing helium. Tomlinson became weightless as he tumbled toward the bottom . . . or tumbled somewhere. He wasn't sufficiently conscious to decipher direction, or even open his eyes to the glare of celestial light.

Light?

The surface was up there somewhere! He began to claw his way toward it. For sustenance, he inhaled another watery breath.

Light faded. Murk displaced all else even as helium buoyed him up into a golden field of wreckage that included a head of cabbage, Styrofoam, the listing tower of a periscope, and green, helpless bottles of Steinlager beer bobbing nearby. His drooping eyes struggled to assemble order from a tableau that was too damn strange to deal with.

Vomiting, however, was familiar. The same with treading water. He had often done both while stoned or half asleep.

Tomlinson felt sleepy now. He could have drifted off, no problem. That's what he was doing, drifting into sleep, when an unseen force grabbed his hair from behind, yanked hard, and began to drag him across the surface. Painful . . . the sluggish lunging pace was nauseating, yet he didn't have the strength to break free, so he lay back and vomited again.

A voice hollered, "Hey . . . Hey! I need help. There's a paddle over there. Swim to the paddle. There's enough of your boat left to hold us both. *Hurry.* We have to get out of the water."

Tomlinson gagged and wedged an eyelid open. What he saw against the setting sun was a hallucination: Julian Solo, his shirt burned off, arms bloody, clung to the tip of the periscope not far away. The tower, which had been leaning, was gone and slowly pulling the periscope down with it.

"Grab one of those beers," Tomlinson croaked, "and breathe in some saltwater."

"Shut up . . . Shut up and look at me! There's a paddle over there." Julian pointed frantically. "Your boat's still floating. Get the paddle and come get me. Please. My sub—my real sub—it's on its way. You'll love it, man. I'll take you anywhere you want."

"Sure . . . Swim over and we'll talk about it. You ever been to Maui?"

Tomlinson's voice was improving.

"I can't, you idiot. There's a shark and I'm bleeding. Just a minute ago, I saw it over there." More frantic pointing, which led Tomlinson's eyes a few points south of the sun. He didn't see a shark, but he did see a low-flying aircraft. It was close enough to reveal colors of orange and white, accompanied by a ceiling fan thrum.

"That's a Coast Guard chopper," he called in reply. "Oh—I get it. You're afraid they're coming to arrest *you.*" Then he winced and said, "Shit, that hurts! Hey . . . let go of my hair."

A heavy tail smacked him in the face when he turned.

It was like being hit with a bullwhip, but the blow levitated him into consciousness.

It was the dog. The dog had towed him to the remains of Ford's monster boat, which had overturned, but its unsinkable inflated tubes were still floating high.

He flipped around, climbed onto one of the tubes, then tried to pull the dog up by the collar. "Damn it, Pete . . . cooperate."

The dog lunged away with a wild splash and swam toward Julian, who was wrapped around the periscope like a pole dancer at a strip joint. He was screaming, "It's coming . . . It's coming back!"

After a moment to clear his head, Tomlinson called, "Pete doesn't bite. Shallow up, man," then checked on the chopper. It was cargo-sized, close enough that the propeller blast roiled the Gulf's sunset colors with an escalating roar.

Loud. It was difficult to hear Julian, who was pointing again, but not at the helicopter. "Do something. Watts, goddamn it . . . help me!"

Tomlinson expected to see the missing crewman. Instead, a dorsal fin appeared from out of the sun, black and glistening against a blazing sky. The fin was cruising toward Julian, then angled abruptly toward the dog, which was okay. The massive wake and dorsal were familiar.

"It's not a shark," Tomlinson hollered, "it's a killer whale." But just in case, he cupped his hands and added, "Pete . . . Hey, get your crazy butt back here."

The animal's head pivoted in response, but he kept swimming. The dorsal fin, which had been zigzagging, increased speed on a straight line toward the dog.

Tomlinson got to his feet, ignored the few barnacles on the hull, and triangulated the distance. The whale would intercept the dog before the dog got to Julian. Those three elements were separated by less than thirty yards.

"It's only a killer whale," he shouted again.

Julian suddenly went silent. The periscope had sunk from his grip, leaving him alone in the water. He looked blankly at Tomlinson for an instant and mouthed the words, *Help me*—or his plea was lost to the roar of the helicopter that passed low overhead.

At the same instant, the dorsal fin sounded. A giant gray shadow lifted the dog from the water and spun him around. The dog responded by tilting his butt and diving after whatever had bumped him.

"Pete. Pete, you dumbass!"

There was nothing Tomlinson could do but watch from his elevated position as a giant shadow, pursued by the dog, made a graceful turn toward Julian.

To the north, the chopper had also banked. A helmeted man appeared in the door, holding what might have been a rifle. Tomlinson looked up long enough to wave his arms in acknowledgment.

When he turned back, Julian was gone. A second later, the dog surfaced. He spouted a geyser of water from his snout and began to swim a circular search pattern.

Searching was pointless. Below, peering into the shaded depths, Tomlinson could see Julian rocketing downward, helpless against the languid strokes of a massive scimitar tail. In counter-sync, Julian's porcelain face appeared, vanished, and reappeared; a descending beacon dwarfed by the gray tonnage of a predator that was not a whale.

Hello, Dolly!

The Coast Guard chopper zoomed in and hovered. The first thing Tomlinson said when he and the dog were aboard was "This is an emergency—I need to use a phone."

26

A PHONE CALL TO THE MARINA OFFICE WAS SIG-
naled by a clattering bell on the wall outside. Mack was
headed there anyway on this tropical eve, with the moon
already up in a dusk-bright sky. It was Friday, the nine-
teenth day of Christmas.

He ignored Jeth and Fast Eddie, who were wrestling with
a keg of beer. Same with Capt. Hannah, who was socializing
with Ransom, Ted Cole, Alex, and some other fishing guides
beneath holiday lights. When Marta, the pretty Cuban, called
to him, "Where's Sabina?" he only pointed to the office window, where he could see the girl sitting on the counter.

Friday was traditional party night at Dinkin's Bay, but the crowd was bigger than usual because of the season. Mack equated population with profit. The more people in attendance, the more beer, hats, and T-shirts he would sell.

Even so, he was in a foul mood. Sanibel cops had spooked away business two hours ago when they showed up looking for a bomb in a music box.

"It's another damn hoax," he'd told them. "Just like the boater who was supposedly attacked by a great white. You didn't hear about that? I was standing by the VHF when it happened and I knew right away it was bullshit."

The cops had cleared the area anyway; wasted a perfectly good sunset, before opening the marina gates again—money down the drain.

The fancy new sound system was another irritant. It had taken hours to set up—a job he had surrendered, finally, to Figueroa. The little Cuban, although not bright, was a savant when it came to wiring and other jury-rigging skills. Worse, after showering and a change of clothes, Mack had returned to the marina only to realize he'd put Rhonda's boat mate, JoAnn, in charge of music.

It was a stupid oversight on his part.

So far, JoAnn had played nothing but weird, sleep-inducing Gregorian chants, as if intentionally trying to piss off him and his not-so-secret lover.

"Do you think she knows?" Rhonda had asked for the millionth time.

"Are you kidding? I guarantee she'll play *Madame Butterfly* just to make you cry," was his response.

Mack was right. When the soprano's first wistful lyrics began in sync with the clanging phone, he took off for the office. He'd heard the damn song often enough to know he didn't have long before the heroine launched into a series of high notes that would reduce Rhonda to tears and quite possibly blow out the speakers.

"Excuse me . . . Make way, please." Mack threaded his way through clusters of people, some of whom were already covering their ears, the volume was so loud. By the time he got to the office, he'd covered his ears, too. "Turn that damn thing down!" he yelled. "Why didn't you answer the phone?"

JoAnn Smallwood was from Old Florida stock, and not a woman to cower. "Answer your own damn phone," she shot back.

Mack did; put the phone to his ear while Madame Butterfly wailed the first notes of an ascending scale.

He said, "What . . . huh? Hang on a sec." He covered the phone and glared at JoAnn. "It's Tomlinson. I can't hear him and he sounds upset. Turn that goddamn thing down."

Sabina, wearing a red felt dress, had sat quietly until then but got involved by demanding in English, "I'm a *children*. Stop swearing, you *pendejos*."

The girl reached for the volume knob, the old amplifier where it had always been, on a shelf near the cash register. As her fingers made contact, however, the Earth shook, a window imploded, and the little girl screamed.

From a speeding Coast Guard helicopter, ten miles out, Tomlinson saw the explosion—sparks atop a rising plume of smoke.

He lowered the phone.

"Oh my god," he said.

27

DAN FUTCH CHANGED RADIO FREQUENCIES AND
tapped the screen of the Garmin GPS while saying, "An
area thirty-five miles west of Sanibel has been declared a
temporary no-fly zone. Same area as the Captiva Blue
Hole. I wonder what the feds have going on?" He
glanced at Ford, who was flying the plane. "I take it back.
Don't tell me a damn thing."

"When we're on the ground," Ford said, "I will. Any
reception?"

Futch checked his phone. "We might have to climb to
pick up a signal. But not now. When we're closer. I want

Fort Myers tower to think we're coming out of the Everglades. Because of the no-fly zone, we'll have to make our approach into Dinkin's Bay from the mainland."

They'd been airborne almost three hours, but, with no tailwind to boost ground speed, Sanibel was still twenty miles away. To the east was a string of lighted dominoes—condos on Vanderbilt and Bonita Beach. Out the portside window, the moon brightened a December sea.

It was nine-thirty p.m.

A few minutes later, Futch activated an electronic responder and the little Maule climbed to a thousand feet. Sanibel Island appeared in the windscreen, a twinkling scimitar not unlike the rubyhandled knife in Ford's gear bag. The knife and $150,000 in cash, presumably counterfeit, would add to his credibility when—and if—a secret debriefing was scheduled.

Something had gone rotten at the highest levels in D.C. He was certain of that now. He also knew they might decide to kill the messenger rather than risk a messenger who, after speaking the truth, would demand the truth.

That was okay—*they* were predictable. A silence of more than a week or two would tell him much of what he needed to know. If it happened, he would turn the tables and target them—or he would have to find a new home. There was no other way. He would never again put people at risk who were guilty only of being his friends.

Ford touched the mic to speak. "I don't think you ought to stick around after we land. It's not that I don't have room, but—"

Futch silenced him by pointing northeast to where

Sanibel was broadened by the expanse of Dinkin's Bay. "Lots of blue lights flashing down there. Looks fairly close to the marina . . . or maybe it's beachside. What do you think?"

The biologist used the windscreen brace to pull himself up for a look. "I've got to get down there."

"With all those cops?"

"It's the ambulances that worry me," Ford said. "Put me on the water, get me close. Just like before."

He exited through mangroves into the parking lot, thinking, *Where the hell is my boat?*

The parking lot was nearly empty, which was also strange, but lights were on at the marina and he could hear static-laced music—Gregorian chants through blown speakers, it sounded like, the volume low.

Nor were there any blue flashing lights. Until then, Ford felt as if he'd been waiting to breathe.

Or maybe it was too soon to be sure.

He threw the gear bag in his truck and jogged to the office, where one shattered glass door was open. He charged inside, expecting to see blood on the walls, but there was none. Nausea transitioned into confusion. He went out the side door toward the docks and nearly collided with Tomlinson, who was coming around the corner with an Igloo filled with ice.

He dropped the cooler. "Doc . . . ? *Doc,* you're alive. Or"—he stepped back—"are you?"

"Why wouldn't I be?"

"For real?"

"Jesus Christ, stop your babbling."

Tomlinson threw his arms wide. "That's all the proof I need, *hermano*. Wow, there are times when reality really throws my ass for a loop."

Ford endured a hug and a flood of questions before pushing away. "Where is everybody?"

"A bomb," Tomlinson said. "Marion—talk to me. You were shot. I saw it happen, man. That snake Vargas—"

"Vargas isn't as bad as you think," Ford cut in. He kicked at some broken glass, and scanned the docks, seeing lights on in a few boats but no people. "How many were hurt?"

"Aside from you? Or did the bullet miss? Vargas sure as hell wasn't shooting blanks."

"Drop it. Geezus, I'm fine," Ford said, but it took a while to convince his pal. Finally, he grabbed one side of the cooler, waited for Tomlinson to heft the other handle, and they walked toward the parking lot. "Get it over with. Tell me who was killed. How many hospitalized."

"Nobody."

"Bullshit. This happened because of me. I know it and you know it. Don't lie."

"Would you just listen? A bomb, yeah, it blew out Figgy's eardrums, and windows for about a mile—you know, windows that weren't up to code—but that's all. No other injuries that I've heard about."

"Impossible. It's Friday night, party night. This place had to have been packed."

"No, it's destiny, man, that's what it is. But only because the bomb went off at Mack's cottages, not here. In the clubhouse. Thank god, the place is built like a bunker;

didn't even damage the cottages, except for the windows. Everyone's there now, waiting for the cops to finish doing whatever it is they do. Then it's party time, so I came back for ice. I've never seen so many unmarked narc cars in my life."

The feds are already involved, Ford realized, but listened to Tomlinson explain, "The bomb was in a new sound system that arrived—it's a long story. Anyway, Figgy went outside to reset a breaker and that's what saved him—you know, no power, then he hit the breaker switch. If it wasn't for those concrete walls—" He stopped, a look of sudden wonderment on his face. "Doc . . . Julian's dead. I saw that happen, too, man. Black karma in the form of a great white shark—"

"No more mystic visions. Just tell me. Julian's really dead?"

"Marion . . . *with my own eyes.* It happened when I was anchored over the Captiva Blue Hole. Today, just before sunset."

"You're sure."

"Am I ever. A great white, I swear. Julian, pieces of him, are passing through her large intestine as we speak—once a shit, always a shit, you know? But I shouldn't joke. The look on that pathetic loon's face when the shark took him under. *Jesus.* The Coast Guard was shooting video the whole time, if you don't believe me—from a chopper. If I call the station, maybe they'll"—Tomlinson hesitated—"That's the good news. The bad news is, it shows wreckage of your boat, too. Julian blew it up. But Pete's fine, don't worry about him. He's at the cottages with Figgy."

"Who?" Ford stared in the direction of Mack's new property. He was thinking about the man he no longer trusted. Maybe the man was there with local police, the FBI and ATF agents, and other agencies that would be hanging around the island for weeks.

"Your dog," Tomlinson said. "I've been calling him Spaceman 'cause that's where he's from—outer space— not what you're thinking. Hang on a sec." He wobbled around with the weight of the cooler and pointed to three vague shapes outside the office. "Those plastic cows showed up a week ago. Tonight, he came back dragging that new one. Crazy bastard's been stealing from the Episcopal church on Periwinkle."

"The dog? Stealing what?"

"One of the Wise Men, obviously. It's sure not Mary, and Joseph wouldn't be jeweled up like a pimp." Tomlinson steeled himself for the maddening question that came next.

"How stoned are you?"

"I knew it, I knew it. From a *Nativity scene*, dude. Are you sure you're okay?"

No . . . the biologist was not okay. Tomlinson recognized the signs. In Ford, impatience could signal a new project, or anger. But it could also signal a glowering obsession too dark to risk inquiry.

"I've got Mack's Lincoln," he added in his cheeriest voice. "I'll tell you the rest in the car—one hell of a story it is, too—but first we have to stop for some beer and goodies." He looked over the Igloo, grinning. "We've got a lot to celebrate tonight. Sweet, huh? All our friends are there primed, ready and waiting."

Friends. The word, and the word's obligations, stuck in Ford's consciousness until the cooler was stowed in Mack's car. When the trunk was closed, he started toward his truck. "I'll meet you there. Not right away, so don't mention you saw me."

"You mean, pretend—"

"I don't want anyone to know."

"Whoa, I don't like the vibe I'm getting here. At least tell me what's going on." Tomlinson watched, expecting his pal to look back. He didn't. "Hey . . . Doc . . . ? Marion! Where are you headed? I mean *really*? And, for christ's sake, don't tell me some science gig in Orlando."

Ford at least chuckled a little at that. "Take care of Pete," he replied but didn't stop.

A legendary charter captain named Tootsie Barlow comes to Doc Ford, muttering about a curse he believes is causing a bizarre series of attacks on members of his extended family. Ford doesn't believe in curses, but as he and his friend Tomlinson begin to investigate, they, too, suffer a series of near-fatal mishaps. Is it really a curse? The answer lies in solving a near-hundred-year-old murder... and probing the mind of a madman.

PUTNAM
EST. 1838

Penguin
Random
House

1

ON THE PHONE, TOMLINSON SAID TO FORD, "WHEN the deputy's wife and kids disappeared, moonshiners might've dumped their bodies in the lake—it was during Prohibition. It wouldn't be the first time karma has waited decades to boot justice in the ass."

"Tootsie Barlow told you that story?" Ford, a marine biologist, was referring to a famous fishing guide who ranked with Jimmy Albright, Jack Brothers, Ted Williams, and a few others as fly-casting pioneers in the Florida Keys.

"His family was involved somehow—the Barlows go way, way back in the area. I don't know how yet, but I will. He's in bad shape, so I need to take it slow, but *you're* the one who told me about the lake—Chino Hole. That's the connection. The access road cuts through Tootsie's property."

"I had no idea. He lives in the Everglades now?"

"Smack dab in the middle. One of those little cross-road villages like Copeland or Carnestown. The property's been in his family for years. I'm driving down this afternoon. Since he quit guiding, it's probably easier for him to wake up and see sawgrass instead of the Gulfstream. The end game, dude, for watermen like us, it can be pretty damn sad."

"I've heard the rumor," Ford said. "But, as far as your story goes, I'm still lost."

"So's Tootsie. How many fishing guides put away money for retirement? He's broke, which is bad enough, but now he's afraid that God has singled out his family for punishment. Like a conspiracy, you know? Not because of something he did, more likely something his father or a relative did. The cops won't listen, his preacher doesn't believe him, so who else is he gonna call but the Right Reverend yours truly."

Tomlinson, an ordained Rienzi Buddhist priest, seldom employed the preface "Right Reverend." The title had been bestowed by a Las Vegas divinity mill after cashing his check for fifty bucks.

"Tootsie wants you to put in a good word with God, I get it. I still don't see what this has to do with us . . ."

"He wants someone to convince the cops he's not crazy. And there's another connection. The deputy who disappeared was J. H. Cox. That ring a bell? It should."

"When was this?"

"Nineteen-twenty-five. A few years earlier, a woman was murdered by a man named Cox. Same area; near Marco Island. I don't know if it was the same man, but *your* Hannah Smith is a direct descendant of the woman he killed."

Mentioning the biologist's ex-lover Hannah was a calculated risk to catalyze Ford's interest. In the background over the phone, Tomlinson could hear a steel drum band. "Hey, seriously. Where are you?"

Ford, who was in the lobby of the Schooner Hotel—Nassau, Bahamas—said, "I'm in Lauderdale. At a convention for aquarium hobbyists. I'll get back to the lab late tomorrow. Hopefully."

"Bahia Mar, Lauderdale?"

"Close enough. Look . . . I've got a talk to give, and I'm still working on my notes." As he spoke, the child porn dealer he'd been tailing stepped to the registration desk. Ford covered the phone, and moved as if getting into line.

When he rejoined the conversation, his boat bum hipster pal Tomlinson was saying, " . . . Tootsie's story is historical fact. I've got the old newspaper stories to prove it. In August 1925, Deputy Cox, his wife and two kids, all disappeared the night before a bunch of bootleggers went on trial. Marco Island, or somewhere at the edge of the Everglades. Get it?—all within a few miles of Chino Hole."

"Moonshiners would need fresh water," Ford reasoned while he watched the clerk encode the porn dealer's room key.

"That's who the newspapers blamed, but there was other nasty crap going on at the time, which I'm just starting to research. You ever hear of the Marco Island War?"

"Come on, you're making this up."

"It *happened,* man. Same time period. A bunch of heavy hitters had their fingers in the regional pie—Al Capone, probably Joe Kennedy, too, but they weren't the worst. The elite rich were stealing homesteads, and smuggling in Chinese illegals to boot." Tomlinson sniffed, and added, "Lauderdale, huh? Dude, the satellite must'a stopped over Nassau, 'cause I swear I can smell jerked chicken."

Ford replied, "Call you back," and hung up as the clerk addressed the porn dealer by name for the third time—standard, in the hospitality business—then handed over a key in a sleeve with the number 803 written and circled.

"I'll be checking out in about an hour," Ford told the clerk when it was his turn.

There were ceiling fans in the lobby and panoramic windows, beyond which sun-baked tourists lounged by the pool. A brunette in a red handkerchief two-piece was sufficiently lush and languid to spark a yearning in the biologist—an abdominal pang he recognized as discontent.

Focus, he told himself, and returned to his encrypted notes. It became easier when the brunette stood and buttoned on a beach wrap. Every set of poolside eyes followed her to the door.

An hour later, the porn dealer reappeared in the lobby wearing shorts and flip-flops, and exited toward the tiki bar.

Ford shouldered his computer bag, and crossed the lobby to the elevators.

From the eighth floor, Montagu Bay was a turquoise basin encrusted by slums and ox cart traffic on the eastern fringe. Spaced along the waterfront were resort compounds: postcard enclaves that were separated from Nassau's realities by armed guards and tastefully disguised concertina wire.

The biologist no longer wondered why tourists came to places like this. People seldom traveled. Not really. Travel was too damn unpredictable. Instead, they contrived daydreams. They chose template fictions that matched, or came close enough to, the vacation they wanted to describe to their friends back home.

Near the elevator was a house phone. He dialed housekeeping, and told the woman, "I'm a dope. Can you please send someone up with a key to eight-oh-three? I locked myself out."

"Your name, sir?"

"James Lutz." That was the name the porn dealer was using.

"When security arrives," the woman added, "show them your passport, Mr. Lutz."

"Have him bring a bucket of ice, too," the biologist replied.

He was palming a twenty euro bill when a kid wearing a name badge appeared, used a passkey, and bowed him into the room. "Hang on, I've got something for you." Inside the closet, as anticipated, was a wall safe which he fiddled with before giving up. "Damn . . . must have punched in the number wrong. What's the default code? I need my wallet."

The kid opened the safe, and stepped back in deference to this solid-looking American who exuded confidence, but in a friendly way that suggested he was also generous.

"Thank you, Mr. Lutz," the kid said, accepting the twenty. No eye contact, he backed out of the room.

"You're supposed to see this." Ford held up one of his three fake passports. It earned only a dutiful glance.

He has no future in the security trade, Ford rationalized when the kid was gone. *I did him a favor.*

On the other hand, probably not. Child pornography was a billion-dollar international industry. Nassau was the ancillary stronghold for a Russian network that branched into Haiti, Indonesia and the Middle East, particularly Muslim regions where daughters were treated as chattel. Children provided a steady income to jihadists who enjoyed beheading infidels. When word got out that a high level dealer had lost incriminating files while drinking at the pool bar, Jimmy Lutz, or whatever his name was, would beg first for his life, then a painless bullet.

If he lived that long.

Wearing gloves and a jeweler's eyepiece, Ford secured an adhesive keystroke transmitter to Lutz's laptop. The translucent tape was two inches long, and thinner than a human hair. Once mounted on the screen's black border, it became invisible, which Ford confirmed before returning the laptop to its case.

Next, the safe. He photographed the contents: a wallet, two passports, a bundle of cash, and half a dozen ultra-secure biometric thumb drives. Three platinum thumb drives; three stealth black. Ford's employer, a Swiss agency, had anticipated this, but had provided him with only four stealth versions. He switched out the three black thumb drives, and repositioned each item exactly as he'd found it before closing the safe.

Ford had also anticipated that Jimmy Lutz was in Nassau on a working vacation. On the bed, a Dacor dive bag lay next to a leather suitcase and a valet parking ticket. He unzipped the bag and removed a buoyancy compensator vest attached to a four-hose regulator.

The gear looked new.

Using a multi-tool, he popped a pin, removed the regulator's cover; next, a lubricating seal and the main diaphragm. A stainless valve seat and plunger were cupped within. With a drop of water-soluble glue, he seated an object that would clog the system when it broke free, but would dissolve without a trace within twenty minutes.

He did the same to the back-up regulator, then returned everything to the bag.

There was no such thing as a zero-signature robbery unless the victim wasn't alive to report the crime. No guarantees when or if it would happen, but a nice touch if the man had booked an afternoon dive.

When he was done, he consulted photos of the room to be sure it was exactly as he'd found it, then cracked the door and eyeballed the hallway.

Shit . . . lumbering toward him was Jimmy Lutz after only twenty minutes at the tiki bar. Maybe he'd left his wallet, or needed cigars. Ford hurried past the bed, pocketed the valet ticket, then exited onto the balcony, closing the curtains and sliding doors.

"You . . . bastard . . . get your hands off me," a woman's voice demanded from nearby. British accent. She sounded startled more than mad. A neighboring balcony was empty, but billowing curtains suggested the woman was in the adjoining suite. Ford's attention wavered until a slamming door told him Lutz was in the room. Lights came on within, then heavy feet flip-flopped toward him as the woman, voice louder, threatened, "I'll call the police, by God, if you don't get out of here right now."

Lutz heard her; curtains parted. Ford hugged the wall while the man peered out, his face inches away through the glass. Satisfied the woman wasn't on his balcony, Lutz engaged the deadbolt, and swept the curtains closed.

Ford was trapped. He waited, hearing a mix of sounds from the adjoining suite: a clatter of furniture; the woman gasping, "Damn you . . . that *hurts*," and other indecipherable noises that signaled a struggle. Or was it a kinky twosome enjoying rough love?

Inside Lutz's room, a toilet flushed. A door suctioned curtains, then banged closed.

The porn dealer was gone.

Ford grabbed his computer bag before testing the sliding doors. Yes, they were locked. He swung a leg over the railing, ignored the dizzying distance to the beach below, and made the long step to the next balcony which was screened by landscape foliage. A potted plant crashed to the tile when he pushed his bag through, then followed. Beyond billowing curtains, through open doors, the room went silent.

Standing, looking in, he was prepared to apologize until he accessed the scene. A fit man wearing medical whites and a name badge glared back—a massage therapist whose table had collapsed on the floor during a struggle. Askew on the table, still battling to cover her body with a sheet, was the brunette he'd seen earlier by the pool.

"Didn't know you was there, sir," the man glowered. "She want to call the constables, fine, but what you think they'll say? She's the one requested my services."

In Nassau, even extortion threats sounded as melodic as a woodwind flute.

"Are you hurt?" Ford asked the woman. He pushed the curtains aside and stepped in.

She was confused, and mad enough to sputter, "I want this bastard fired. If you work for the hotel, I want to file a—"

"That man don't work here," the therapist interrupted. Until then, he'd been backing toward the door. Now, looking from Ford to the broken pottery outside, he figured out the situation. "Yeah, what the police gonna say? This guest hire me, take her clothes off her own free accord. I already know who they gonna believe."

"You cheeky son-of-a-bitch." The woman tried to scoot away; the sheet fell. She folded her arms to cover herself until Ford yanked the sheet free, and tossed it over her. He wore a baggy white guayabera shirt, tails out to cover the waistband of his khaki slacks. Again he asked the woman if she was hurt.

"Who are you?" she demanded. "For Christ's sakes, call a manager . . . or do something. This man tried to rape me."

"Naw, come on," the therapist said in a soothing way. "That ain't true. You want to know the real problem? This fella come here to rob you, that's what they'll figure out. Why else he climb over that balcony? You being such a wealthy lady, they'll know a poor boy like me wouldn't do nothing so stupid."

"Bastard," the woman said while the man grinned.

"Ain't you a pretty one," he said. "I'm not the type to make trouble, so tell you what. Mister, I'm willing to leave polite-like—but I want compensation for all the fun I missed, plus the coin you lost me. Sound fair?"

"Very fair," Ford said. He reached back as if for a bill-fold, but came up with a 9 mm pistol and leveled the sights at the man's nose.

"Where do you want it?" he asked.

The massage therapist, no longer smiling, said, "Shit, man. What the . . . don't make me stick that gun up your ass."

Staring over the sights, Ford cocked the pistol and spoke to the woman. "Get some clothes on and call the police if that's what you want. But not from here. There's a house phone near the elevators."

The therapist turned to her. "See there, Miz Cobourg! He plans to shoot me 'cause he don't want witnesses," he said, while the woman asked Ford, "Is it true? The con-stables won't believe me?"

"Not a chance," Ford said. "You made the appoint-ment through the concierge?"

"Of course," she said, then understood the implica-tions. "Oh hell. Yes, it was a damn fool thing to do." She got to her feet with the sheet around her, no longer afraid, just angry and undecided.

"It happens a lot in places like this. If you're worried about headlines, I'd pack your things now, and not look back. Or forget this ever happened."

"Who *are* you?" she asked again.

"In my bag, there's a roll of duct tape," Ford replied. Then, to the therapist, said, "Get on the floor, or I'll shoot you in the knee."

The woman, kneeling over a tan tactical bag, said, "I shouldn't have come. I didn't think I'd be recognized here."

He waited for the elevator doors to close before dialing valet parking. "This is Mr. Lutz, room eight-oh-three, would you bring my car around? A lady friend will be there in a minute. Please load her bags."

When Ford stepped out into the salt-dense heat, the brunette, wearing sunglasses and a scarf, was in the passenger seat, left side, of a raven-blue Range Rover. He folded a twenty euro note around the valet ticket, and confided to the attendant, "If a man shows up claiming to be me, it's the lady's husband. Understand?"

"A jealous one, yes, sir," the attendant agreed.

Ford added another twenty. "Can you blame him? I'll double this if you give us time for a quiet dinner."

The woman didn't speak until they were heading north on East Bay Road. "Did you shoot him?"

Puzzling, the cool way she was handling this, both

now and in the room. Instead of hysterics and pointed questions about why he was armed, she remained subdued; no . . . distracted, as if she had more important matters on her mind.

"I taped his mouth, that's all. I can drop you at another hotel, but that might not be smart. Depends on how the police deal with it."

"Then what was that noise as I was walking to the elevator? I heard something, a sharp bang or thud. It came from my room. For God's sake, please tell me you didn't."

Ford pretended to concentrate on the road. "If there's no reason to stay in Nassau, there are daily flights to Cuba. It's a lot more scenic—and safer."

She lowered her window, saying, "Dear Jesus, you did. You shot him."

"You wouldn't have gotten in the car if you believed that." He looked over at her profile, the wind tangling her hair. "Or maybe you would've."

"I was unaware I had a choice. A man with a gun comes over my balcony, I assume you've been paid to shadow me. A security agent of some sort—who else carries a role of tape and three passports in his bag?"

For a moment, she made eye contact; an up-down sweep, then she was done with him. "I'll admit you don't look the part. More like a math prof I fancied at university. The type you surprise in the stacks at a library, who spills soup on his tie." She touched a button, and lounged back. Her window slid into place, sealing out the monoxide din of traffic. "Aren't those always the ones who fool you?"

Ford braked left-footed, swung around a pedicab, and

turned abruptly onto Baillou Hill Road before consulting his mirror. It was four miles to the south side of the island. He drove for a while. "Cobourg—I'm not familiar with the name. What should I call you?"

"I'd prefer you didn't."

"For now, at least. He said you're wealthy. Are you an heiress or an actress?"

Cynical laughter was the response. "Come off it, please. You know precisely who I am. Who hired you?"

He'd been wrong. Her aloofness didn't signal distraction nor was she subdued. It signaled *indifference*. A woman who didn't care what happened. It suggested she was very rich, or had powerful connections . . . or was teetering on an emotional ledge.

Ford's eyes darted from the mirror to his phone. He touched redial and handed it to her. "A friend of mine should answer. When he does, tell him to book two seats for us to Lauderdale, and two seats to Havana. The earliest possible flights; doesn't matter which airlines. He's got my name and AmEx number. You can text him the rest of your information. He's not the type to carry a notebook."

"Just like that, huh? Four seats, only two people. Are we traveling separately?"

"Stay in Nassau, if you want. Keep in mind police don't report sexual assaults here—not if a tourist is involved. It's bad for the local economy."

Her window scrolled halfway down, then up again. "Filthy little island, isn't it? I was shocked when that clod recognized me. I certainly didn't register under my real name." She paused. "The boy at the valet called you 'Mr.

Lutz.' I assume that's not your name, either. You nicked some poor fool's rental car, didn't you?"

Tomlinson's phone was ringing. Ford heard it while he studied the mirror where a beat-up white van had joined a black Nissan.

Before putting the phone to her ear, she asked, "Why don't you speak to him? He's your friend."

"I need both hands to drive." He downshifted and accelerated; made a sharp turn onto Cowpen Road, then swung abruptly onto a sand trail that ribboned downward through a landslide of shacks, the Caribbean Sea beyond.

"We're being followed," he said. "Keep your head down while you talk. One of them has a gun."